Wild Wind

Also From Kristen Ashley

Rock Chick Series:
Rock Chick
Rock Chick Rescue
Rock Chick Redemption
Rock Chick Renegade
Rock Chick Revenge
Rock Chick Reckoning
Rock Chick Regret
Rock Chick Revolution
Rock Chick Reawakening
Rock Chick Reborn

The 'Burg Series:
For You
At Peace
Golden Trail
Games of the Heart
The Promise
Hold On

The Chaos Series:
Own the Wind
Fire Inside
Ride Steady
Walk Through Fire
A Christmas to Remember
Rough Ride
Wild Like the Wind
Free
Wild Fire
Wild Wind

The Colorado Mountain Series:
The Gamble
Sweet Dreams
Lady Luck
Breathe
Jagged
Kaleidoscope
Bounty

Dream Man Series:
Mystery Man
Wild Man
Law Man
Motorcycle Man
Quiet Man

Dream Team Series:
Dream Maker
Dream Chaser
Dream Spinner (coming Summer 2021)
Dream Keeper (coming Winter 2021)

The Fantasyland Series:
Wildest Dreams
The Golden Dynasty
Fantastical
Broken Dove
Midnight Soul

The Honey Series:
The Deep End
The Farthest Edge
The Greatest Risk

The Magdalene Series:
The Will
Soaring
The Time in Between

Moonlight and Motor Oil Series:
The Hookup
The Slow Burn

River Rain Series:
After the Climb

The Three Series:
Until the Sun Falls from the Sky
With Everything I Am
Wild and Free

Wild Wind

A Chaos Novella

By Kristen Ashley

1001 DARK NIGHTS
PRESS

Wild Wind
A Chaos Novella
By Kristen Ashley

1001 Dark Nights

Copyright 2021 Kristen Ashley
ISBN: 978-1-951812-45-4

Foreword: Copyright 2014 M. J. Rose

Published by 1001 Dark Nights Press, an imprint of Evil Eye Concepts, Incorporated

Sign up for the 1001 Dark Nights Newsletter
and be entered to win a Tiffany Key necklace.

There's a contest every month!

Go to www.1001DarkNights.com to subscribe.

As a bonus, all subscribers can download
FIVE FREE exclusive books!

Dedication

This book is dedicated to two kings.

Chadwick and LeBron

Acknowledgments from the Author

Thank you to the greatest team in publishing, Liz, MJ and Jillian. The process of writing is personal, sometimes brutal and always challenging. After all of that, it's a sigh of relief to submit a book to you, knowing it will be handled with the utmost of care in the gentlest of hands.

One Thousand and One Dark Nights

Once upon a time, in the future...

*I was a student fascinated with stories and learning.
I studied philosophy, poetry, history, the occult, and
the art and science of love and magic. I had a vast
library at my father's home and collected thousands
of volumes of fantastic tales.*

*I learned all about ancient races and bygone
times. About myths and legends and dreams of all
people through the millennium. And the more I read
the stronger my imagination grew until I discovered
that I was able to travel into the stories... to actually
become part of them.*

*I wish I could say that I listened to my teacher
and respected my gift, as I ought to have. If I had, I
would not be telling you this tale now.
But I was foolhardy and confused, showing off
with bravery.*

*One afternoon, curious about the myth of the
Arabian Nights, I traveled back to ancient Persia to
see for myself if it was true that every day Shahryar
(Persian: شهریار, "king") married a new virgin, and then
sent yesterday's wife to be beheaded. It was written
and I had read, that by the time he met Scheherazade,
the vizier's daughter, he'd killed one thousand
women.*

*Something went wrong with my efforts. I arrived
in the midst of the story and somehow exchanged
places with Scheherazade — a phenomena that had
never occurred before and that still to this day, I
cannot explain.*

Now I am trapped in that ancient past. I have taken on Scheherazade's life and the only way I can protect myself and stay alive is to do what she did to protect herself and stay alive.

Every night the King calls for me and listens as I spin tales. And when the evening ends and dawn breaks, I stop at a point that leaves him breathless and yearning for more. And so the King spares my life for one more day, so that he might hear the rest of my dark tale.

As soon as I finish a story... I begin a new one... like the one that you, dear reader, have before you now.

Prologue

Jagger

When Jagger first saw her, it was eleven years ago.

On his sixteenth birthday.

His brother Dutch had let Jagger use his truck and Jag drove by himself for the first time.

Where'd he go?

He went to his father's grave.

That was another first.

The first time he'd been there by himself.

And it was the only time Jag could remember that he and his dad had been alone together.

Well, kinda alone.

She was there.

Not with him and his dad.

She was at a funeral that was happening across the way.

When he first clapped eyes on her, she was in one of those chairs they set up, right at the front, staring at the casket.

Jag sat, and he was supposed to be sharing part of his sixteenth birthday with his dad, but he couldn't help himself.

He kept glancing over at her, mostly because she was pretty.

But he looked her way so often, he knew, eventually when he did it, she'd be looking at him.

And eventually, she was.

She was so pretty, he didn't think about what she was doing there, he just thought about how pretty she was.

But when they caught eyes over those thirty yards dotted with headstones, he felt the look on her face in the back of his throat.

Only then did he take in her surroundings.

There was a man sitting beside her and a guy maybe Jagger's age sitting on the other side of the man.

But there was no woman.

So…

Yeah.

He wasn't surprised.

He knew that look on her face.

He felt it.

Still.

Fuck.

Even though it was his birthday, and he was finally legal to drive, and there were a million other things he wanted to do, he didn't do any of them.

He hung there until the service was over.

He didn't get why. Maybe it had to do with the fact that, once she saw him there, she kept glancing at him. Maybe she knew what he knew, and they both just got it. So, if she was looking his way, he needed to be there for her.

Or maybe it was that she was just that pretty.

Jag had guessed it before, but he figured it out for sure when the service was over. The way people were with her, the guy who looked like her brother, and the man who was probably her dad.

God, Jag had had that shit shoved down his throat for as long as he could remember.

He was barely old enough to talk when his dad was murdered, and to that day, he got those looks. Especially when folks found out his father was murdered. And more especially when they learned Jag was barely able to talk when his old man got whacked.

The looks she and her brother and her dad were getting right then.

Looks that Jag knew the person intended to be nice, but they made you just want to punch them in the throat.

Or shout in their face.

Just be real! I'm not dead, he is!

I barely knew him!

I don't even remember him!

My real dad is alive. He's always been there for me. So you can just chill!

It was not the same for that girl.

Nope.

She was probably fourteen, fifteen, and Jag was guessing it was her mom who was gone.

That was a lot of time to have in before you lost everything.

He didn't know what he'd do if his mom kicked it.

Or Hound did.

Or something happened to Dutch.

No, he did know.

He'd go off the rails. He didn't even care. End up dead or in prison.

But his birth dad? Graham Black?

Jag didn't know the man.

So, yeah.

When it came to Jag, people could just chill.

Her though?

That girl?

For her, even on his birthday, able to drive by himself, he stayed at the cemetery.

He wanted to go over there, take her aside, say to her, "Yeah, just look like you're listening, nod and move on. It'll be over soon. They'll go away. And then it's just your family. It'll always be just your family."

He wanted to save her from that shit or at least shield her from it.

But he couldn't do that.

Still, he stayed.

He stayed while everyone came over and fucking touched her. Her arm, or shoulder, her hair, her hand.

And it was tough to sit through that. It was tough not to haul his ass over there and stop that shit.

Christ, why did they do that?

Like, your mom was gone, and you wanted people pawing you?

But he sat where he was and stayed through all that.

He stayed, watching her walk with her dad and brother to their car.

The dad held her hand.

He had his other hand wrapped around the back of his boy's neck.

Jag couldn't even look at the dad's face.

He knew what he'd see.

Jag had been looking at that for as long as he could remember.

But seeing it new? Fresh? Raw?

Nope.

He wasn't looking at that dude.

Jag also stayed after they drove away.

After everyone was gone.

And he stayed to hold vigil as the cemetery workers took care of things.

Put her mom under dirt.

Did right with the process. Laid the flowers on just so.

Yeah, Jag stayed through all of that.

Only when her mom was all good did Jag look at his father's tombstone.

"Later, Pops," he said, getting up, brushing off the ass of his jeans, and making his way to Dutch's truck.

And it was fucked in the head.

But to this day, he would swear it happened.

Swear that he heard *You're a good kid, Jag,* in a voice that was totally familiar. At the same time it was not.

* * * *

It was a couple of months after when he saw the tombstone go up.

He was in Dutch's truck again, alone, visiting his dad.

And he was pissed because Hound and his mom were just not getting it on. Seriously with that, what the fuck?

Hound was, like, wasting his whole damned life waiting for his mother to snap out of it.

But did she?

No.

Hell, everything she needed was right there.

In her boys.

And in Hound.

Jesus.

But yeah, Jag saw the new headstone, which was good. Seeing that, he could think of her, the pretty girl, and not think about why he kept coming to his dad's grave, especially when he was frustrated that his father's wife wasn't hooking up with a man his father considered a brother.

And Jag didn't know why, but when he saw that new gravestone, he turned right around, drove to the store, bought some paper, envelopes and Ziplocs, as well as duct tape. He found a pen in Dutch's glove box and drove back to the cemetery.

He sat on his father's grave and wrote her a note because he knew, that headstone was up, they'd come back for certain to check it out.

The note read:

Hey,

I'm the guy from across the way. Just to say, it sucks now and people are gonna be weird about it for a long time. Just ignore them and do your thing. You got her in your head, you know? That's not going anywhere. Ever.

And you got your dad and your brother. That's big.

I got my mom and my brother. And they're like, everything, you know? We look out for each other. We're a family. Totally.

I can't say it's all good, because it's not.

I can just say you get on with it.

So let people do their thing, you do yours, and stick tight with your dad and brother. You'll be OK.

Hang loose,

-J

He'd then folded it up, put it in an envelope and wrote *For the Girl Across the Way* on it.

When he was done with that, he'd taped it to the base of her mom's headstone.

Her mom's name had been Bryn.

Pretty.

He wondered what the girl's name was.

At the time, he figured that he'd probably never find out.

* * * *

It was a week or so later when Hound caught up with him.

"Reckon this is for you," his stepdad-not-stepdad had grunted, handing him an envelope in a Ziploc.

Hound said nothing more.

That was just like Hound. He always knew what to do, say, how to be.

So he took off and left Jagger to it.

Jag never asked him when he was there, or why. It wasn't a surprise Hound visited his father's grave.

They were brothers, after all.

Jagger pulled the envelope out of the baggie and saw it said *For the Guy Across the Way*.

The writing wasn't girlie. Each letter was straight up and down, deep impressions in the strokes, taking space. It had personality but it was so perfect, it was a little eerie. Like it wasn't handwritten, but instead some font pretending to be handwriting, printed out on a printer.

It said:

J-
Thanks for the advice.
Dad says you're right.
And you're wise.
You hang loose too.
        -A

Jag really wanted to know what "A" stood for.

But he'd have to wait a while to find out.

* * * *

The next time Jag saw her, it was two, three months later, outside an Arby's.

She was with her family.

Or what was left of it.

Jag was going in.

She was coming out.

He stopped dead the second he saw her.

She did the same.

Her father and brother didn't notice and kept walking to their car.

Jag moved to her where she was standing on the sidewalk, waiting for him.

"Hey," he greeted.

"Hey," she replied.

"How's things? You hangin' in there?" he asked.

She nodded.

"Cool," he said, feeling something he'd never felt before.

Uncomfortable.

Unsure.

Like a dork.

Man, she was pretty.

And man, he was a dick, when all he could think was how pretty she was, and her mom hadn't been under dirt for a full year.

"Thanks for the note," she said.

"I get it," he told her.

"Yeah, I saw your dad's stone. I get that you do," she replied.

"Honey!"

They both looked in the direction of the call.

The dad was looking impatient and not too hip on his daughter chatting with Jag.

The brother had the same exact look.

"Be right there," she yelled back.

"I'll let you go, but you know how to get me, you need me, yeah?" Jag asked.

He was talking about exchanging notes.

What he wanted to do was get her number.

"Yeah," she answered. "Thanks," she said, tucking her black hair behind her ear.

And he wondered about her mom. The dad was tall and blond.

She was not either.

Nor was her brother.

She stepped off the curb and said, "Later?"

This was the time he should ask for her number or give her his.

But how did he do that when her brother and father were right there?

"Later," he said, though he didn't know how that would happen, unless she left him a note, which could be intercepted by someone other than Hound, like Dutch or his mom, and they wouldn't be as cool about it.

He watched her walk to her dad and brother, thinking he shouldn't.

But he just couldn't stop.

She said something to her pops when she skirted him to get in the backseat, and after she did, the man looked right to Jag.

He then dipped his chin Jag's way.

Well, shit.

She'd told him that Jag was Note Guy.

And the dude was cool.

Jag gave him the salute he'd seen Hound give every once in a while, finger to temple and out.

The man quirked a grin, lifted his chin this time, and angled into his car.

The brother glared at him.

Jag ignored that, tried to catch sight of her in the car, but couldn't.

So he walked into Arby's, hoping like hell there was a "later."

* * * *

Later turned out to be *later*.

The next time Jag saw her, it was at a party, and well over a year had passed.

She hadn't left him a note.

Since she hadn't, he hadn't left her one either.

And he hadn't because he didn't want to be that jerk, creeping on some girl who'd lost her mom, doing it by leaving notes on her mom's tombstone.

The party where he saw her was a party she shouldn't have been at.

He knew her the instant he saw her, even though she'd grown up—*a lot*—in the time in between.

He'd never forget her, though.

Never.

And the second she locked eyes on him, he knew she hadn't forgotten him either.

The minute she saw him, she immediately looked guilty.

As she should.

He was eighteen. He was the son of a biker (actually two, but only one was blood). It was a rough crowd, and a big one, everyone (that he knew) was of age (or at least, not a minor). There was definitely booze, some drugs, some folk who he knew could get rowdy, and not in a good way.

Jag could be there.

She was maybe sixteen, at most, seventeen.

She had no business anywhere near there.

He went right to her, fighting his way through the crowd to get where she was.

And when he got close, he saw she'd already started tatting up.

Shit.

Not huge tattoos, little ones here and there on her arms, her fingers.

He had no problem with tats. He had some of his own.

But at sixteen?

Nope.

The first thing he wanted to talk about when he saw her again was to ask her name. It seemed like forever since that birthday, their note exchange, running into each other at Arby's, and he'd thought about it a lot.

Was she an Ann? Or Amy? Andrea? Amanda? Abby? Audrey?

He didn't ask her name or say hi.

He said, "You got a lift home?"

"Yeah," she'd muttered.

Mm-hmm.

She knew she had no business being there.

"Then get them and get outta here," he ordered.

He saw right away some attitude start surfacing.

"I'm just havin' fun."

"You can have fun. Just not here."

"I'm all right here."

Jag shook his head decisively. "No, you're not. You're too fuckin' young to be here. Can you even drive yet?"

Chin tilt and, "Yeah. And by the way, I'm my own lift. I don't need anyone to drive me around. I can take care of myself."

Oh yeah.

The attitude was surfacing, and he sensed she was digging in.

So it was time to blow past this and get her safe.

"Your dad is probably worried like fuck about you."

That did it.

She looked away.

Hung her head.

Caught herself doing that and looked back to him, trying to keep her chin high.

"A, go home," he urged.

"J, you're a pain," she retorted.

She remembered his initial.

That felt good.

It also spoke to their connection.

So, it wasn't all in his head. It wasn't only on his side.

It was on hers too.

He put his hand out toward her. "Let's go."

It didn't take real long before she put her hand in his.

He led them through the crowd like he was her bodyguard.

He took some shit along the way from friends and acquaintances about showing and then immediately nabbing the prettiest girl there.

Jag stopped once through this, when some asshat called her "talent."

He was in staredown with the asshat when A put her hand on his back and said, "He's a douche. Let it go. I don't care. I *am* talent and he's never gonna get that lucky."

She was right.

Still, Jag gave it a couple more seconds to make his point before he broke contact and kept moving.

Her car was parked at the curb and it was nice. A solid Honda a dad would think his girl was safe in.

She beeped it and he opened the door for her.

"So, you're, like, a gentleman?" she teased.

"My dad is dead, I was raised by my mom, so yeah. A woman raises you, you got no choice but to learn to treat women right, unless you're a moron or born a dickhead."

She kept eye contact with him all the time he said this, but when he was done, she looked away.

"A—" he started.

"You know it hasn't gotten better," she told the road.

He felt like an imposter.

Because, yeah, he knew that.

But she'd been fourteen (fifteen?) when her mom died.

He'd been three when his dad was gone.

He still said, "It doesn't get better. You just get used to it."

She looked back to him and she looked pissed.

Or hurt.

He'd get it when she said, "My dad's dating someone."

For her, it was a betrayal.

For him, if his mom got her shit together and started moving on, it'd be a relief.

Which was why he said, "That's good."

And now she was definitely pissed. "No, it isn't. She died, like, *yesterday.*"

"It wasn't yesterday, A," he said softly.

She got that stubborn expression on her face before she turned her attention to her toes.

He got closer to her.

Not too close, but close.

She looked up at him.

Perfect height, even if she had on heels.

He was tall, he wasn't into short women.

But he wasn't into tall women either.

She was neither.

Yeah.

Perfect.

"My mom isn't over my dad and we'll just say my dad's been gone way longer than your mom has, and it sucks," he shared. "It fuckin' hurts. Every day, wakin' up and seein' her in pain. I get it doesn't feel good seein' him with another chick or thinkin' what that means about how he felt about your ma. But trust me, the alternative is way fuckin' worse."

"It just...makes me remember, not that I'd forget. But the pain comes back, you know?"

He shook his head. "I don't know, seein' as Ma hasn't gone there. But I just want her to be happy. That's, like, the only thing in this world I want. Because she's the mom who made it so I want for nothing else, so it's more like, I *need* that for her. You get me?"

She nodded and said, "I'm sorry, J. That does sound like it sucks."

"Don't be too hard on your dad and don't make him worry about you. It's not cool."

She nodded again and started to fold into her car.

He was about to ask her name, get her number. She was underage, but *just*.

And they'd just had the deepest conversation he'd had since Hound sat him down to share about the birds and the bees and how he'd knock Jag's block off if he took a girl ungloved.

But someone called his name and he looked to the house they'd exited.

Some dude he knew was shouting something he couldn't hear.

Jag called, "What?"

And in that time, she got in her car, closed her door and her Honda started.

When he heard the engine catch, he looked down and through the window at her.

She waved, gave him a smile she didn't really mean because she was sad and had learned too young how big life could suck.

And he stepped back wide when she pulled her car out of the spot and drove away.

* * * *

The next time he saw her was maybe a year later. At a concert. At the Gothic.

She was coming his way when he spotted her. She'd seen him before he saw her.

She smiled and waved.

She looked good, happier.

He still saw the weight she carried, something he carried too.

But yeah.

Happier.

And he was glad to see that.

He waved back and started her way.

But since it was a punk act they were catching, and they were in the mosh pit, a surge hit the pit, they both got caught up in it, he lost sight of her, and even if he looked (all night), he didn't see her again.

That was a serious bummer.

Though, he was glad to know they liked the same kind of music.

He was glad just because they liked the same kind of music.

But also because it meant they might run into each other again.

* * * *

He saw her a few months later at Taste of Colorado downtown.

They caught up then.

She was with a dude.

He was with a chick.

But she dragged that dude right to Jagger, smiling big.

And Jag stood next to his chick, watching her do it, smiling big right back.

"Hey, J," she greeted.

"Hey, A," he'd returned.

And Christ.

Yeah.

She just got prettier and prettier.

She barely glanced at his chick when she started up their convo, which did not go over well with his chick.

Or her dude, who Jag felt no remorse about the fact it seemed she forgot he was even there.

"So cool to finally run into you again," she started it, still smiling big. "I was gonna leave you a note at our place, but the last time I went to visit Mom, there was this other dude who looked like you there and I didn't want him to get it."

And he knew what she meant.

Our place.

Reaching out using his dad's grave.

"That's my brother, and yeah, no." He shook his head, for some reason, the thought of Dutch knowing about her, getting her note to him, not understanding what it was, reading it.

Yeah…

No.

"Babe, we're supposed to meet Slammer, we're already late," her dude said, pulling on her.

Another barely-there glance, this time at her guy while she said, "A second," and looked back at Jag. "He dumped her."

"What?" Jag asked, his chick grabbing his hand and tugging on it to get his attention.

"Dad," she said. "He dumped the woman he was seeing, and you were right. It made me sad because it made him sad too. So I should have just chilled and let him have it."

"Hey, baby," his chick murmured to Jag, "you said we'd go to that ice cream booth and you'd get me a cone."

He glanced at her, "A sec," then back to A. "Sorry, but he'll move on again. You'll get it this time when he does and give him that." After she nodded, he went on, "Anyway, you look good."

When he said that, her dude got closer to her.

So did Jag's chick, to him.

"We gotta *go*, babe," her dude said.

She spared him another glance and then to Jag, "We have to meet a friend, but you want to hook up later?"

Her dude made a noise.

Jag ignored it and smiled at her.

"There's a band coming on that's rad," she told Jag. "You gotta see them play."

"We're in," Jagger decided.

His chick made a noise.

"Okay, four o'clock? Right here?" she suggested.

"We'll be here," he replied.

She smiled huge, bopped forward, and gave him a hug.

It was the first time they'd touched.

She felt good.

She smelled good.

He pulled his hand from his chick's to wrap his arm around her waist.

"Four," he whispered in her ear, giving her waist a squeeze, and feeling really good that they were finally going to get the opportunity to get to know each other better.

"Yeah," she replied, returning that squeeze to his shoulders, and he knew she felt the same way. "Four."

She bopped back, her dude claimed her, Jag's chick claimed him, and they were both tugged in opposite directions.

But they kept eye contact over their shoulders as they walked away. And right before she disappeared from sight, she shot him a devil's horns, and the way she did was funny, cute and cool, so it was also totally hot.

Needless to say, Jag's chick was not happy about this even a little bit.

So, needless to say, around four, she pitched one helluva fit and he had to deal with her ass.

This meant he missed the meeting with A. By the time he got back to the area where they met, she was long gone.

And he was so pissed that she was, he broke shit off with his chick.

He never saw that girl again.

As for A, it went so long, he thought he'd lost her forever.

And thinking that, he felt it.

Deep.

* * * *

It was four years before Jag saw her again.

She was in a car.

He was on his bike.

They were stopped at a stoplight.

He looked over to her, she looked at him, and when she recognized him past his shades and his longer hair and his Chaos Motorcycle Club cut, she grinned.

He frowned.

Because there she was, driving down Broadway like years hadn't passed.

Where the fuck had she been?

No notes?

No sightings?

Nothing?

She made hand motions and he jerked up his chin because, fuck yes, he was gonna follow her.

And he did.

To the parking lot at the Albertson's by the Blue Bonnet.

They parked.

He swung off his bike.

She got out of her car.

Her hair was longer too, she was thinner, but somehow with that, her ass was rounder, her tits bigger.

And she had more tats.

He gave himself seconds to take her in, and in all that, it wasn't lost on him that she was even fucking prettier.

And then, no other way to describe it, he bore down on her.

"What the fuck, A?" he growled when he was deep in her space.

She pressed back to her car, but he just moved into the opening she created when she did.

Through all this, she stared up at him, demanding, "What the fuck, what, J?"

"You've been gone for fucking years," he pointed out.

Her head ticked. "Yeah, I went to college out east."

Well...

Shit.

But...

Still.

"And you didn't leave me a goddamn note?"

She blinked.

"You were gone, like, every fuckin' day for the last four fuckin' years so you couldn't leave me a note?" he pushed it.

"Well, no, but mostly, yeah, 'cause Dad had two kids in college, both out of state, we're not rolling in it so I couldn't exactly fly home every weekend. And anyway, J, you stood me up at Taste."

And again.

Shit.

But still.

"My chick got up in my shit, I had to deal with her," Jag explained. "We were late, you were gone."

"Yeah, well, my guy got up in mine too. He wasn't a big fan of me hugging on a hot dude in front of him. We had words. I told him he could relax and deal or he could take a hike. He wasn't relaxed, but he was ready to deal, and then you didn't show. After that, I had to put up with him being smug, which was worse."

Hang on a second.

She thought he was hot?

"So, that's the only excuse you have?" she pressed. "That your girl threw a tantrum and that's why you stood me up?"

That was twice she'd used those words.

Stood her up.

But they'd both been on dates.

"A, I—" he began.

She didn't let him get any further.

"So no, J, I didn't leave you a note because you blew me off and I'm not feeling this." She motioned between them, but explained it anyway. "I see you for the first time in years, and you get all up in my face because I didn't keep connected after *you* didn't connect with *me* and I was just off, *living my life*."

"You gotta know I'd never leave you hanging unless something came up I couldn't avoid," he told her.

"I don't know that because that's what you did. You left me hanging."

"My chick was throwing a hissy fit."

She shrugged. "So walk away."

"If you were throwing a hissy fit, would you want me to walk away from you?"

"Brother, I would not ever throw a stupid hissy fit."

She said these words like they were gospel and her face registered nothing but disgust at not only the idea of chicks who did, but that he'd think she would.

Jag found that interesting.

As well as promising.

But again…

Still.

"So you're telling me it wasn't a four-year long hissy fit that was the reason I got no fuckin' note after that happened?" he demanded.

That hit.

He knew it when she hit back.

"In case you haven't noticed, we're not anything to each other, J," she informed him. "I don't even know your name."

He stepped back.

She watched him do it and winced.

But no fucking way.

Maybe he'd screwed up, and then she'd screwed up.

But she knew that went too far.

"You're right, we're not," he agreed. "Sorry to fuck up your day."

He headed to his bike.

She moved with him.

He was firing it up when he felt her hand over the leather on his forearm.

He looked at her standing beside him.

"J, hang on a sec," she requested.

"Do your thing, A, live your life," he threw her words back at her. Then he finished it. "Hope it's a good one. Later."

With that, he opened up his bike and glided away.

* * * *

Jagger lost track of how many times he saw her after that.

At concerts, mostly.

Also at some bars.

Couple of times, out to eat.

Even at the mall once.

She'd been with guys.

He'd been with girls.

She'd been with friends.

Ditto with him.

Also alone.

She kept her distance.

He did too.

Eye contact and then avoidance.

Through all this, over the years, even though he was born there and he knew a lot of people and there was more than a rare occasion he'd run into one of them, it was the first time he realized how small of a town Denver was, even if it was a big city.

But it wasn't lost on him they had the same taste in music, food and social life.

It also wasn't lost on him that was way cool and it way fucking sucked because she was enjoying it, so was he, but never together.

He knew he should boss up, apologize for acting like an asshole and getting in her shit after she got back from college.

That said, she was the one who lowered the hammer, so on one of those occasions they were in each other's space, she could have bossed up too.

She didn't.

And the longer she didn't, he got to the point where he just wouldn't.

So he didn't either.

* * * *

In the end, it wasn't about bossing up.

In the end, it was about the fact he was on his bike and he saw some kid motoring down the sidewalk, totally being chased.

And seconds later, he saw it was A doing the chasing.

So yeah.

No hesitation.

He waded right into that.

Fuckin' A.

In both ways he could mean that.

Chapter One

Touché

Jagger

The kid took a turn at the end of the block, and Jag took that turn on his bike.

He passed the kid, pulled up into a drive to cut him off, and to avoid Jag, the kid jetted right into the street.

Fuck.

Jag parked quickly, swung off and saw A racing across the street, following him.

In his motorcycle boots, Jag took off after her.

It was good he did.

She was losing steam.

The kid was not.

Jag passed her, sparing her a glance as he did, through which she wheezed, "*Thief.*"

Shit.

Great.

He kept motoring.

The kid was twelve, maybe thirteen, he had a little extra weight and was carrying a backpack, but he was twelve, thirteen.

He had legs that could go forever and the same kind of energy.

He darted around another corner, then, halfway up that block, he shot into an alley.

Jagger followed.

Bad luck for the kid, someone was moving, and the alley was plugged by a massive truck it wouldn't be easy, even for the kid, to get around. Jag didn't know how they got that behemoth wedged back there in the first place.

But there it was.

The kid decided to double back and take a shot at evasive maneuvering, but as he tried to cut past Jagger, Jag caught him by the backpack.

The pack was important, he knew this because the kid wasn't losing it. He grabbed hold of the straps and twisted vigorously to get away from Jagger. In order not to lose hold, Jag had to catch him by the back collar of his shirt.

That was when the kid started shouting.

"Help! I'm being attacked! Pedo! Pedo!"

"Cool it, kid. I know more cops than hopefully you'll meet in your life, and they know me, so trust me. That's never gonna fly," he advised.

Desperate times called for desperate measures, apparently.

"Help!" the kid kept shouting, pulling at Jag's grasp. "Pedo! Pedo!"

At this point, A rounded the corner, jogged up to them, stopped about four feet away and immediately went hands to knees, head bent, her long black hair falling forward, her torso moving as she hauled in deep breaths.

"Shit," he heard her rasp. Then her head jerked back, hair flying, and she squinted at the kid. "You little turd."

"Fuck you," the kid spat back.

Hmm.

No.

"What'd I hear you say?" Jagger asked.

The kid looked up at him. "Fuck you too."

In an effort at control, Jag turned his attention to A.

"What we got here?" he asked.

She sucked in another big breath before she straightened and stated, "He's a thief, and that's why he's no longer in the group. He was kicked out. But until now, it was never big. Cash register stuff. Candy. Gum." She homed in on the kid and her eyes narrowed again. "Today, it was big. You take off with what you grabbed, I lose out and my consigner loses out and it's never been cool, Mal, you lifting stuff. It's *really* not cool now."

The group?

What did that mean, *the group?*

"I didn't take that shit you said I took to get me kicked out of group in the first place," Mal retorted.

"Brother, I saw you do it with my own eyes," A shot back.

"Did not."

"Did too."

"Did not!"

"*I did!*"

Christ.

To move this along, and stop the back and forth, Jag waded in. "What'd he take this time?"

A turned her gaze to him.

"Game controller bundle. Never been used. It's worth two hundred bucks," she shared.

Keeping a hold on the kid, Jag jostled the backpack.

"That bundle in here, kid?" he asked.

"You shouldn't be touching me, and you can't search me," Mal sniped. "Let me go and fuck off."

"Language, bro," Jag replied.

"Fuck you, *bro*," Mal returned. Jag sighed and turned his attention back to A as Mal lost it and shouted, "*Let me go!*"

Jag again looked down at the kid, saw his grip had loosened on his straps, and said, "Sure," let his shirt go but did it stripping him of his backpack.

"*Hey!*" he cried, whirling and jumping on Jag as Jagger held it high and out of the kid's reach.

Jagger ignored him and asked A, "You want me to look in it or you want it?"

"*Give me my pack! You can't take my pack! You can't search my pack!*" the kid shrieked, still jumping on Jag.

"Everything cool here?"

Jagger turned and saw the movers were now in the mix.

"Yeah. It's cool. This kid stole a game controller from my girl here," he told them, jerking his head to A.

The movers looked from Jagger, who was in jeans, a black tee, and a motorcycle club cut, to A, who was wearing a T-shirt with *The Blob* movie poster on it, a high-waisted corduroy miniskirt, white ankle socks and Doc Marten Mary Janes.

The movers visibly relaxed.

Then again, Jag was the kind of guy who made a lot of men tense.

And A was the kind of woman who undoubtedly made a lot of men relax.

She looked like a seriously toned-down Harley Quinn, but still with that grown-up schoolgirl vibe that was cool as hell and hot AF.

"We have this covered, it's all good. Unless…should we ask them to call the cops, J?" A asked, and he knew with how she did it, she had no intention of phoning the police.

The kid didn't read that.

"*No!*" Mal shouted, stepping away from Jagger, shaking his head. "No cops."

A leveled her eyes on him. "Mal, this isn't candy. This isn't stickers. This isn't a Lionel Richie koozie."

A Lionel Richie what?

"This is serious," A continued, "and I think maybe the cops should be involved." She looked to Jag. "So maybe leave it in the backpack. The cops can search it when they get here."

"Arch, come on," Mal said, his voice now whiney. "Take it back, I don't care. Whatever. I just nabbed it 'cause I was pissed you kicked me out of group."

Arch?

Was her name Arch?

Or was that a nickname?

No one was named Arch.

It had to be a nickname.

"So you took it," A noted.

The kid bit his lower lip.

Yup, not that Jagger doubted it, but that controller was in the kid's pack.

"We've got an issue here, Mal," A said to the kid, her voice softer. She turned her attention to the movers and called, "We're good. We'll work it out. Sorry to disturb."

"Right, you need any help, we're right here," one of the guys said.

Yeah, they'd lost sight of him *and* Mal and they were all about "Arch."

Jag looked heavenward.

The movers shifted away as A said to Mal, "You know I'm gonna have to tell your mom about this. And gotta remind you, we made a deal. I didn't tell her about the other stuff you stole, you didn't pull any more hijinks. And here we are, more hijinks. You reneged. I'm on the phone the minute I get back to the store."

His mom?

Okay, was she a teacher or counselor or something?

And if she was, what was the store?

"*No!*" the kid cried again. "No, Arch. All right. I stole it. Okay? All right? I admit it. Take it back. No beefs. Just don't talk to Mom."

"I can't have you coming into the store and stitching me up, Mal," she said to the kid. "I've got things to do that don't include chasing you through Denver."

Mal turned his head away.

"What's the deal?" she asked him.

Mal kept his head turned away.

"What's the deal, Mal?" she asked again. "We never had any problems before. Why are you suddenly being a pill?"

Mal said nothing and kept his gaze averted.

"She asked you a question, bro," Jag prompted.

Mal turned his head at that, tipped it back, and glared at Jag. "Who are you?"

"Who he is isn't relevant," A stated.

Well, fuck me very much.

Jag scowled at A.

"*He* thinks he's relevant," Mal muttered.

"He's not relevant *to you*," A amended. "Or this situation. Now, what's the deal, Mal?" she kept at him.

"You're right. Mom doesn't know I'm kicked out of group. I didn't tell her," Mal spat out like the words didn't taste good.

A leaned back and crossed her arms on her chest.

"Right," she said slowly. "So what have you been doing after school?"

"None of your business," Mal replied.

"It's my business, you want another shot at group," she said.

Mal's gaze darted to her hopefully.

He wanted another shot at group.

"Seriously?" he asked.

Jag also looked to her, and when Mal was finished, he repeated, "Seriously?"

"Stay out of this, J," she muttered.

"If the kid's stealing from you, babe, just sayin'," Jag returned.

Her head ticked and she focused on him. "Babe?"

"Babe," he confirmed.

That was when A looked heavenward.

"Are you guys, like, together?" Mal asked, his gaze darting between them.

"Mind your business about J, Mal, and answer my question," A demanded.

But Mal was still busy looking between "Arch" and Jag.

"It's weird, he's biker, you're punk, but I see it," he decided. Then he said to Jag, "I'd call her 'babe' too, because she's totally a babe."

"*Mal!*" A snapped.

"Nothin'," he whispered, and Jag wasn't a huge fan of his sudden change in tone or the look on the kid's face. "Nothin'. Just messin' around, keepin' to myself. Hangin' at the laundromat sometimes. But the Harris brothers—"

And Jag did *not* like the way "Arch" responded to the words "the Harris brothers."

He shifted in a way he was closer to her and the kid.

"They know I'm loose and they've been givin' me shit," Mal finished.

"Why don't you go home?" A asked.

The kid hung his head, and if there was a rock to kick, he would have.

"Mal," she pushed.

He looked up at her. "Mom'd know I was home if I went home, you know?"

Oh shit.

"That was part of our deal that I didn't share what went down for it to happen," she said low, also now visibly seriously pissed. "I trusted you, Mal. You promised and I trusted that you would tell your mom you'd left group."

"She'd be disappointed, Arch."

Christ, with the way he said that, now Jag felt for the kid.

It took all of two seconds for A to say her next.

"You're back in group, but I swear to God," she pointed at him, "you blow it again, I'm going right to your mom. Do you hear me?"

Mal nodded.

"Give me the backpack, J," she ordered Jagger.

Jagger handed it to her.

She unzipped it, took a big box out of it that had a picture of a game controller on it, complete with carrying case and other shit (Who needed a carrying case for a game controller? What? Did folk take their controllers on vacation?).

She handed the backpack to Mal.

"Back to the store, brother, your mom's not home for at least an hour."

Mal nodded to A, swung his head to Jagger, then he looked back to A.

"Why hasn't your man been at the store?" he asked.

"Back to the store, Mal," she demanded. "*Now.*"

"Whatever," he replied, but he didn't move.

"That's backtalk, not walking back to the store," she pointed out.

Mal rolled his eyes.

A crossed her arms, still holding the big box in a hand.

"Whatever," Mal repeated, then started walking out of the alley.

A and Jagger watched him.

But A did it shouting, "And I'm not punk! I'm not anything but me!"

Mal said nothing in response before he turned the corner and disappeared.

When he did, afforded an opportunity he hadn't had in a very long time, and not about to waste this one like he did the others, Jagger got right in her space.

"First, what's your fuckin' name?" he asked.

"Archie," she returned, bellying right up to him in return.

Archie?

"What's *your* fuckin' name?" she asked back.

"Jagger," he told her. "Your name is Archie?"

"Yes, my name is Archie. Your name is Jagger?"

He grinned at her. "Touché."

She didn't grin back.

"Now...store?" he continued.

"I have a shop, about seven what I've recently discovered are very long blocks from here."

"A shop?"

"A shop."

"What kind of shop?"

"Albums. Books. Home stuff. Gifts. Local artisan things. Shit I like. That's why it's called S.I.L."

"Your shop is called Sil?"

"S.I.L. on the Hill."

He'd heard of it.

He'd also heard it was fucking awesome.

But he wasn't a shopper so he'd never been there.

"Okay, then," he went on. "Lionel Richie koozie?"

"It has his picture and 'Hello, is it me you're looking for?' on it."

Jag busted out laughing.

Yeah, he'd never been there, but it definitely sounded like her shop was awesome.

"Jagger," she called.

He pulled his shit together, doing this primarily because he liked how his name sounded in her mouth so much he couldn't focus on anything else.

He gave her his gaze, but before she could say anything, he asked, "Group?"

"There's folks in the 'hood, where I live, where my shop is, who can use a break. I give 'em a break."

"What kind of break?"

She shifted, and her body language shifted with her.

She also vocalized this change.

"Jagger, you don't get twenty questions."

"I just chased a kid into an alley for you and got called a pedo. Repeatedly."

"I would have caught him."

He shot her a look.

Then he vocalized that look.

"Babe, you were goin' down. I saved you two hundred bucks."

"I guess that's the least you could do after you left me high and dry for four years."

His eyebrows shot up. "Say what? High and dry?"

"You know, not being there when I needed you."

The back of his neck started tightening.

"When you needed me?"

"Are you gonna repeat everything I say?"

"Are you gonna fill in the blanks?"

She stared up at him.

But now she was doing it like she'd run into an ex who she'd fallen head over heels for and he'd cheated on her.

And yeah, his neck was constricting something fierce.

He dipped his face closer to hers and said quietly, "Archie."

"You know it doesn't end, Jagger," she replied curtly. "It never ends."

Oh yeah, he knew that.

He knew when you lost a parent too early, that hurt never went away.

Even if you didn't remember that parent.

It just never went away.

But she knew her mom.

So that had to be worse.

"Talk to me," he urged.

She shook her head and took a step away. "I gotta get back to my shop."

"I'll walk you there."

"Don't bother."

She made a move.

He caught her arm.

She stopped moving, glanced at her arm, then aimed her eyes to his.

"We're done talking," she informed him.

"We haven't even started and we shoulda started ten years ago."

"Yes, we should have, but we didn't and now it's too late."

"What's too late?"

"Jagger, let me go."

"Archie—"

"Is your brother good?"

At that question coming out of the blue, the contraction in his neck got a whole lot worse.

"Yeah," he said carefully.

"Well, my brother went off the deep end, man. He and my dad barely talk. He's constantly an asshole. He hurts people with seemingly no remorse. My family fell apart. And it would have been nice to have you around so you could tell me how you all kept yours together."

With that, she yanked her arm free and jogged away.

Jagger let her, not because he was done talking to her.

Not even close.

But because, clearly, she needed space.

So he'd give it to her.

And he would because now, he knew how to find her.

Chapter Two

Jagger

Tomorrow, cool?

Jag stared at his brother's text, thinking it was not cool.

But it was what it was.

And what it was, was that Dutch and his woman Georgie wanted Jagger over for dinner.

That would never be a problem, both his brother and Georgie were good cooks, and if they got busy, they had a fantastic relationship with DoorDash.

Not to mention, Dutch loved his big brother and Georgie was the shit.

The problem was, Carolyn was going to be there.

Carolyn was Georgie's sister.

She was also Jagger's ex and things had not ended copacetic with them, mostly because, for years, Carolyn had been snorting coke when she said she wasn't.

And, oh yeah…

Begging money off him so she could do her blow *and* get herself into a hole with all the designer-gear shopping she was doing.

Jag didn't give a shit about the Chanel.

But drugs were a no-go and the thought his money went to that pissed him off.

Huge.

But now she was family, in a way, and he had to suck it up and put up with her.

Like at dinner tomorrow night.

Sure, what time? he replied.

7:00 Dutch sent.

Jagger returned the "ok" hand gesture emoji which pretty much said it all with how enthusiastic he was about this dinner.

Then he stared at his phone, moved down two in his text list, and sent another one.

You open to have a drink at the Compound tonight?

That one, he sent to Hound.

What he was trying to figure out right then was why he sent it to Hound, and not to Dutch.

Dutch was his brother of the blood and of the patch. They were both Chaos.

As their father, Graham Black, had been Chaos.

And as Hound, their other father, was Chaos.

Jag and Dutch were close.

But he'd never wanted Dutch to know about Archie.

And Hound had never brought it up, but Jag knew he knew about her because of the note he'd passed.

He didn't *know*.

But he knew.

And Jagger was totally okay with that.

But not Dutch.

And with that…

Why?

His phone binged and he got, *Yep. Time?*

Jag smiled.

Hound wasn't a man of a lot of words.

Though he knew how to use them when he needed them.

What he was, was always there for Jag and Dutch.

Always.

Nine good with you? he asked.

See you then, Hound answered.

That made Jag feel better.

Then again, Hound always did.

* * * *

Shepherd "Hound" Ironside was already sitting at bar in the Compound of the Chaos MC when Jagger strolled in.

Hound was in his usual position when he sat a stool in the common room—hunched over a bottle of beer cradled in both hands.

But his eyes were on Jag.

"Yo," Jag greeted.

"Yo," Hound replied.

Jag passed Hound at the back to get to the end of the bar, and then he went behind it, because Hound was the only one in the common room, there wasn't a Club prospect to serve them, so Jag had to get his own beer.

He did that, popped the cap, and then turned to stand opposite where Hound was sitting.

He took a drag from his beer and then leaned into his forearms on the bar, cradling his bottle the same way Hound was.

"You good?" Hound asked.

"Yup," Jag answered.

Hound stared right at him.

Jag took another pull from his beer.

Hound spoke again.

"Right then, if you're good, why am I here when I could be at home in a house where my kid is asleep, and my wife is pretty much always in the mood to fall on my dick?"

Jag flinched and reminded him, "Dude, you're talking about my mom."

"Yeah," Hound agreed.

Even if it was totally gross, Jag couldn't stop his chuckle.

"Jagger," Hound said in a warning tone.

"Okay, there's this girl," Jag started.

Hound didn't move, didn't say a word.

He also didn't take his gaze from Jagger's.

He was there. He was interested. He was listening.

He was all Jagger's in that moment.

Something about that made Jag feel great.

At the same time it totally fucked him up.

"I've known her for ten years," he continued. "And the only things I know about her are, she has a dad and a brother, good taste in music, she dresses great, runs a store, her mom is dead, and today was the day I learned her first name."

"Sounds to me like you're takin' things slow."

Jag chuckled again before he handed that shit right back.

"You'd know all about slow, brother."

Hound nodded his head once. "Yup, you don't push a woman when important shit is at stake. Like her heart. Her emotions. Her loyalties. Her sons. And your brothers."

Jag was no longer chuckling.

"Why're you not pushin' this woman?" Hound went on.

"Timing's never been right," Jag lied.

"Cut the shit." Hound knew he was lying.

Jag sighed.

Then he gave it to him.

"We're completely connected and we're totally not."

Hound's brows drifted up. "Why's that?"

Jag looked down at his bottle.

Then he looked at Hound.

"The first time I saw her, she was at her mother's funeral, and I was sitting on Dad's grave."

Hound said nothing, just held Jag's eyes.

"That's how we're connected, Hound," Jagger pointed out.

"That's an important connection, Jag. Now explain to me how you never knew her name until today."

"We'd connect, it was always brief, and then we'd miss connections that were meant not to be brief."

"This is the girl across the way."

Jag straightened from the bar.

Christ.

Hound always had his finger on the pulse of his boys.

So it shouldn't surprise Jag that, even over a decade since that note was passed, he remembered.

It still surprised him.

"Hound—" Jag began.

"And you dicked around for all this time, not learnin' her name?"

"I don't have what she has," Jagger told him.

"What's that?"

"Any time in with my dead dad."

Hound got quiet.

"She needs me, Hound. She's always needed me. And I'm an imposter," Jagger told him.

That made Hound straighten from his hunch over the bar.

"You are the fuck not," he returned.

"Today, she told me she's got troubles. All this way down the line from her mom passing, she's got trouble in her family. And she's pissed at me because I wasn't there when she needed me, and her family fell apart. I got nothing for her. I didn't keep our family together. Mom did. You did. Dutch did. I…"

He trailed off because he didn't know where he was going with that.

"You don't have to have the answers, Jag. You just gotta be there to be a sounding board as she finds them. Or stand strong for her if she doesn't."

Jag took another drag from his beer.

But he didn't say anything.

"Now, the thing she's gonna help you with is figuring out why your ass was on Black's grave and you don't think you lost what she lost."

Okay.

No.

They were not going there.

Jag didn't share that.

He rolled his head on his neck and he felt three things pop.

And Hound heard them.

"You stretchin'?"

This was a thing.

Jag could get wound up.

He worked out, with the brothers in their weight room, at the boxing gym Hound got them working in years ago, and he started doing that young.

Or Hound got both him and Dutch into doing that young.

It was smart and not just as a way to teach a couple of kids how to stay fit.

It worked out other shit too.

But Jag could get tense, and when he got tense, he got tight.

Sometimes it would manifest in some not insignificant pain in his neck and shoulders, also his upper back.

So he could go at a bag, a sparring partner, jump rope or hit the streets and run.

But Hound always made sure he was all over doing a good stretch after.

"It's all connected, bud," Hound would say. "You can't just focus on your neck and shoulders, your hammies, big shit like that. You gotta work the tension outta your hips and abs, triceps, lats, delts, calves. You gotta get *loose* or anything could pop off."

Yeah.

Hound was always on the pulse.

Always there to listen.

Always there to advise.

Always there to teach.

Always there to look out for his boys.

Always there.

Like right now.

The woman Hound loved who he waited twenty years to have was at home with the kid they made and where was Hound?

Right there.

"No," Jagger answered his question.

"Boy," Hound said with disapproval.

"I'll get a run in tomorrow morning and a stretch in after," Jagger promised.

Hound nodded.

"And this girl?" he prompted.

Jag shook his head. "I can't go there unless I know I'm gonna *go there.*"

"Yeah, that's why she's pissed."

Jagger blinked. "Say what?"

"Because you're fuckin' around and you either need to stop fuckin' around or cut her loose."

Jag said nothing.

Hound did.

"And just sayin', son, she doesn't wanna be loose. I don't know what's happenin' with you two, but no woman gets pissed at a man she wants loose from. She gets pissed at a man she's tight with, or wants to be tight with, or wants to be *tighter* with. You got years under your belt with this one and only asked her name today, however the fuck that works, one thing I know, however it works, it means you're jackin' around. She needs you to stop jacking around, Jagger. She needs you all in or to get the fuck out. That's your decision. That's why I'm sittin' here across the bar with you. To figure that out. Are you all in, or are you tapping out?"

Annnnnnnnd…

This was why Hound was right there, and not Dutch.

Because Dutch was a together dude. Smart. Wiser than his years.

But he might not get there, to what Hound just said.

And if he did, if Dutch laid it out like that, it'd get under Jag's skin and Jag wouldn't get where he needed to go.

Because Hound was right.

That was why they were both there.

"I want in," he said quietly.

"What's holding you back?" Hound asked, but before Jagger could answer, Hound went on, "And don't give me more of that imposter shit. She's the one, right?"

Fucking *fuck*.

It wasn't like Hound ever delayed cutting to the chase.

But Jesus.

"Hound—"

"You knew that when you were visiting with your dad and saw her across the way. And it wasn't about your dad bein' dead and her mom bein' the same. You just knew."

That was crazy.

"I was sixteen and she was maybe fifteen, tops."

At that, Hound's brows snapped together. "Who gives a fuck how old you were?"

"You can't know a girl's the one when you're sixteen and you never spoke to her."

"Well, your dad knew, and he wasn't sixteen, but he knew, no doubt about it. He saw your mom and that was it. He was done. And you are his boy. It's just how it is with the Black men. You watched it happen with your brother and Georgie, do you doubt it?"

That was the rub.

Because his last name was Black.

But he wasn't a Black.

"Answer me, Jag, do you doubt it?" Hound pushed.

He gave Hound what he was looking for.

"No, I don't doubt it."

Hound watched him closely.

Then, unusually, he read Jagger wrong.

"You got oats to sow, you cut her loose, and pray like fuck when you're done wasting your time doin' shit you woulda preferred doin' with her, that she's still there."

Having that day in the alley with Archie, knowing her name, seeing her with that kid, knowing something deeper was happening between Archie and Jag, having known that for a long time, and knowing she needed him, the idea of doing anything with anyone other than Archie did not appeal to him.

Not anymore.

He knew how to have a good time and spent a fair amount of it doing just that.

And now…

Christ, was she the one?

Was he a Black?

At least with this?

"When'd you know Mom was the one?" Jag asked.

"Second I laid eyes on her," Hound said before throwing back a swallow of beer. When he was done, he finished, "But she was your dad's then."

"Yeah," Jagger replied.

So he could also be like the man who raised him.

He could be an Ironside.

Jag dropped his head and focused on his bottle.

"You wanna know what I think?" Hound asked.

Jagger tipped his head back to look at his dad.

Then Hound told him what he thought.

"I think you're in. And I think if you walk away from this girl, you'll regret it for the rest of your life. And I think I'm here to tell you that because you need another voice sayin' something you already know."

"That's what I think too," Jagger admitted.

Hound nodded, and again he did it only once.

"Then I'll look forward to havin' her over to dinner and celebrating with your mom that she can finally stop worrying about you because she's feelin' you shoulda been done sowin' those oats about five years ago."

Jagger grinned at him.

His mother had never been at one with the way Jag tackled life, considering he'd always been about wresting as much of it as he could for his own.

Dutch was the quiet, responsible one.

Jag was…

Not.

Hound reached out and caught Jag by the neck, gave him a squeeze, a shove, then let him go.

And Jagger felt better.

"So, what's her name?" Hound asked.

"Archie."

Hound looked him right in the eye.

Then he burst out laughing.

He settled back into the bar, his fingers cradling his brew, and he was shaking his head.

"Archie and Georgie. Fuck," Hound said.

Jag hadn't thought of that, both him and Dutch finding girls with boys' names.

He grinned, leaned back into the bar himself, and replied, "She doesn't have red hair and freckles, and I seriously doubt her best friend's name is Jughead, but I think she might have a bit of tomboy in her."

"Well, son," Hound picked up his beer and tipped it toward Jag, "you're about to find out."

Jag grabbed his beer and tapped necks with Hound.

And he was grinning again.

Because Hound was right.

He was.

Chapter Three

Jagger

The next day, Jagger went out for a morning run, made sure to take his time stretching, then he had shit to do at the garage at Ride, the business Chaos ran that was half a big auto-supply store and half a garage that built custom cars and bikes.

Jagger was a certified mechanic, both cars and bikes, and he wasn't skilled with design, but his Chaos brother Joker was (like, award-winning, get-magazine-articles-written-about-you and have-TV-producers-come-to-you-to-do-reality-shows skilled).

And they worked well together.

On the build they were doing, Joke needed Jagger that day, and with what had to get done, Jag couldn't cut out until mid-afternoon.

And he couldn't go straight to Archie after six hours at the garage without going home and having a shower first.

So he couldn't get to S.I.L. on the Hill until late afternoon.

He was pissed at the delay.

Now that he knew where she was, and his decision had been made, he wanted to see Archie, talk to her, get some shit sorted, learn other shit and make it clear he was done dicking around, and whatever it was that connected them, they were going to explore.

But when he walked through the door to her shop, which was right on Colfax in the Capital Hill area, he learned his timing couldn't have been better.

There was stuff all over the floor, the area close to the door and in front of the cash register, was a disaster, and Archie was standing between two kids who had their backs to Jagger, and Mal, who was on her other side, was facing Jag.

Her arms were up like the referee holding two opponents from each other in a ring.

Jag had a feeling he was about to meet the Harris brothers.

And with one look at the expression on Mal's face—and the kid was openly freaked and upset—he knew how he was gonna play it.

He didn't delay doing that.

"*What the fuck is going on here!*" he barked.

Archie's attention shot to him, Mal jumped a foot, and the two little shits he knew were there for no reason but to cause trouble, whirled around on him.

He took them in.

Bullies.

Twins.

Twin fucking bullies.

Jesus.

They were Mal's age. One needed to lay off full-sugar Coke and the other was skinny and weaselly.

But even if their bodies couldn't be more different, they were the same height, had the same face, and the same beady eyes.

That said, only one pair of those eyes was mean.

However, the belligerence shifted when they got a load of a pissed-off biker standing between them and the door.

"You two do this?" he asked them, stabbing a finger at the mess.

The skinny one's stance adjusted like he was going to make a break for it, so Jagger turned, walked the three strides that took him back to the door and flipped the lock.

He retraced his steps and announced, "Not gonna ask again." He threw out a hand in a repeat of indicating the mess all over the floor. "You do this?"

No one said anything.

He looked to Archie. "Babe, these two fucks do this to your store?"

"Jagger, I've got this," Archie replied.

But the Harris twins didn't miss the "babe" part of what he said.

They were looking at each other with identical "oh fuck" expressions.

Jag crossed his arms on his chest, glanced between them and stated, "Yeah, motherfuckers, I'm in this mix, I do not like what I see, so what I see better change right fuckin' now. Clean this shit up."

The boys looked at each other again, then to Jag, and the skinny one, who Jag was tagging as the leader of their two-man crew, said, "You can't lock us in here."

"Choice one," Jag retorted, ignoring what the kid said. "You clean this shit up. Choice two, you leave and me and my brothers will find something you care about and we'll mess that up so you'll get how it feels. You got five seconds to make that choice. One…"

The skinny one spoke up again.

"No Chaos bro is gonna mess with a twelve-year-old."

"Two…"

"Let us out man."

"Three…"

"Fuck you! Let us out!"

"Four…"

The heavy one nudged the skinny one and said low, "Aaron."

"Shut up," Aaron hissed back.

"Five." Jag shook his head. "Wrong choice, boys," he finished, turned on his boot, went back to the door and unlocked it.

But since he stood in front of it with his arms crossed, when both boys raced to him, they had to stop and skim by him to get out.

"I hear any word my boy Mal here has trouble with you two fucks, the shit you just bought escalates, do you get me?" he said as they slid by.

The heavy one looked away.

Aaron held his gaze before he took off.

Yeah, Aaron was trouble.

Shit.

Jag turned his head to watch them race down the sidewalk.

When he turned it back, Archie was in his space.

"Let me guess, the Harris brothers?" he asked.

Making a noise he liked a lot, because it was frustrated, but it was cute, she dug into the crook of his elbow to grab his hand, forced him to uncross his arms and then started dragging him.

"Dude, that was bad...*ass*," Mal said as Archie pulled him abreast of Mal.

It was then, Jag saw others accumulating, all of them around the same age as Mal, boys and girls, different races, maybe a half dozen of them, all staring at him like an explosion happened in S.I.L. on the Hill and he'd formed like a god from the force of the blast.

"Help her out, bud, start pickin' this shit up, yeah?" Jagger asked.

"Yeah!" Mal cried, like that was his most fervent wish, then he jumped to it.

"You know him?" one of the other boys asked Mal.

"Sure," Mal replied casually.

Archie had no comment on any of this, mostly because she was fully involved in continuing to drag him.

Jagger let himself be dragged and he took the place in while he did.

It was not what he expected.

He expected a record store vibe with some kitschy shit thrown in, bargain basement-type décor that was cool because of some album cover posters tacked haphazardly to the walls with some vintage shit intermingled just to shake things up.

But mostly cool because Archie was cool, and it was hers.

It wasn't that.

Oh, it was cool.

But it was a lot more.

First, it was big. Way bigger than he expected.

Second, the floors were covered in large, overlapping rugs and the overall feel was of a massive living room that was filled with a ton of dope stuff.

Helping this feel was the fact that there was some lounge lizard jazz playing not discreetly over the sound system, and if someone walked up to him and handed him a chilled martini he wouldn't have been surprised.

There was a vinyl section with a sign over it that just had musical notes on it that hung cockeyed. Against the wall of that section was tailored shelving filled with old CDs.

Across from this, there was a section of freestanding shelves that had its own sign over it that was an opened book, and the section itself looked like a library with places to sit and read.

There were racks of clothes that surrounded a setup of a bedroom area (but was really a bed and a bunch of stuff for sale), one side with a big picture of Amelia Earhart over what had to be the women's section, the Dos Equis guy over the men's on the other side.

The rest of the place was filled with more stuff for sale, from furniture, glassware and lamps to gifts, candles, jewelry, kitchen stuff, and more.

Some of it was new.

Most of it was used.

Apparently, there was a lot of shit that Archie liked.

The way it was laid out was unique, appealing, and comfortable.

This was a store you hung out at and not only because there seemed to be a working, vintage soda fountain that had been either restored or resurrected against the side wall opposite to where they were going.

The place reminded him of Fortnum's Used Books, which obviously had a shit ton of books, not to mention sold vinyl. But it had a coffee counter at the front. And you didn't go to Fortnum's unless it was to hit the coffee counter and grab the best coffee in the city...or to hang around because it was the kind of place where you wanted to hang.

And Jag wanted to hang at S.I.L., walk around, check shit out, and maybe get a cherry Coke.

Archie wasn't gonna let that happen.

She was pulling him to a door that had no window, but there was a big square one in the wall beside it.

He was guessing it was her office.

He was pleased to see she didn't leave it open, she had to dig in her pants to get the key (no mini-skirt, movie T-shirt and Doc Martens today (fuck him running)).

Nope.

She had on bright yellow oversize pants that hung sexy on her hips and were rolled up in wide cuffs at the hems, a tiny, white, ribbed tank that fit her like a second skin, and a pair of vivid green, spike-heeled pumps that he just noticed and the sight of them he felt in his dick.

Which was what he was concentrating on when she unlocked her office, tugged him in, shut the door, then pushed him up against it and got close.

Okay.

Yeah.

He needed her to back off.

More accurately, his cock needed her to back off.

Pronto.

He didn't get the chance to say that.

She got there before he did.

"First, we have a rule here at S.I.L. We don't call the young 'uns 'fucks' *or* 'motherfuckers'."

She left that a beat, and when he didn't respond, she continued.

"And tied for that top spot on the don't side of our do's and don'ts list, we don't threaten them."

Even if all he could see was her, he could still feel the glimpse of her sexy shoes in his crotch, and he could smell her and she smelled like pepper and moonlight and flowers (the only way he could describe her scent was "luminous," and Jag was not a poetic person, but there it was).

He still started laughing.

"Jagger, I'm not being funny," she said into his laughter.

"Babe, you could have a neon sign coming from the ceiling pointing to them that said 'bullies' and those two would still scream that shit louder than neon. And the only way to handle a bully is to be a bigger bully."

"Yeah? Do you have years of juvenile counseling and study of adolescents under your belt to back that wisdom?"

"No, but I was a kid once." Then, out of curiosity, he asked, "Do you?"

"Jagger," she snapped.

And even pissed, he serious as fuck liked the sound of his name coming from her mouth.

So he said, super low, "Baby, I know we are nowhere near here, but I really dig what you're wearing and you smell great, so do a man a solid, and take a couple steps back."

Her eyelids straight-up fluttered in a sexy version of surprise and she took a gigantic step back.

Now he could see the whole package, which didn't help, but he couldn't smell moonlight and her lips weren't a duck of his head away anymore, so that was good.

For more than one reason, he moved to the window, and looked out of it.

There was stuff in the way, but he saw all the kids were cleaning up the mess, and it looked like some staffers were helping them.

The cash registers—and there were two, one on either side of the front door—were up high, with a view to the whole of the space.

And from what he could tell, there was ice cream at the soda fountain.

He still wanted a cherry Coke.

"You got real cherry Coke at that fountain?" he asked the window.

"Jagger," she called.

He turned to her.

She was leaning a hip against a messy desk, her hair was piled on top of her head, a lot of long tendrils floating down, some of them she'd braided, and yeah.

He should have continued looking out the window.

"I was handling that," she said.

"Yeah?" he asked. "How? Mal looked like he was about to piss his pants, the only thing stopping him was how upset he was that your store was fucked up."

She pressed her lips tight together.

Nope.

She didn't miss that Mal was messed up about whatever happened out there.

"Why do you have a boatload of kids hanging out at your store?" he asked. "And don't tell me they're customers."

He turned his head to look out and watched how the kids were moving while they helped clean up.

This was their space.

He returned his attention to Archie. "They're here a lot."

"They're group."

"What's group?"

She pushed away from her desk and started, "Jag—"

He turned fully to her, lifted a hand, dropped it, and cut her off, saying, "Okay, this is where we are."

She looked surprised.

Then she appeared to be settling in and she did this putting her hands on her hips.

She had thin, long, elegant fingers, she varnished her nails and shaped them into ovals. They were painted white. And he wanted to spend some time looking at the tats she had there and on her wrists, which were tiny, but they looked cool.

That would have to be later.

For now…

"I'm done dicking around—" he began.

"Well, it's good you are, but—"

"Listen to me, A, and don't interrupt," he ordered.

"This may have escaped you, J, but you're in my office, in my store, and you can't tell me how shit is gonna go down here. Or, really, anywhere."

"Okay," he crossed his arms and leaned a shoulder against her window, "you tell me. How's this gonna go down?"

"First, I'm not a big fan of being called babe."

"Noted."

He said it.

He didn't mean it.

She was totally *a* babe and he hoped she would soon be *his* babe.

So that was sticking.

She could find that out later.

But for now, they needed to move this along.

"Second, it actually doesn't matter if you call me babe or not. The window where we could have been something to each other has closed. I've moved on. You need to move on."

"What are you, twenty-four? Twenty-five?"

"Twenty-five, who cares?"

Whoa.

"You're only twenty-five and you made all of that?" He jerked his head to the window to indicate the store beyond.

"Jagger!" she snapped. "Focus."

He grinned. "Babe."

"Oh my God," she said quietly, her stare hinting at being a glare. "Are you really this annoying?"

"Just to say, you're only twenty-five, I'm twenty-seven, there are no windows that are closed for us. Unless you haven't stanned for a boy band. I think for any cool chick like you, at your age, your window is closed for that."

"You can be cute," she was still talking quietly, but her tone was completely different, "but you're still too late."

He was talking quietly too, when he asked, "Too late for what?"

"Me."

Shit.

"You married?" he asked.

She shook her head.

"Engaged?" he went on.

"Jagger—"

"Are you taken, Archie?"

She held his eyes.

Hers were black.

She had mixed blood, that was obvious, and everything she got out of however that fusion came about was perfection.

Including her deep-set eyes that dipped down at the inner corners.

But she didn't answer his question.

Which was an answer to his question.

So he kept going.

"I wanna know what's happening with your family. And I wanna know why you got a bunch of kids hanging at your store. And I wanna know about these Harris brothers, and how much trouble they're causing you, but mostly Mal. I also wanna take you out to dinner. I wanna see a picture of your mom because I've wondered what she looked like, considering how pretty you are, since the minute I set eyes on you. I want you to meet my dad who isn't my real dad and I wanna share a drink and a game of pool with you in my MC's compound. I wanna be your friend, Archie. I wanna take this where we should have taken it years ago. But to be clear, I also want more. I'm attracted to you. I wanna know how you taste and what you feel like and the noises you'll make when I turn you on. That's where I'm at right now and I want you to be there with me."

He took a breath and she didn't utter a word.

Which was good.

Because he wasn't done.

"So last, you gotta know, I refuse to accept that our window is closed. If you believe in God or fate or destiny or karma or whatever, I was there for you the day you needed me the most. And I may have fucked up along the way, but I'm standing right here telling you, unless shit goes south in a way neither of us can turn that tide, I'll always be there for you."

When he was done with that, she turned her head away.

It was a sharp movement, and the way it was, was concerning.

"Archie, baby," he called.

She turned back to him and said, "She was the best mom in the world, Jagger. She was…she was…I am *everything* I am today because of her and she died when I was fourteen. But boys with their moms, that's another thing. And her being gone fucked my brother up. *Fubar. Huge.* And Dad was okay with it for a while. And then he got fed up with it. And now shit is dark, Jagger. And she would hate that. She'd really fucking *hate it.* And I have no idea what to do about it."

For his part, he really fucking hated hearing the emotion tremble in her words and not be close to her, at least, holding her, better.

"Can I come to you?" he requested.

She visibly tensed.

Then she jerked her head up and down.

He went to her.

And carefully, he pulled her in his arms.

She didn't commit to it, just rested her hands on his waist.

Though she did twist her neck and put the side of her head to his chest.

He breathed her in and tucked her as close as he could without being gross and pervy in doing it.

She didn't say anything, and he didn't have anything to say.

He just kept her folded in his arms until he felt the time was right to say, "Choice placement of the word 'fubar,' babe. Well done."

Her fingers tensed into his flesh, but she didn't remove her hands as she tipped her head back to look up at him.

Yup.

Not too short.

Not too tall.

Just right.

Mm.

Though, it was good to see a light shining in her pretty eyes, and she wasn't pissed or hurt he'd made a joke.

"So, is this Jagger-style being there? You being a smartass?" she asked.

He faked looking insulted. "I wasn't being a smartass. That was totally choice placement of the word 'fubar.'"

Her body moved a little with her humor.

It felt too good, so he gave her a squeeze then stepped away from her.

She moved her head in a way it was both a cute tip and a sexy-flirty duck and asked, "You wanna catch dinner tonight?"

Right the fuck on.

There it was.

They were on the same page.

Goddamn *brilliant.*

"Fuck yeah," he said, then immediately had to say, "Ah, hell. No."

"Pardon?"

"I'm supposed to go over to my brother's tonight for dinner. He and his girlfriend are in this zone to get me to sort my shit with her sister, who's apparently cleaned up her act. She's also my ex, which is problematic to their goal of all of us stomaching each other for family shit since Dutch and Georgie are breaking the land-speed record for most committed relationship in the shortest period of time."

She looked both freaked and amused when she inquired, "Which one is Dutch and which one is Georgie?"

"Dutch is my brother. Georgie is his girl."

"I should have called that. And…your ex is her sister?"

"I had the sister first. Dutch is the copycat on that."

She was nodding at the same time still looking amused.

"Though, he got the better one," Jag continued.

"This definitely would make things uncomfortable, you gotta put up with the ex at family affairs."

"Yeah, especially when she fleeced me, repeatedly, for money that was supposed to be helping her out paying rent because she said her landlord kept jacking her around, when really she was snorting my money up her nose and buying three thousand dollar purses. Her sole purpose for being with me was being on the grift. She supposedly fell for me sometime through that, but that's not my problem. My problem is, I'm told she's found the road to redemption and I gotta sit at a table with a woman who pissed away thousands of dollars that I earned."

"Holy fuck, Jagger," she whispered, horrified, but also, he sensed, angry.

"Yeah, so I'd actually wanna say yes to dinner with you and then take you over to Dutch and Georgie's, because I want time with you, and it'd be cool they met you. Though, full disclosure, also because Carolyn would fucking hate that. But I wouldn't do that to you because that would not be fun for you and we should have time for ourselves before we get to shit like that."

"I hear you, but I'm game."

Jagger stared at her.

"Seriously," she went on, "if they've got enough food to feed me, I could totally play girlfriend to get in the face of some grifter who conned you out of your hard-earned cash."

"I didn't say my cash was hard-earned. I dig my job. It isn't like every day's a trip to Disneyland, but I love what I do."

"You still earned that cash and gave it to her to be a decent guy, not for her to use you and blow money you could be using to buy more motorcycle boots with."

He grinned down at her.

She grinned up at him.

And she asked, "So, we on?"

He stopped grinning and asked back, "Are you serious?"

She shrugged. "Why not?"

"Maybe I should take you out on a proper date before I take you to my brother's house for dinner."

"Why?"

He opened his mouth.

Closed it.

Opened it again.

But he said nothing.

Archie spoke. "In case you didn't get it, I'm over my snit of you being a big baby about our tiff a few years ago."

Uh...

Hang on a second.

"*Me* being a baby?" he asked.

"And we'll need to work on your apparent addiction to the word 'babe'—"

"Archie—"

"But I wanna know you too. I've been waiting a long time. So we're doing this. And I'll warn you, I'm not conventional."

He was getting that.

"I'm not either," he pointed out the obvious.

"So who cares if our first date is at your brother's?"

"With his woman and my ex," he reminded her.

"With his woman and your ex."

It was then, Jagger got serious.

Very.

"Honey, that might be a lot and you gotta know you're ready for it."

"Jagger, I wouldn't tell you I'm good to go if I wasn't good to go. Something to know about me, I don't bullshit. I don't lie. I don't play games. I don't have time for any of that. I became a mom and a wife when I was fourteen. It sucked but I learned a lot. And that's part of what I learned."

There was a lot to unpack there, but now was not when they should get into it.

Now was for him to say, "We've waited a long time to be here, and I'd like our first date to be something special."

The area around her mouth got soft, which brought his attention to it, and how gorgeous it was, and she used it to say, "So he can be sweet."

He tore his focus from her mouth and said, "I'm a lot of things."

Another light hit her eyes as she started, "If you don't want me to go—"

He cut her off, fast. "I do."

"I have a feeling, whatever happens, dinner at your brother's might not be special, but it'll be memorable."

He couldn't argue that.

"Come pick me up before. We can talk on the way. And we can talk on the way home. That'll be our special," she offered.

"Right, I'll need your address," he told her.

She pointed up.

He looked up.

Then he looked at her. "You live over your shop?"

She nodded. "I semi, kinda own the building."

"What's the 'semi, kinda' part of that?"

"My mom's folks owned it. When they passed, they left it to us. So my brother owns half."

He wasn't loving the look on her face.

"I see this is a story," he noted.

"Yeah," she muttered.

"You gotta get back to work?"

She nodded.

He needed to let her get to it.

"I'm not leaving here without your number," he stated.

"Phone trade."

He dug his out, engaged it, handed it to her, and took hers.

He entered his info, then took his phone back.

He called her immediately and her phone rang.

She smirked at him. "So you're a tester."

"Never did before."

"Right." She was unconvinced.

"Only had one girl put in the wrong digits. Her loss," Jagger shared.

"Right." Still unconvinced.

"But you're different and you know it, so quit fishing."

She stopped smirking, held his gaze, and whispered, "Right."

She knew what he was saying.

"I'm glad you could quit being a big baby and give us a shot," he teased.

"Jagger?"

"Right here," he noted.

"Be good or I'm not going to make our first date special by laying a *really* hot kiss on you when it's over," she warned.

Immediately, Jag held up three fingers.

Her gaze slid to his hand then to him.

"You ever a scout?" she asked.

"Hell no," he answered, lowering his hand.

She did another head tip that wasn't cute, it was just sexy, and drawled, "See, baby, I knew it. I like you more the more I get to know you."

"You got a problem with scouts?"

"Not at all. But I'm not a joiner. And I always had the feeling you weren't one either. And it's good to know I was right."

"I always had a feeling we had a lot in common, and not just what we know we got in common," he replied.

"Is dinner gonna be caj?" she asked.

Annnnnnnd she could be a dork, calling "casual," "caj."

"Georgie knows how to turn herself out, but it's at their place and neither of them are up themselves, so you do you and they'll be cool."

"Your ex, is she gonna be gunning for your attention?"

He shrugged but said, "Probably."

"Hmm…"

Through all this, she had a semi-flirty look on her face.

And then suddenly, she didn't have a flirty look on her face.

"Notwithstanding you cursing at and threatening children, I'm really glad you showed at my shop, Jagger."

And with the expression on her face, the tone of her voice, he knew she really meant that.

"I am too, honey," he replied.

And he really meant it too.

Chapter Four

The Sopranos

Jagger

Jag could have called it.

That "it" being that he got two competing responses to his text to Dutch and Georgie that he was bringing someone to dinner.

Georgie: *Awesome! Can't wait to meet her!*

Dutch: no text. He phoned.

Jagger considered letting it go to voicemail but decided if there was going to be any awkward with Dutch about Archie, he wanted it out before Archie was in the mix.

So he picked up.

"Yo," he greeted.

"C'mon, man, you cannot be that petty."

Oh shit.

Dutch was not a big brother who was constantly riding your ass.

But that didn't mean Dutch hadn't ridden Jagger's ass.

Even rare, Jagger fucking hated it.

"Wanna say that again?" Jag invited.

"Listen, Carolyn isn't my favorite person either, but she's trying and we both know it isn't cool you bring some rando chick in order to—"

Okay, there we go.

That was precisely why he hated it when Dutch started riding his ass.

Because he usually did it when he didn't know what he was talking about.

"She's not rando," Jag bit out.

"So you're seeing some woman who you've never mentioned to anyone and she's important enough to bring to a family dinner?"

"I met her the day her mother was put into the ground. It was a day I was visiting Dad's grave. And that day was my sixteenth birthday."

That shut Dutch up.

Jag kept talking.

"I haven't said anything because we haven't pulled our shit together. Now, we're pulling our shit together. She wanted to have dinner tonight. I told her I had plans, told her about Carolyn and she wanted to be there. So she's gonna be there."

There was stuff he left out and Dutch didn't miss it.

"You've been seeing someone for over ten years and I've never heard of her?"

"It's a long story," Jagger replied. "But bottom line for you is, this isn't about Carolyn. You want this not to be weird for Georgie. And you want what Georgie wants. Family sitting down together and breaking bread and you want it to go well for her. Now, the bottom line for me is, you and Georgie are going the distance and I'm eventually gonna end up with someone and Carolyn is gonna see that and she's gonna have to move on with her own life. If she's not ready to do that, then I should not have been invited to this dinner."

"I'm still not feeling the fact you've known some woman who clearly means something to you for ten years and I've never heard her name."

"How 'bout you let me have my shit, and I'll let you in on it when I'm ready, like you have your shit, and I hang tight and wait for you to let me in on it, if you're ever ready to let me in on it."

"When have I had shit that isn't yours?" Dutch demanded.

Was he for real?

"Uh...Carlyle. And you and Georgie investigating his dad's murder," Jag returned. "And, say, you and Georgie being hot and heavy *at all* and we only found out because we showed at your house as a surprise and she showed at your house and it was a surprise to us, but it absolutely was not to you."

"Fuck," Dutch muttered.

"Unh-hunh," Jag returned.

"That was going on days, not a decade, Jag," Dutch shot back.

Okay, he was done talking about this.

"Listen, there's something between me and Archie and there's something Archie is dealing with and something I'm dealing with and it's ours. Just lay off. And be cool with her when she comes over. Or if you can't be cool with her, and me, tell me now and we just won't come over."

"What are you dealing with?"

Fuck, fuck, *fuck*.

"Did you not hear me when I was talking about shit that was mine and I'll let you in on it when I'm ready?"

Dutch went silent again.

"So, Archie and me good to come over tonight, or not?" Jag pushed.

It took a second before Dutch spoke again.

"I'm always there for you, man, you know that, don't you?"

Jag felt that in his throat.

So much, something he was not allowing himself to lock onto, he locked onto.

He *was* dealing with some shit.

Some major shit.

And Archie triggered it.

"I know," he said to Dutch.

But that was all he could say.

For now.

"You're always welcome, Jag. Look forward to meeting Archie. And it'll be cool," Dutch assured.

"Thanks, brother."

"See you in a while," Dutch said.

"Yeah. Later."

"Later."

They disconnected and Jagger took in a big breath, because he didn't know what was up with him, he didn't know if he wanted to know what was up with him.

But he had a feeling whatever it was, it was about to come out.

* * * *

Before he left her at her shop, Archie told him that the way to her place was the door to the side of the store.

So when he showed at six thirty, he went there.

There was a call box with four buttons, and Jag guessed the one that had a picture of Grace Jones next to it was Archie's.

In other words, he was grinning when he hit the button.

There was a speaker on top of the call unit, and through it came Archie's voice.

"I'm door number two, brother."

And then the door buzzed.

He opened it and it was heavy, no window, steel enforced, which was good, considering it was on Colfax.

He went in and was in the outer vestibule that was cut off from the inner by a code-lock door.

He saw color-block floors in big squares of white, black, gray and yellow, and the mailboxes were there, built into the wall. Four across, tall, but narrow with a large USPS lockbox underneath for the postman to lock bigger packages.

His phone buzzed with a text that was from Archie.

9768, it said.

The code for the inner vestibule door.

He punched it in, the lock clicked, and he moved beyond the second secure area, seeing more color-block flooring, an orange tub with some umbrellas sticking out of it, and under the stairs was caged storage that had a couple of bikes locked behind it.

The walls were white, as were the stairs. The treads black. So were the doors.

And there was an all-weather mat that said *Hola* on his side, and upside down on top of that (so if he was coming from the other direction), it read *Sayonara*.

The area was clean. It was nice. It was stylin'.

It was Archie.

He jogged up the steps and found himself in a hall that led down the middle of the building.

Her door was to the back of the building, on the left.

He barely knocked before it was opened.

And then he was knocked out.

Archie had on a Chinese embroidered, pink miniskirt and a creamy blouse that had a high neck and ruffles down the front, no sleeves. There was a hidden slit coming down from the throat that he knew, with movement, would hint at the goodness underneath. Rounding this out were her vibrant green pumps.

Her makeup was dark and smoky around her eyes, just the top of her hair was pulled back in a spiky mess at the back of her head.

And she smelled like Archie.

He'd changed into a dark blue button down and nicer jeans.

And before he could tell her how gorgeous she was, her fist was in his shirt, she'd hauled him in, slammed the door, lifted her other hand, caught him by the back of his head, and pulled his mouth down to hers.

Her lips were soft and cushiony, but he didn't get to enjoy them long before her tongue spiked into his mouth and took all of his attention.

Fucking *fuck*.

She tasted as dark and smoky as her eyes and he liked that taste so much, he couldn't stop himself from rotating her, shoving up against her at the door, going for her ass with one hand and bunching her hair against the back of her head in the other to give himself something while he let her have her way with his mouth.

She broke their kiss by sliding her tongue out and nipping his lower lip with her teeth, so he lifted his head and stared up close into her gorgeous eyes.

"Hey," she said.

The word was kinda breathy, but mostly it was just cool, confident and Archie.

"Hey," he replied.

"So I decided I didn't wanna sit down with your ex for dinner without knowing what you taste like," she shared. "Hope that's cool."

"You wanna memorize it?" he offered. "'Cause, if you do, I'm totally down with that."

She grinned at him.

Then she said, "You still got a handful of my ass, boyfriend."

He started to slide his hand up at the same time apologize.

She stopped him by saying, "Just making an observation, no need to react."

Jag chuckled, but in the middle of it, he suddenly stopped because what he said next was serious.

"You look gorgeous, Archie."

Her fingers in his shirt went up to brush along his jaw, and she whispered, "Thanks."

"But even if the world deserves to see you in that getup, I gotta admit, I got no motivation to go to dinner now."

She smiled and shared, "No pressure, but my fourteen-year-old self, and fifteen, not to mention sixteen, seventeen, you get the picture, up until just now fantasized a lot about what it'd be like to kiss you."

He felt a lot, hearing those words.

But he didn't know what to say.

"Good those versions of me didn't know how good it actually is or I'd be even more pissed you were such a big baby about our falling out," she finished.

That made him move his hand from her ass to give her ribs a rebuking squeeze. "It wasn't me being a baby."

"So was."

"Totally wasn't."

"*Soooooo* was."

Jag wasn't doing this.

So he kissed her again.

Yeah, it wasn't a figment of his imagination.

She tasted *that good*.

He broke it that time, saying, "Okay, baby, even if I have zero motivation to go, this is my brother, so we gotta get going."

She nodded, pressed up against him in a way that wasn't meant to be sexy, just sweet, then she slid away.

He turned and watched her walk to a sofa that was in the middle of the room.

Then he took in the room.

Her place was mostly open loft space. Wood floors with some rugs. At the back, a bar with stools delineating the kitchen. Walls behind which he guessed housed a bath. Open racks that held her clothes. Windows at the back and side that had alley views, her outdoor space was a fire escape where she had a bunch of potted plants and flowers.

It was eclectic and groovy. Like her store. Like her skirt. Like the welcome mat that had Spanish and Japanese on it. He saw a hint of a lot everywhere. Moroccan. Native American. A big chandelier that looked made of gold leaves hovered in the center of the ceiling that gave a slap of Italian. Old West. Boho.

Asian. African.

It was cluttered but still felt roomy, schizophrenic but it made sense.

He dug every inch of it.

When he stopped inspecting it and looked at her, she was standing, holding a compact in front of her face, and putting on lipstick.

Seeing that—and feeling the velvet smack of the extreme femininity of it—he wanted to tackle her and fuck her on her tapestry-draped, emerald green velvet couch.

He didn't.

He asked, "What's Archie short for?"

"Nothing," she answered, rubbed her lips together, slapped the compact closed, wound the lipstick down, capped it, and bent to her couch to grab a bag made entirely of fuchsia pink fringe.

She shoved the stuff in and turned to him.

"Nothing?" he pressed. "Your birth certificate says 'Archie?'"

"It isn't funny, and it's funny." She started walking to him. "They made a deal. Mom got to name the first kid. And Dad got to name the second. My brother's name is Elijah. Dad always wanted a boy named Archie. Thing was, I came out a girl. Dad said it didn't matter. Archie was a cute name for a girl. Mom was having none of it. Sucks for Mom, but she was out of it from giving birth and falling in love with me after, so she was all about that, and he hijacked the birth certificate. Named me Archie."

She stopped in front of him still talking, but now she raised her hands at her sides, the fringe of her bag falling over the one that held it.

"So, I'm Archie." She dropped her arms. "Mom was livid at first. Then it got to be a joke, her giving him shit about it. But she admitted to me, she wanted him to have what he wanted. So once she calmed down, she was glad he got what he wanted, even if she wanted to name me Emilia."

"You are so totally not an Emilia."

Her expression was amused, but also nostalgic, and not the good kind.

"I like that I'm what he wanted, but also I'm her giving that to him. I remember that happening a lot, both ways, when she was with us."

"Yeah," he said softly.

She tipped her head to the side in that curious, flirty way he liked a fuckuva lot.

"Jagger? And I'll just add for sake of time, Dutch?"

"My dad was a biker. My mom was and still is a biker babe."

When he stopped speaking, she laughed, low and sultry, "I guess that's enough said." Her focus on him changed when she went on, "Though, I knew he was a biker. And not just because you're walking in his footsteps. I go to his tombstone almost every time I visit Mom. And the epitaph there made it pretty clear."

And again, he got that feeling in his throat and it was such a bitch, he couldn't hold her gaze and fight it, so he turned his face away.

She put her hand on his chest and called, "Jagger?"

He cleared his throat, swallowed, and looked back to her.

"I bet he likes that."

This head tip was not flirty.

It was concerned.

"You okay?"

He nodded and said, "We should go."

"All right, boyfriend," she murmured.

He didn't know what this "boyfriend" business was about when they'd had two kisses and zero dates.

He just knew he liked it.

He took her hand, they paused outside her door so she could make sure it locked, and he noticed what he didn't notice on the way up, such was his intent to get to her. The color-block flooring was up here too, but the tiles were smaller, and instead of the contrast color of yellow, it was orange.

There was also a lot of light from kickass sconces in the walls and two sunlights that were throwing late summer sun.

"Seems you're a good landlord," he noted, still holding her hand as he led her to the stairs.

"Place was a *just-a-hint* shy of a slum. Not purposefully. My grandparents just got old and lost track of it. When we got it, we took it in hand. Dad owns a security company. Because of that, he knows a lot of contractors. We got some castoffs, overages, stuff that was dinged and dented. He called in some favors, owed some more. Got the common places cleaned up and secured, new kitchens and baths in the units."

They were shoving through the inner front door when he noted, "Better to charge more rent, I suppose."

"Didn't raise the rent."

That caught his attention and he stopped and looked down at her before he pushed through the outer door.

"It wasn't about regentrification," she told him. "It was about safety and pride. This is a cool, old building. There's history here. The tenants who lived here then, live here now, save one, in the unit I have. A couple of musicians. An older lady who's been a schoolteacher for decades, she's also an artist. This is their home. I didn't want to take away their home. I just wanted to take care of them."

"That's cool, Archie."

She grinned. "I know, Jagger."

He squeezed her hand.

Then he pushed out and led her to his truck.

"Bummed you're not on your bike," she said when she saw it.

"You're in a skirt," he pointed out.

"So?" she asked.

Yeah, this girl, not conventional.

He beeped the locks, got her in, strolled around the grill and angled in himself.

He was about to start her up when Archie wrapped her fingers around his wrist.

He turned her way.

"I need to know something, and I need to share something. I'll go first. Fast. Band-Aid. Then you go. Same way. Then we're done. For now. Okay?"

He had no idea what she was talking about.

He still said, "Okay."

"Car wreck."

That was when he knew.

"Murdered."

She made a noise that was little, but came from deep, and he felt it through every cell of his body.

"I'm sorry," she whispered.

"Me too," he replied.

They sat there, staring at each other in the cab of his truck, her fingers still wrapped around his wrist.

They tightened before she him let go.

He started up the truck and pulled out of his spot.

"We have parking in the back," she shared. "It's parallel, against the building, but it goes along the entirety of it and there are six spots, so two guest spots. Though one of my tenants doesn't have a car, he bikes everywhere. In other words, usually, there are three spots for the taking. I have signs. Own that space. So I totally tow if anyone takes them that shouldn't be there. If there's a spot open, you can park back there from now on."

From now on.

"Gotcha," he said.

He drove.

She rode.

They said nothing.

He had a million things to say and a million more to ask.

All he could think was *car wreck.*

One day her mom was there.

The next, she wasn't.

No warning.

No prolonged illness.

No time to come to terms or bargain with God or sulk about bad luck.

There.

And gone.

Her laughter took him out of his thoughts.

"What's funny?" he asked.

"Well, from the minute you left my store today, I had a thousand and one topics of conversation to introduce with you. The ride to your brother's house would have to be three hours to get to it all. And now I can't think where to start."

He started laughing too, through it saying, "That was what I was just thinking."

"Okay, in brief. Red. Cream, no sugar. *Cat's Eye. Insecure.* Tie *Cinema Paradiso* and *Rear Window.* I got the idea for my shop from one in Boston where I went to school at Boston College, I just had more space to work with and made it bigger. I opened two years ago. Yes, my dad thought I was crazy and worried like hell. He's remarried. Has been for nearly seven years. I dig her. My brother detests her. Okay, now, you go."

"Uh..." he said, smiling at the windshield.

"Favorite color, coffee," she prompted.

"Red too. One sugar, no cream. *Fight Club.* And..."

"Book, TV."

"*The Stand* for books. I don't watch much TV. I'm a mechanic, both car and bike and work at the garage at Ride on custom builds. My mom's remarried to the guy who helped raise us. He's a Chaos brother too. There was shit around that and it took them a while to get it together. But now they're together and I got a little brother who is the absolute best. His name is Wilder."

"I don't have any half siblings, though I have two step-sisters."

"Right."

"I dig them too. Elijah thinks they suck and treats them like that. This is the biggest part of how he's an asshole, because he does that and doesn't hesitate to hand that to our stepmom too."

"Shit."

"Unh-hunh."

He reached out a hand.

She took it.

"We can get into that later, okay?" he said.

"Yeah." Then, "You don't watch much TV?"

"When the weather's nice, I like to be on my bike. It was my dad's. It's the only thing of his I have that's tangible, outside his blood. My stepdad is awesome, and my mom is happy, genuinely happy, for the first time since I can remember. So I dig being with them. As mentioned, my baby bro is the shit and he cracks me up. So I get time in with him too. Ditto my big brother. We're tight, always have been. He's my bottom-line ride or die. I have a lot of other brothers, and there is not a one of them who I don't enjoy his company. So there's that. I like to play pool. I like to get loose. I know my way around a dart board. If I get a wild hair, I follow it, even if it takes me to Montana. And if my ass is ever in front of a TV, it's usually to completely unplug and I have no clue what I'm watchin', and don't remember it when I'm done."

He paused.

Then he finished, "Though, I happened onto *The Sopranos* once and binged that motherfucker even if it took weeks. So I guess that would be my favorite, because it rocked."

She didn't say anything when he quit talking so he glanced her way to see her staring at him.

He looked back at the road and asked, "What?"

All of a sudden, she was in his space.

He could feel her nose brush his skin and her breath against his jaw and neck when she said, "That is the fucking coolest thing I've ever heard."

"Yeah?"

"Yeah."

"Do I need to pull over?"

"Maybe."

Her "maybe" was Jag's "no maybe about it."

He found his shot, a parking lot outside a Little Caesar's.

He pulled into a spot and barely got the truck in park and turned his head before they were making out.

In the middle of it, she stopped kissing him long enough to ask, "Are we gonna be late?"

"Yes."

"Do you care?"

"Fuck no."

He watched her eyes smile.

Then they started making out again.

And yeah.

They were totally late.

Chapter Five

It Just Is

Jagger

An hour and a half later, Jagger didn't know what to do.

He was leaning toward laughing his ass off.

Though, that was only because he couldn't drag Archie's ass out of there, take her to her pad, and make out with her with every intent of eventually making love to her.

And this was because she'd played him.

Major.

The thing was, she did not want to go to dinner that night at his brother's because they were sorting their shit, getting to know each other, she was unconventional and self-possessed and wanted to know him and maybe was a little curious about his brother.

Uh.

Nope.

She wanted to go to dinner that night to fuck with Carolyn.

He'd noticed when he'd shared what Carolyn did to him that Archie had seemed a little pissed.

And right then, he was making certain to tuck that away because her "little pissed" hid "totally pissed way the fuck off."

He didn't know if she was angry on behalf of the sisterhood that a woman would do the dirty on a guy and make them all look bad.

Or if she was pissed that Carolyn did that to Jagger.

He was guessing it was part the first.

But mostly it was the last.

He should have known with the skirt, the blouse, the fuck-me green pumps and showing a lot of leg, toned arms, hints of cleavage and lush, chic, assured style and beauty.

Though apparently, he didn't know her well enough.

But seeing her in action, he knew now that was totally OTT and in your face when everyone else there was in jeans, except Carolyn, who had on a tight-fitting tank dress that showed serious cleavage, and not to be a dick or anything, but it also showed no imagination.

Carolyn was dressed like she thought a biker would want her to dress.

Archie was dressed like Archie liked to dress, even if she had a point to make.

Carolyn was miserable.

Archie was calm and comfortable and deep in vengeance mode.

That night, Jagger had never been touched so much in such a casual, affectionate way that it came off just like that, instead of over-demonstrative or clingy.

She didn't stick her tongue in his ear or lay her hand on his leg near his crotch as an overt way to stake her claim.

She touched the pulse on his wrist.

She'd smile in his eyes and squeeze his knee.

She'd stand beside him while she was laughing and bump hips.

She'd fiddle with his fingers, pressing her thumb into the center of his palm, totally engrossed in this for about long moments, like his hand was the most fascinating thing in the world and she couldn't help getting lost in it, before she shook herself out of it and looked around apologetically.

She hit it off with Georgie right away, partly because Georgie had been to her shop and loved it, partly because Georgie was a journalist and Archie thought that was cool.

But mostly because Georgie and Archie were sisters of the same ilk.

They knew what they were about and were good in their own skin.

It was clear Dutch wanted to play the "You've Gotta Win Me Over" Big Brother, but in the face of Archie, not to mention Georgie bonding with her, that lasted fifteen minutes.

She was just interesting and interested. Complimentary without being effusive. Curious without prying.

But when they sat down to dinner, and she scooted her chair so close to Jagger's, their thighs were pressed together, and for part of the meal, simply for comfort, he had to drape his arm around her shoulders, he knew shit was real with her rubbing it in with Carolyn.

Hell, when he put his arm around her, she just tucked her body to him and ate and sipped wine and chatted like they were physically attached since birth and she was good with that.

Only a seriously cool chick could get away with that, making it seem as cool as she was.

And that was the way being with Archie was.

She was into him, she'd not made that a mystery.

Though, it was just her.

And it was her way of stating plainly to Carolyn that he'd scraped off the shit and come up smelling like roses.

Carolyn was helping Georgie and Dutch clear after their main, and they assured Archie they didn't need any more help after she'd offered, and that was when he took his shot.

"Babe," he called low.

She was in the tucked-close position.

This meant when she turned, she had her shoulder under his arm, her hand was on his thigh, and her face was close to his.

"You can cool it," he said quietly.

"Mm?" She pretended not to know what he was talking about.

"All you had to do was walk in, and you had her," he informed her.

"Had her?"

"Babe," he said on a chuckle.

His chuckle didn't last long.

Because her expression didn't change.

He stared at her.

Christ.

This wasn't about Carolyn.

She was being that way because she was that way.

And she was being that way with him because that was who he was to her.

Christ.

While he had these thoughts, she was examining his face.

So before he could react to what he'd just learned, she spoke.

"It goes without saying, no one fucks with you, Jagger, and no one fucks you over. And should it become necessary I communicate that information, I won't hesitate to do it. But I wasn't here then. That was the message you sent and you're still sending it. That's not on me to communicate."

Even though she seemed pretty laidback about that, there was an edge there he felt he needed to address.

"You should know, I'm not hurting money-wise, I never have. And I wasn't in deep with her emotionally. It wasn't cool what she did, but it also wasn't that big of a deal."

She nodded. "I hear you. But letting you in on the girl side of things... that dress is for you, Jagger. You said you're not going back there. I believe that. But you and I are exploring things, so straight up, a bitch needs to know where shit stands."

And there it was.

"Right then, so you know, when I thought you were Vengeance Archie, it was hot."

She smiled.

"Staking Her Claim Archie might be hotter," he continued. "I haven't decided. I'll be sure to let you know when I do."

She started laughing.

He cupped her jaw and bent his face to hers.

"Now that you made your point, and since I already made my point, I think we both need to cut her some slack. She's miserable."

"I noticed that, baby," she murmured. "But honest to God, I don't know how to make it better. It is what it is. Her bed, she's lying in it. But I'll try to come up with something."

Her eyes that close, her mouth that close…

Shit.

"Christ," he grunted. "I wanna make out with you, like, all the time."

"That isn't gonna help her be less miserable," she pointed out.

"No," he was grunting again.

"We gotta be good, boyfriend."

He just shook his head, grinning, but said, "Yeah."

She shifted away, but not too far away, and Dutch was at the table, grabbing the salad bowl.

"You sure I can't help?" Archie asked Dutch.

"There can be too many cooks in the kitchen, not too many to clean up, though," Dutch replied. But on a glance to the sisters and back to the table, he said, "Maybe give them some time, yeah?"

"For sure," Archie replied.

Dutch looked to Jag, to Archie, gave her a tight smile, then moved to the kitchen.

She turned to Jag. "Something there I'm missing?"

"He's pissed he didn't know about you."

"Until today, there wasn't a lot to know."

"Yeah, there was."

She conceded that point with a dip of her chin and then said, "Fair warning, the family stuff is probably gonna be stepped up a dozen notches. We get too deep before I take you to see him, Dad's gonna be pissed. He's mentioned you, like, five hundred times."

Say what?

"He has?"

She reached for her wine, nodding, took a sip, then slid her eyes to him and said, "Yep."

"How does he know who I am?"

"Your note."

"Oh, right," Jag muttered.

"He was…I was…" She set her glass back down. "The timing was perfect. I needed that. Elijah did too. Dad didn't know what to do. He was in it with us. Not down the road where he knew what to say. You knew what to say and that helped all of us. Even Dad. So, in the meantime, considering he's hated every guy I've dated, he would say things like, 'I don't see why you're with this schmuck. What about that Arby's guy?'"

"Great," Jagger sighed. "I'm 'Arby's Guy.'"

She grinned at him. "Hey, don't knock Arby's. And bee tee dub, that's Dad's favorite fast food joint. So you scored points you didn't know you were scoring."

He grinned at her, doing it thinking he hadn't smiled this much in…

Well, ever.

And he was a pretty happy guy.

"I fear the meal wasn't all that great if you guys are talking about Arby's," Georgie joked as she rejoined them at the table. "More wine?" she offered Archie, extending the bottle.

"Yes, please," Archie answered, extending her glass. "And we're talking about my dad, not Arby's," she corrected.

Dutch and Carolyn were also back, and it seemed they were going to sit and gab, instead of having dessert and then he and Archie could get gone.

Which sucked.

This wasn't comfortable, but it wasn't entirely uncomfortable.

He just wanted Archie to himself.

"And Dad semi-met Jagger outside an Arby's. We had a lot of fast food after Mom died," Archie carried on.

And with that, she got the acute attention of everyone at the table.

"She's buried, I don't know, twenty, thirty yards from your dad's grave." She said this to Dutch. "Jagger was hanging out with your dad during Mom's funeral. We caught each other's eyes and," she shrugged, "we got each other right away. Didn't know his name. Didn't know if I'd ever see him again. Still, with that, he was my person for the rest of my life, you know? It's just the way that shit works." Pause for a sip, then, "I'm just really freaking happy I saw him again. And the first time was at an Arby's."

Again, this was casual.

But it packed a massive punch.

It said to Dutch, *Don't worry, I got this and he means something to me.*

It said to Georgie, *We're on the same team.*

And it said to Carolyn, *Sorry, but he was meant to be mine.*

For Jagger, she'd just announced to two of the most important people in his life that he was her person.

So yeah.

A massive punch.

Awesome all around.

She returned her wineglass to the table.

When she sat back, Jagger tucked her tighter to his side.

Dutch cleared his throat.

Carolyn was twisting her wineglass back and forth by the stem.

It was Georgie, who had a flair with laying things out in an honest but thoughtful way, who stated, "That's one of the coolest things I've ever heard."

"I know, right?" Archie replied.

It was then, Carolyn rallied. "Sorry about your mom."

Archie looked her right in the eye and said from the heart, "Thanks, sister."

"I haven't been to your shop, I heard it was great, but I'm kinda, you know," her eyes darted to Jagger, then back to Archie, "on an epic money diet. But maybe the three of us girls could go out for coffee or something."

"Hell no."

That was Dutch.

And everyone looked at him.

He didn't hesitate to explain.

"You are not instigating a Black Brothers Gossip Club right under our fuckin' noses."

Georgie burst out laughing.

Archie laughed too, but low.

Carolyn finally got some of the Carolyn Jag liked back, grinned unrepentantly at Dutch, and said, "You can't stop us."

"Girl, that was not the response," Archie chided. "You just gave it all away. You should have said, 'This is not all about you,' when it would totally be all about them."

More woman laughter.

Dutch looked at Jagger. "You got anything to say?"

He did.

"I have nothing to hide."

"Do you have something to hide, darlin'?" Georgie asked her man.

Dutch made his point.

"If I did, it'd be only you I'd tell."

"Right," Georgie replied, giving the other women big eyes.

"Well, Archie's cool, and obviously Georgie and I are cool, so can we have your permission to get together and *not* talk about the Black Brothers?" Carolyn requested.

"Knock yourselves out," Dutch granted.

"Thank you, oh master, my master," Georgie teased.

"That's for later," Dutch returned.

Georgie burst out laughing again.

Archie leaned further into him even as she reached for her wine again.

He couldn't see her face, but he knew she wasn't laughing this time, so he gave her a squeeze.

She glanced up at him.

"Family," she said softly.

She didn't have this.

Not with her brother.

He gave her another squeeze and mouthed, "Later."

She nodded, looked away and took a sip of her wine.

* * * *

They were on her fire escape.

She had a bunch of pillows on the ground by the window to it that she tossed out so they could sit on them and lean against them.

It was late September, nights getting darker earlier, but regardless, it was late, dark, and they were outside, sitting and leaning.

Jagger against the building.

Archie, between his legs and against him.

She had his hand in hers and was fiddling with it, but her eyes were aimed through the railing, where you could see a sliver of the deep purple hues of the Rocky Mountains silhouetted against the night sky between some buildings.

She also had double stamps of approval.

Between then and now, Georgie had texted *I'm in love with her! I want her to be MY girlfriend!*

Dutch had texted *She's cool, brother.*

He didn't need the approval, but it was good to have.

Now, they were in a weird zone.

Not a bad weird, but still weird.

Before they went out, she'd got him a beer, made herself a vodka tonic, they settled in, and again they had a million things to say.

But neither of them was saying anything.

And it was…

Right.

Jag didn't know if he'd ever been like this with a woman. He was always up for tying one on, working toward getting it on, then getting it on.

In other words, having a good time one way or another.

If he'd ever had quiet time with a woman, it definitely wasn't on the first date.

Then again, he'd never taken a first date to his brother's for dinner.

He took a slug from his beer, set it aside, then gently pulled away from her fiddling and took control of her wrist.

Evidence was suggesting she hung out there a lot, because she had a lamp on the floor by the window that she'd switched on and set outside.

And with that light, he traced the tiny drops inked into her skin that fell from her shoulder, down her biceps and inner forearm to her wrist, where there was a slightly less tiny puddle with an extremely tiny splash coming up from it.

"Probably don't have to guess with that means," he murmured in her ear.

"No," she agreed.

He swept the pad of his thumb across the puddle of tears.

She turned her head and pressed her temple into his collarbone.

Jag went after her hand.

On the side middle joint of each finger, there were miniscule words, one for each finger, from index to pinkie: *Live, Love, Laugh, Rock*.

Fuck.

He was into this girl.

He ran his thumbnail under each like he was underlining them.

Jag then turned her arm, and on the outside he saw the diminutive but decorative arrows pointing every which way in what seemed like a random pattern.

When he touched one, she said, "I wanna go everywhere. I wanna do everything. I want to skateboard in Iceland like Walter Mitty. I want to spend the night in an elephant hide in Zambia. I want to do a wine and cheese tour of Paris. I want always to remember I shouldn't be going only in one direction. I need to head out in all of them."

"What directions have you gone?" he asked.

"This year's big one, I stayed in a Rajasthani tent in Portugal. Went to the beach, took surfing lessons, sucked at it, but it was fun. Mostly, I walked around the lake where the tent was, hiked in the wood there, and hung with the other people staying at the site or chilled outside my tent by myself and read."

"Hang on a second, you went alone to stay in a tent in Portugal?"

"Yeah," she said, not like it was an answer to his question, but like she was talking to herself. This would be explained when she finished, "Dad is gonna dig you."

She wasn't fifteen.

He had to chill.

Still.

She took over his hand, pressed her thumb in the center of his palm and remarked, "They rent Harleys pretty much everywhere, you know."

He had his other arm resting on her midriff, but when she said that, he moved it to wrap it around her upper chest and then used it to tuck her closer.

She pressed harder into his palm and said, "I want you to spend the night, but I don't wanna fuck. I just want you beside me. And I want to wake up next to you. Will you stay?"

"Fuck yes."

She curled her fingers around his hand and held on.

"What you said about me being your person—" he started.

She cut him off.

"It just is, Jagger, no pressure. Seriously. It just is and you can just let it be that. It's cool."

"No, it's that…I think you're my person too."

She didn't say anything.

"Being yours feels good. And I know it's fucked, because it doesn't make sense, but I think you being mine freaks me."

"I get that."

He was surprised, because he did not.

"You do?"

She adjusted, letting his hand go but wrapping the fingers of both of hers around his forearm at her chest and tipping her head way back to catch his eyes.

He helped by tucking his chin in to catch hers.

"Our disconnect, seeing you around, but you didn't come to me, and you were mine, you know? That hurt. It hurt a lot. And I didn't get it at first. I mean, I didn't even know you. Why did it hurt so much? But it did. And that freaked me too."

Fuck.

He slid his free hand up her cheekbone, gliding his fingers over her hair at the side of her head.

"Okay, maybe I was being a baby," he admitted.

"We both were," she replied. "This is big, and we know it. It makes it scary, and we understand that. You can't have this and lose it. You can't get it and then fuck it up. So our response was to back away from it at every opportunity."

"Yeah," he agreed, because they for sure did that.

He felt the big breath she took.

And then she said, "I'm glad you quit backing away."

"I'm sorry it took so long."

"You shouldn't apologize. I didn't take that step, you did. So, I'll amend. I'm glad you quit backing away and I'm glad you made me quit doing it too."

In response, he swept his thumb along her cheekbone.

"Do you want to go to Iceland?" she asked.

"Sure," he answered.

"Zambia?"

"Definitely."

She smiled up at him, twisted and fit herself to him so she was lying sideways on his chest, her arms around him, cheek to his shirt, cuddled in.

"It feels better, being freaked with you here," she whispered. "Rather than freaked and not knowing where you were and who you were with."

He again agreed, "Yeah," because that was the God's honest truth.

"I like your brother, he's protective of you and it's sweet."

"Mm-hmm."

"And Georgie is rad."

"She really is."

"And I don't know what Carolyn's gig was, but she's obviously pulling it together and she loves her sister, and cares enough about you to change where you guys are."

That had become apparent as the night wore on.

"I think we'll get there," he said.

"Yeah. That says a lot about you, you know, that you'd be willing to get past that for her and for your family."

He wasn't sure what to say about that except, "Well, it's family."

They got quiet again.

Archie broke it.

"I felt, like, locked."

Jag didn't know what that meant, so he asked, "Sorry, baby?"

"In my grief. Like, I was with Dad, and he was lost. And Elijah was a mess, but he was there physically. They were going through the same thing I was. But I was locked in my grief. I had all these people around me, but I felt totally alone. And I couldn't get out of that feeling, because I didn't think anyone would get it, where I was at. Not even Dad and Elijah."

He curved both arms around her and held her tight.

She continued.

"And then I was at the funeral. I looked across the cemetery and you were sitting there with your dad, and this opening started forming."

Fuck.

Fuck, fuck, fuck.

"And you came in," she went on.

"Honey," he murmured.

"And I wasn't alone in there anymore."

Jag turned his head and put his cheek to her hair.

"I haven't made up my mind about fate and destiny, what god there is, if there is one," she stated. "I just know that day, however it happened, you were put there for me. And that might not be true in someone else's reality. But it is in mine."

"It's true," he confirmed.

"Okay."

"I've never sat quiet and talked with a woman like this before," he told her.

"It's good to be quiet," she replied.

"Maybe for some. I don't think so. I live loud."

It was cautious when she said, "All right."

And he knew this was cautious because it seemed from what she was saying that Archie lived wide, not loud.

But Jagger felt that was a match.

"But for this, you and me," he carried on, "I think it's okay, it works for me, because we have time and it doesn't seem like…there's no race to…"

He couldn't figure out how to finish that.

"Get it all in before it all ends?" she suggested.

He closed his eyes.

She cuddled closer.

"We have time, Jagger," she assured.

His voice was thick when he said, "Yeah."

"That's the difference, you know, for us?"

"Uh…" he said, because he didn't know.

She tipped her head back and he lifted his.

"My arrows, your race. That's how we are. That's what we learned to be. They taught us the biggest lesson we'll probably ever learn, and it's a lesson they would never have wanted to teach. We now have no choice but to live like that. But with each other, we can have quiet. With each other, we can slow down. With each other, we can be right where we are. That's the difference. That's me for you and you for me. Do you feel that?"

Oh he felt it, all right.

He nodded.

"That's why I don't wanna fuck. Because I really *do* wanna fuck. But that's not us. It's not for now. We have time for that. We need to wait for that time. Yeah?"

He could not believe he was doing it, but he nodded again, and he meant it.

"We'll know when it's right," she said.

"Totally didn't agree with not making out with you, though," he pointed out.

She smiled up at him.

Then she slid up him.

He took her mouth.

It was slow and warm and wet, and it lasted a long time.

And he couldn't believe it was him who did it, but it was him who eventually ended it and said, "Ready for bed?"

"Yeah, baby."

They grabbed the drinks they didn't fully drink, the pillows and the lamp.

They took turns in the bathroom, her last, and he was in her bed, which was a mattress and box spring on the floor with some kind of carving on the wall at the head, a fitted sheet, no top sheet, and a ton of pillows and blankets. The nightstands were wooden trays on the ground on each side.

He was in his boxer briefs.

She came out in a tank and panties.

He'd turned out all the lights but the one on a tray by the bed.

She left it on when she slid into him, so he pulled her close, rolled into her, reached and switched it off.

You could hear the traffic on Colfax, city lights were coming in the windows, but Archie pulled the covers up over their heads and suddenly, they were alone in the world.

"Locked here, with me," she whispered.

With her words, it felt like his entire chest was banded iron tight.

But the second he had that feeling, it released.

So Jag tangled up with her, kissed her shoulder and settled in.

"Sleep, Archie."

"Okay, baby."

She shoved her face in his throat.

And as she drifted off to sleep, Jagger wondered.

He wondered if his dad laid awake with his mom pressed close and he thought, being just like that with her, that the world was completely right.

And he really hoped his dad had that.

Even just once.

He hoped his dad had that at least once.

Before he died.

Chapter Six

Since Eternity

Archie

The next morning, Jagger turned and sprawled over onto his back when Archie slid away from him in bed.

She sat on the side and took him in.

His messy, thick, overlong, dark hair.

The heavy stubble on his strong jaw.

Those damned lips that were perfect.

He had a smattering of hair on his chest and belly, it wasn't thick or long, though it got dense where it led into his boxers.

He was cut in a lean way.

He was really tall.

He had some tats on his arms, but the one that took her attention was over his heart.

It said *K.D.H.W.G.*

She had no idea what that meant, but she could guess "D" was Dutch, "W" was Wilder and "G" was Graham, his dad.

So the others: Mom and Stepdad.

Stepdad got better billing.

Real dad coming up the rear.

They'd be getting into that.

She sat at the side of the bed and she wanted to touch him, but she didn't.

If she did, she wouldn't stop.

She might not ever stop.

Archie was not afraid of that thought.

He gave her peace.

She was at one with anything, because of him.

She wanted to crawl into his lap like a little girl.

She wanted to ride his face like an Amazon.

She wanted to press against his back on his bike.

She wanted to stand by his side on the edge of the Grand Canyon and stare at forever.

She wanted to trade shots of raw spirit with him in Nepal like Marion in *Raiders of the Lost Ark.*

She wanted him to make her dad know she was okay and always would be so her father could stop worrying about her.

She wanted to sit on a mountain and watch the sun set then fuck and talk until they could turn the other way and watch the sun rise.

She wanted to bow before him and let him fuck her cunt like he owned it.

She wanted to mistress his hair and make him ask her permission if he ever wanted to cut it.

She wanted to watch him gnaw meat from a bone.

She wanted to bake his every next birthday cake.

She wanted to argue with him over which new couch to buy.

She wanted him to pull her over his thighs and spank her then shove her between them and fuck her face.

She wanted her symbol tatted into the palm of his hand, because that was where he had her.

She wanted his symbol in the palm of hers, right under her puddle of tears.

She wanted to get their tarot read together.

She wanted to listen to his heart with a stethoscope.

She wanted his cock up her ass.

She wanted to claim his.

She wanted him to paint her toenails.

She wanted every inch of him.

Every centimeter.

Every thought.

She wanted to give him every inch of her.

Every centimeter.

Every thought.

And none of this frightened her.

She felt nothing but peace.

Because he was hers.

And he had been since she was fourteen.

And she was his.

She knew this.

Because she had been since eternity.

And finally.

He was right there.

Chapter Seven

The Village

Jagger

It was safe to say, Jagger was not a morning person.

So after he spent the night at her place, Jag did not wake up with the dawn.

He woke when he woke, refreshed, and since he was at Archie's and the sun had no direct shot at getting into her pad, he had no idea what time it was.

But when he turned to the side, saw the bed was empty save him, and got up on an elbow to scan the space, he saw her in the kitchen wearing the white tank she went to bed in and a pair of wide-legged satin pants that were a rosy color.

She had a mug of coffee cradled in both hands and her hip against the counter.

"Why are you over there?" he groused.

She lifted her mug as answer.

"Get over here," he ordered.

She didn't move.

She said, "You're almost irresistible, watching you sleep in my bed."

"I'm not a fan of the 'almost' part of that," he told her.

She grinned into her mug before she took a sip.

Watching her do that, his cock, semi-morning-hard, got harder.

"Archie," he warned.

"Baby, I wanna suck your cock, like *bad*," she declared.

You could safely say his woman was honest and direct.

Annnnnnd…

Yup.

Now his cock was harder.

"I don't see a problem with that," he told her.

"I want candles and wine and good music and munchies on hand for energy, and time, lots and lots of time, and nothing at all edging in, just you and me, when I first take your dick in any part of me."

"Fuck," he muttered and dropped to his back, because he wanted that for her and for him too.

It was just difficult to want that for either of them when his dick wanted something else.

He stared at her ceiling, which was mostly beams and ductwork painted black, and took pains with trying to control what had quickly become a raging hard-on.

This endeavor was significantly hindered when he heard a thump, looked left and saw Archie bent over the tray by the bed.

She'd deposited two mugs of coffee there.

And then, no hesitation, and lithe as fuck, she put a knee to the bed and swung over him so she was straddling him.

Again, no hesitation, she settled on top, tits to chest, pussy to cock with too damned much in between.

"Are you trying to kill me?" he asked.

"Okay, this was a mistake because that feels nice," she told his mouth.

Her eyes had gone dazed, and, moving like she couldn't control it, she squirmed a little against his dick.

Since that burned through his balls and up his ass, he put his hands to her hips and called, "Archie."

She lifted her gaze, focused and said, "You don't snore."

"Neither do you."

"I thought you'd go little boy on me when you slept, your face all soft and vulnerable, but you didn't. When you sleep, you look like a badass who would call a couple of bullies motherfuckers even if they're only twelve."

"That's because I *am* a badass who would do that," he returned, then took over. "Let me guess, you're a morning person."

She shook her head, some of her hair brushing across his shoulders and chest.

Annnnnnnd...

Yeah.

Staying hard.

"Nope," she contradicted verbally. "I'm a whatever-the-day-brings person. I can be morning. I can be night. I can be lazy. I can be energetic. I just go with the flow. I have staff to open so the flow goes with me too."

"Good being boss," he noted.

"Let *me* guess, you're *not* a morning person."

Jag nodded. "Total night owl."

"Even being boss, I have to work today," she announced.

"I do too," he shared.

"So what's on for us? Work then you want me to cook for you? You cook for me? Or we go out to eat? Then movie? Hit a club? What?"

He slid his hands to the small of her back, letting one keep going up her spine, the other he wrapped around her waist, and teased, "I see you're already taking me for granted."

She copped to it immediately. "Absolutely, and going with that theme, you cook for me. I wanna see your space."

"It isn't as cool as your space," he warned her.

"I don't care."

"It also isn't as *clean* as your space."

"So you *can* be a boy, because a grown man looks after himself."

He started laughing as he said, "Life is too short to spend time cleaning. I do laundry and hate every second of it. And that's all I got in me to waste on that kind of shit."

"So you cook here."

He shook his head. "My baby wants to see my pad, I'll make sure shit is picked up and presentable and so you don't run screaming into the night when you see the bathroom."

She got a smug expression. "I see how deep you are for me."

"No, Archie, I'll send prospects over to clean my place. Though, just to say, I'm in deep, but another reason I don't waste time doing that shit is because of how much of it I had to do when I was prospect. So I earned bustin' the guys' chops and I won't hesitate to do that, especially when something as important is going to happen as you coming to my crib for dinner."

"Works either way."

It did, it was just that this way, without him scrubbing toilets, was better.

"There'll be clean sheets, sweetheart," he told her. "So come with whatever you need since you're spending the night."

Her eyes warmed.

He moved his hands to either side of her waist and gave her a squeeze.

"Now, slide off, I need coffee."

She slid off, and he pushed up to rest his shoulders on her mountain of pillows. But being Archie, she rolled from him in a way that she was up on a forearm in the bed beside him with her pelvis pressed to his hip and her leg thrown over his thigh.

He twisted at the waist and reached for the mug she'd been drinking from, and he did it back to fighting his rock-hard dick that hadn't gone soft because after last night, this morning and now her message couldn't be clearer.

He was owned.

However, he didn't fight the warmth that thought burned into his gut, because when that happened between people, it went both ways.

He handed her the mug, got his own and lay back against the pillows.

They both sipped and then he asked, "How worried do I have to be about these Harris brothers?"

She caught the side of her bottom lip with her teeth, and Jag was not a big fan of that.

So he muttered, "Terrific."

"Okay, they were in group. And you're right. They're bullies *and* motherfuckers. They got kicked out. But they don't need close proximity to rain havoc. The kids all go to school together so they have a captive audience there for whatever shit they want to pull."

"Backtrack," he demanded. "Explain group."

She sipped and said, "So, you know this 'hood is not in a high-income bracket."

He nodded.

She nodded back.

"Freya, the teacher that lives up front," she tipped her head toward the wall that separated her apartment from the next, "she teaches at their school, has lived in this area for years, knows everyone. We were out on the fire escape, having some wine when I first moved in. She shared about some of the issues people face. I had an idea, I told her my idea. She thought it was a great idea, so with her help, we did it."

"And?" he asked when she didn't follow through.

"Childcare isn't cheap. If it's a double-parent household, to get by with still mostly just basics, both parents have to work. If it's a single-parent household, things are a whole lot tighter and sometimes that parent has two jobs. Some of the kids were latchkey. Some of the parents were hanging on by their fingernails, some sliding off. The kids suffered. Parents did. Families..."

Was she saying...?

"So, I take the kids in that age group," she declared.

Yes.

She was saying that.

"Twelve, thirteen years old, one girl is fourteen," she went on. "They hang at the soda fountain. I have an area in the back for them to do their homework. They also have a TV back there. I give them stuff to do to help out around the store, and when they do, I throw some cash their way. Nothing huge, but enough they know their time and energy isn't taken for granted. And this surprised me, but they like that the best. Guess it shouldn't surprise me, though, because anyone likes to feel useful. They also like having cash in their pockets. I also think it makes them feel grown up. Sometimes I come up with fun shit they can do. Or my staff does. Like they play DJ and spin tunes for the shop, shit like that. Sometimes we do field trips."

She shrugged.

And then she kept talking.

"The Ethiopian restaurant up the way is run by a big family. They pay a couple of local teenagers to clean, bus, do dishes, but the kids also watch a few of the younger ones. They have some space above the restaurant, and since they have a big family, there are lots of people to keep an eye on them. Gina, my fourteen-year-old in group, sometimes she'll go down and stay with them if they're busy in the restaurant and there isn't anyone that can be around for the kids. Not for long, though. They usually have five or more kids, that's too much for Gina for too long. Those kids also sometimes come here if there are too many of them. And if there's overflow, or if one of the kids isn't feeling well, the dry cleaners across the way is run by a couple, and her mom lives with them. She's too old to work the machines, but she isn't too old to look after kids and she loves doing it."

She took another sip.

Jagger stared at her through that sip.

Then she kept going.

"Obviously, to be included, the kids have to behave. They have to do their homework and follow rules. That's how the Harris boys got kicked. It sucks, but I had to do it. They were messing up the others. Behavior problems sparking through all of them because the Harrises didn't have their shit together and wouldn't get it together. Then again, their parents are fucked up, don't care where their boys are or what they're doing. This is why I think Mal started acting up and he also had to go. He was stealing. There was backtalk. He was being ugly to the other kids. I worried that something was happening at school. Freya said she wasn't seeing it. I asked Mal, he wasn't talking about it. I asked the others, they don't snitch. I had no choice but to let him go. Now I know those boys are screwing with him."

She definitely knew that.

"So, I'm at a crossroads," she continued. "I'd lose his trust if I told his mom, and I need his trust. But his mom needs to know. I have him back now, and I can work on him. And I just have to see where that leads me."

"So, you're the village," he stated.

She tipped her head to the side in a silent, *What?*

"Any of the parents pay you guys for looking after their kids?"

"That's the point. They have mouths to feed, roofs to keep over heads, and that's hard enough. They needed to make decisions that no parent should make. And this lightens the load, sometimes just the worry, because most of the kids were looking out for themselves. But for the others, it lightens it financially and that's significant."

Oh, he got it.

"You got all these people to look after their own," he explained. "You're the village."

She was quiet a second.

Then she said, "Everything is monetized, even stuff that shouldn't be. At least not to the extent it is. Healthcare, childcare. And it's no skin off my nose to have those kids hang with me for a couple of hours between school and their parents being home. Occasionally, there's a headache. Martin brought the flu in once, everyone got it, and that was a drag. But when I moved here, I moved into a community. For the most part, folks looked after each other already, but it wasn't as organized. Now it's tighter. And it's appreciated. I can't say Mal's mom is a good friend of mine. I can say she saw me and Elijah fighting and she came over that night with a bottle and we hung out and bitched about family stuff. I needed that but didn't think to reach out to anyone to ask for it. So…"

She was done talking because she said no more.

He wanted to get into her fighting with Elijah.

But they both had days to get on with and they were already into something deep and he suspected that'd only take them deeper.

So Jag stuck with the subject.

"How do you not have problems with a bunch of middle schoolers?"

She surprisingly had a ready answer.

"Because kids know things. You can't protect them. They know. Every one of them knows they're either alone in their house and their mom and/or dad is worried about them the entire time. Or they feel like a drain because their folks have to pay someone to watch them and they don't have the means to do that without everyone feeling it. I can't say they're angels twenty-four seven. They're humans. They have moods. They can act like dicks. I think it was a shock, in the beginning, that they had someone who understood that and didn't get up in their shit about it. The road was bumpy starting out. Then respect formed. So mostly, now we all get on with it."

"You do know how fucking cool this is, right?"

Those pretty black eyes shifted to his shoulder.

"No. I know that I had a dad who was clueless, a brother who was pissed off at the world and I needed to step up when I should have been able to be a kid. I don't blame either of them. It was what it was. But did I want to be doing laundry and cooking food and vacuuming and running interference and making sure my big brother did his homework? No. I wished I had someone to step in and let me be a kid. So these kids get to be kids at school. And they get to be kids after school. And they know someone gives a shit. And then they get to go home and be part of a family. I didn't have that. No one stepped in for me. I didn't feel like a part of a family. I felt like I was the only thing holding my family together. It's not like I'm Mother Teresa. I'm just a good neighbor."

Oh yeah.

They had a lot to go over when they had more time.

"Right, well, whether you get it or not, it's fucking cool. And just saying, that's what my Club is about. We look out for each other. We do all right now, money is good, no one is hurting. But there were times, and when those times came, the brothers and their old ladies had each other's backs." He took a sip of his coffee and reiterated, "It *is* really cool, Archie. More people should think like you. No, not just think like you. Think like you and do something about it."

She sidestepped the compliment again, and said, "So the universe as we know it is what we think it to be, and things work out with us, I'm gonna be your 'old lady'?"

"Yup."

Her lips tipped up, her eyes went hooded and that was how she shared her approval of that before she sipped more coffee.

"Now, back to the subject, the Harris brothers," he prompted.

She gave a nod.

"Their parents suck. I'm no counselor, I don't have years under my belt dealing with kids, but I talked with Freya and I tried a number of different ways to get through to them, and nothing worked. I'm not going to go so far as say they're bad seeds. Especially Allan, he's mostly a good kid, but he sticks to Aaron like glue, to his detriment. But dealing with them is beyond my scope."

"I hear you," he said when she paused.

So she kept going.

"What I do think is, they give Mal shit. Mal's mom and dad have split. His dad is military, he's deployed a lot. His mom's going to school, online courses she does at night, she works during the day. His grandma is sick, and that puts a strain on things. A lot is going down with him and bullies, they scent blood. But I think it's more. Mal's parents may have split, but they're both in his life. They care. They're loving. He goes to visit his dad a lot when he's not overseas. The twins don't have that. Nothing near it. I think the twins deal with drugs, alcohol, their parents not keeping good company and just overall neglect."

"Jealousy."

"Yeah."

"And the scene yesterday?"

"I'm not a bully, I don't know, but I think they wanted to communicate that Mal isn't safe from them anywhere."

"And they picked you, because they aren't gonna fuck with him at home and rub up against his mom. She might get the school and cops involved. You're a soft target because they've already tested you and know you'll put up with a lot before you lower the hammer."

"Yeah. But that was before my future held me being some biker's old lady."

Jagger chuckled.

Archie smiled through her sip of coffee.

Jagger quit chuckling.

"They got the only pass they're gonna get, Archie," he warned. "You need to call the cops on them if they show and start trouble like they did yesterday."

She looked massively unhappy when she said, "I know."

"Or, you call me, and either I'll come, or if one of my brothers is closer, they can come and share with those boys that they had their time and now's the time to get their heads out of their asses because that time is up. They fuck with you or Mal again, there'll be consequences."

"How about I share that info with them, and only if things get out of hand or I get the vibe they're not receiving the message, I call badass biker backup?"

He would prefer to be on the way to her the second shit kicked up.

But he said, "That works."

"How hard was that?" she asked.

"Sorry?" he asked in return.

"To let the old lady claim her own shit."

He studied her through swallowing some coffee, wondering if he was that easily readable or if she was just that tuned to him.

Then he answered, "Hard."

She pushed up to a hand, leaned in and touched her mouth to his.

She didn't pull back very far when she asked, "What's for dinner, boyfriend?"

"Smashburgers."

Her brows went up.

It was then he realized Dutch and Georgie's baked ravioli that night was veggie. Inadvertently veggie, they were both meat eaters, but it was veggie.

"You eat meat?" he asked.

"Yep," she answered.

"So, smashburgers. And don't get excited. I cook, but I cook simple. My mom's a biker babe, but she's a mom. A mom with three sons. She took and continues to take care of her boys. We did not have at-home home economics time at Casa de Keely."

"Keely is your mom's name?"

"Yup."

"Pretty," she murmured.

"Hound cooks too, mostly breakfast."

"Hound?"

"My dad."

Something moved over her face.

She didn't comment on it.

Jag didn't push it.

He didn't want to ask his next, but he had to ask his next.

"What time is it?"

"It was closing in on seven-thirty when I brought you your coffee."

"Shit, I gotta get going, sweetheart."

She didn't look like she liked that, but she nodded.

He didn't like it either.

What he did do was take their coffee mugs and set them aside, then pull her in his arms, roll over her and make out with her hot and heavy.

Because they had to get on with their days.

But there was always time to make out.

Chapter Eight

Original Gangster

Jagger

Early that afternoon, Jagger was on his ass on the floor of bay two at the garage at Ride, his wrists to his cocked knees, and Joker was sitting beside him in the same position.

Both of them were staring at the vehicle that was right then currently kicking their ass.

It wasn't a build.

It was a restoration.

An old Ford Bronco that was totally worth the effort, seeing as it was a Bronco, and Joker's vision for it was epic.

But everywhere they turned, they found rust.

Which was a pain in the ass and it was making the budget skyrocket.

"Remind me not to do this again," Joker said.

"Dude," Jagger replied, because Joker said that a lot, but when he got something in his head, he didn't listen to anyone. So a long time ago, Jag had quit trying.

"Every time we take on a restoration, we get kicked in the ass," Joker told him something he knew.

"But, brother, it's a Bronco."

Joker sighed, knowing like Jagger did, at least this time, that made it worth it, just as a child called out, "Daddy!"

Both Joke and Jag looked to the mouth of the bay where they saw a little girl with black hair racing their way.

Joker and his wife Carissa's first.

Though, if you counted Carissa's boy from her previous marriage, which Joker did, their girl was their second.

She was called Clementine.

Coming up behind Clementine was Wyatt, Joker's first blooded boy, and trailing was Carissa, with their last, a baby girl, Raven, on her hip.

Since he wasn't there, Travis (their first) was probably with his father.

But even with this parade, Clementine was determined to take all her dad's attention, considering she little-girl tackled him.

Joker pretended it was a major hit, groaning and rocking deeper with the blow than was necessary.

Wyatt ignored both men, seeing as he was his father's son, and way more interested in the Bronco, so he went right to that.

Raven was all about her dad too, reaching out to him, and Carissa was all about her husband, heading straight to him.

But the shout that Jag would put money on all of them hearing even before they heard it came from the door to the office.

"Get that baby up here!" Tyra yelled.

Tyra, their former president Tack's wife, also the garage's office manager, was a baby monster. It was hilarious. And luckily, with all the brothers busy procreating, she got her fix regularly.

"Coming!" Carissa called.

But she stopped at her husband first, bending low, touching mouths, sharing smiles, shifting so that Joker could get a wet buss from Rave, then, with a smile and, "Hey, Jag," she took off toward the office.

Clementine was having none of this and declared just that before her mother was even out of eyesight.

With a scrunched-up, little-kid-pissed face, her hands to his shoulders, she stated, "I pin you, Daddy!"

"All right, baby," Joker muttered then fell to his back.

She squealed with triumph.

Jagger pulled out his phone and took a snap after Joker took control, wrapping his arms around his daughter and kissing her face all over.

This caused more squeals.

"Selfie, brah."

Hearing this, Jagger looked to his left and Wyatt was already posing with two fingers in front of him in V position.

Christ, the kid was barely four.

Totally Joke's kid, and not only due to the jet-black hair and steel-gray eyes and preoccupation with vehicles, but also the inherent cool factor.

Obediently, Jagger shifted, reached the arm with the phone long, did the V with his other hand, and took a selfie.

After this, Wyatt again lost interest in him and went back to the Bronco.

Yeah, *so* his dad.

After the cool, all about the cars.

By the time he did, Joker had sat up, Clementine was in his lap and her attention had turned.

To Jagger.

She launched herself at him and he did his best to pretend it was a valiant struggle, but she did a great job at pinning him.

"Got you!" she yelled in his face.

"You sure did, cuteness," he told her.

She didn't waste time exalting in victory.

Her head snapped to the side, she then shouted, "Hoppy!" jumped off Joker, making him grunt for real when one of her feet hit his gut, and she took off after their brother, Hop, who'd just walked in the garage.

"I see a future in GLOW for your girl," Jagger said as he did an ab curl back up to sitting.

"It's her new thing," Joker told him. "Last week, she wanted scissors to cut all her dolls' hair. The week before that, she made me sit on the couch and put gunk on my face because she saw her mom give herself a facial. This did not go great for her since I have a beard and that fucked with her vision of how comprehensive she wanted to get with my skin, but her mother put her foot down in a negatory when Clem demanded I shave it off. The week before that, she was karate chopping and kickboxing everything. We had to put a stop to that when she roundhouse kicked a table and broke a lamp. I saw it. It was a solid kick. I was impressed. Carrie was *not*."

Jag shook his head, chuckling low while watching as Clementine screamed in (fake) frustration, considering Hop hadn't proven as easy of a target as Joke and Jag were and now she was hanging upside down on Hopper's back.

"Never thought I'd say this, man," Joker continued, "but I hope we go back to the facial thing. She attacks everybody at random, she's an early riser, her brother and her parents are easy targets, and it's messing with her mother and my morning alone time."

Jagger kept chuckling.

"Carrie's pregnant again," Joker announced abruptly.

Jag stopped laughing and focused on him.

He was watching (and listening to more girlie shrieks) since Hopper had flipped Clem forward into his arms and begun tickling her.

"Say what?" Jag asked.

Joker turned to Jag. "Yep."

"How many are you two gonna have?"

"She wants this next one and one more."

"Dude, that's six kids."

Joker shrugged.

"That's also nuts," Jagger carried on.

Joke caught his eyes. "Right, Jag. When you find a woman, and she's your woman, and then you find out what she wants, I'll let you show me the way in denying her."

Jagger had a feeling he found that girl ten years ago, hooked up with the woman she became yesterday, and he was already in that place.

"Text me and Carrie those snaps, would you, brother?" Joker requested as he hauled himself off his ass, got to his feet and called to his son, "Yo, boy, you want a tour of the Bronco?"

"Yeah, Dad!" Wyatt cried.

Joker strolled to his kid.

Jagger texted him and Carissa the pictures.

Then he pulled up another name and put the snaps in a new text.

He sent it to Archie with the words *Some of my village.*

It took two minutes before he got a reply.

Rad. With about seventeen heart-eyes emojis.

About ten seconds after that came, *Is that selfie with your baby bro?*

He sent back, *No, my brother Joker's boy. Joker is in the other pic with his girl.*

To this, she returned, *Your brother is hot.*

The rest of them are dogs, he replied.

She sent a gif of some woman pursing her lips and rolling her eyes.

Which meant, when Jagger headed toward the Bronco, he was smiling.

* * * *

At six-thirty that night, his doorbell rang.

Jagger left his kitchen, went to his front door, opened it, saw Archie outside wearing a pair of faded olive jeans shorts and an oversized V-neck tee she'd knotted at the waist. The tee was white, a little see-through, and what he could see through it was a red bra. She also had on flat sandals with a bunch of braided straps around her feet and ankles.

Seriously, he dug how she dressed.

That was the only thought he had, outside he was pleased as fuck she was there, before he returned the favor she gave him the night before.

He hooked her at the waist, pulled her to his body, dropped his head and took her mouth.

Kissing her deep, he shuffled her in, shut the door, shuffled her around, and then moved them in further.

Only when she was pressing close and had a hand fisted in his hair, did he break the kiss.

"Hey," he greeted.

"Hey." She smiled.

Truth.

She was beautiful.

But when she smiled, she was all kinds of pretty.

That might seem a demotion in compliments.

But it was seriously not.

She let his hair go but only to rest her hand on the back of his neck, remained snug against him, and looked around.

And even if she was close, she still managed to collapse against him with her laughter.

He knew what was funny and grinned down at her while she did it.

When she was getting control, she drooped a shoulder and dropped a beat-up leather backpack to the floor.

She did some head turning to take more in before she slapped both hands on his shoulders and said, "Thank God, finally, you do something that's cute. I mean, could this *be* more of a bachelor pad?"

He looked around his space that was totally and unapologetically a bachelor pad.

He *was* a bachelor. And it was his time to have this kind of pad.

So that was what he made it and he went all in.

Even if it was a freestanding, his house was considered a condo since his complex had thirty identical ones built in three sections, one around a small park, another around an outdoor workout space and the last around a communal pool. His condo was in the workout space section.

The grounds and pool were maintained really well, this meaning the HOA was a bitch.

But it was totally worth it.

The front room of his crib was L-shaped with living room to the left, big open kitchen to the right, off the front of kitchen a dining area that led to a wall of windows with French doors that led outside to a decent-size, fenced-in backyard.

The bend of the L contained an office that also had French doors that led outside.

The hall led to a powder room and the master, with stairs that went up to the second floor that held two bedrooms that shared a bath.

The furniture in the living room was sectional, slouchy and comfortable.

The TV was ginormous.

There was a black pool table with gray felt in the dining room space.

His décor consisted of two neon signs, one a vintage *Stroh's* and the other was a martini glass with a woman in it, legs high and wide, red pumps on, blonde hair streaming over the side of the glass.

Added to this was his prized collection of boy-perv vintage posters, framed meticulously and mounted on the walls. These included the famous Farrah Fawcett in the red one-piece sitting on the blanket, the tennis player scratching her ass, Tyra Banks's yellow bikini *Sports Illustrated* cover, a black and white Jayne Mansfield and three Lottie Mac Corvette posters.

Considering it was a special occasion, he'd turned on the neon for Archie.

"Do you really need a beverage fridge by the pool table when the kitchen is right there?" she asked.

"Babe, I have a seventy-inch TV and I don't watch TV. Dudes buy shit with plugs regardless if they need shit with plugs. If you didn't know that, learn it now. It's likely never gonna stop."

She laughed softly then suddenly squinted at the wall. "Are those Lottie Macs signed?"

"I got an in with Lottie."

She looked up at him. "No shit?"

He shook his head. "No shit. She's a friend."

"Whoa," she murmured. "Cool."

"Have you seen her dance?"

She nodded. "Me and my crew go to Smithie's on occasion. The new revue is da bomb."

It really was.

Yeah.

He so fucking liked this girl.

"Want a drink?" he asked.

She nodded, he let her go, but only to take her hand and lead her to the kitchen.

He bent and nabbed her backpack on the way and tossed it to his couch.

Archie took off the little purse she had hanging cross-body to her hip and set it on one of the counters.

Jag then opened the door to his liquor cabinet.

Archie peered in and busted out laughing again.

And again, Jag grinned at her while she did it.

"Are you a mixologist?" she asked.

"No, I just never know what mood I'm gonna be in."

She surveyed the contents of the very stocked cabinet then told it, "I'm an amateur, but I dabble in the mixological arts." She looked up at him. "Prepared to be adventurous?"

"Always."

She gave him a look that was both hot and approving before her eyes skidded through the cut potatoes he had on the baking sheets and came back to him.

"I'm on drinks," she declared.

"Gotcha," he replied, taking her hint, moving to the baking sheets and grabbing the olive oil. "You hungry? Or you wanna wait?" he asked to be certain.

"Hungry," she answered.

"Cool, dinner in around twenty-five," he muttered, and got to it with the olive oil, salt and pepper on the oven fries.

He was sliding them in when she was sliding a glass next to the stove.

"I went with a pear base," she shared.

"Pointing out the obvious, since I had a can of juice, I dig pear," he told her and picked up his drink.

She held hers out.

He grinned at her and clinked.

He tasted it.

She'd gone with spiced rum, some lime, a ginger ale float.

"Nice," he said.

Her black eyes twinkled before she tipped her head to the side and stated, "Right, so, my girl Joany, who's a friend, but she's also on staff at S.I.L., got a load of you when you made your presence known at the store. And when I told her we were a thing, she told me I have some viewing to do."

The cocktail she made kicked ass.

But when she said that, all he could taste was bitter because he knew exactly what she was talking about.

She didn't miss it.

"Jagger?"

"Yeah," he cleared his throat, took another sip, tasted the pear, lime, ginger and spices again, and that was much better. Then he went on, "*Blood, Guts and Brotherhood.* Our president, Rush's old lady, Rebel is a film director. She did that documentary on my Club."

"Didn't you like it?"

"It was great."

"Then why, from when I mentioned it, to right now, do you look like you wanna throw up?"

He put his drink down, moved to her, and caught her at both sides of her neck.

Then he dipped his face close to hers.

"Can we eat smashburgers, drink, play pool, make out, take a trip to get ice cream before we're too fucked up to drive, then come home, drink more, play around more, and I call adding some groping and maybe, depending on how that goes, some fingering, and then pass out?" He paused before he finished, "And all that without any heavy?"

"We can avoid what you want to avoid," she agreed. "But before we do that, are you okay with me watching that film?"

"Yeah, I just don't want to see it again."

She took a second to consider that, using that second to study him closely, before she noted, "The tat on your back is carved in your dad's headstone. He was Chaos too, right?"

"Yeah, I'm a legacy."

She took another second to ponder this before she set her drink aside, fit herself to his front, and wrapped her arms around his middle.

"All right, Jagger. I'm good with shifting from the emotional to some fun and physical, if that's what you want. But just saying, I've been waiting years to know you. I'll wait for you, baby. Just, please don't make me wait too long."

He nodded.

Archie pushed up on her toes to kiss him.

He kissed her back.

Then he let her go to get out the hamburger because his girl was hungry.

* * * *

"This is not right. You go Heath. You go Butterfinger. You go Reese's Peanut Butter Cups. Or the ultimate," he lifted the cup in his hand, "Oreo. You *never* do a limited edition, *ever*," Jagger decreed.

"I see my guy is a Blizzard purist," Archie noted, before shoving more of her blasphemous Blizzard in her mouth.

"You gotta know I like you, considering I paid for that sacrilege you're eating," he told her.

Her eyes were twinkling again when she looked at him at the same time reminded him, "Jagger, it's a Wonder Woman Blizzard. It's an impossibility I'd say no to Wonder Woman, unless she sported pineapple or something fucked up like that."

Jag burst out laughing.

Archie leaned a shoulder into him where they were sitting side by side on the table part of a picnic table in front of a DQ, their feet on the seat.

Jagger spooned more soft serve with Oreos in his mouth.

"Your smashburgers were great," she remarked. "I'm impressed you know how to make oven fries. I stand behind this Blizzard choice. And I won't mind if you kick my ass in pool...*again*...when we get back, because it's awesome watching you work that table, you're so good at it. But the best part of the night was being on your bike with you."

Yeah.

That was the best part of the night.

Absolutely.

Now, was he gonna say it?

Yeah.

He was.

"That's my dad's bike."

Her tone had changed when she said, "You mentioned that."

"He never put a woman on the back of that bike, except my ma."

Archie said nothing.

"I've never had a woman on the back of that bike, Archie."

She kept her body mostly in the same position, but she moved just enough to push her forehead deep into the point of his shoulder.

She stayed that way through two of his spoonfuls of ice cream.

Then, without a word, she shifted, resting her head against his shoulder, and she resumed eating.

He was grateful she didn't dig, make a deal about it, just shared she got how huge that was and it meant something to her and then went back to her ice cream.

He was grateful, because it made it perfect.

* * * *

"You're high," she declared.

"I am not high. Everyone knows Disney World is better than Disneyland," he reiterated what he'd said five seconds before.

"Everyone does not," she retorted. "For instance, *I* don't know that. Disneyland is the OG Disney theme park. As such, it is and always will be the best."

He couldn't believe his ears.

"Did you just refer to Disneyland as OG?" he asked.

"Yes," she answered.

It was much later that night.

Archie was in panties and another tank.

She was also straddling his lap in his bed where he sat, legs stretched out, head and shoulders to the headboard, hands moving randomly on her hips and on her skin under the tank at her waist, ribs, sometimes belly, sometimes ass.

It wasn't about sex.

It was about touch.

The warmth of her skin, the smoothness.

It being hers.

And they were discussing some very important shit.

"Your argument is Disneyland is the original gangster of Disney theme parks?" he pushed.

"Dude, don't *even* try to argue that the OG isn't the best of everything."

"We don't have time for me to share the many examples of how faulty that logic is."

She disagreed with this, obviously, since she kept arguing it.

"Right, the Beatles are the OG boy band. Then came the Monkees. Now, 'Daydream Believer' is a kickass song. Just the title kills it. But The Monkees are no Beatles. And the Beatles are *Disneyland* whereas the Monkees are *Disney World*. Good fun, but not the best."

"Wrong," he stated. "In that analogy, The Beatles are OG and therefore Disneyland and *The Stones* are Disney World. Do I need to go on?"

"My point still stands," she declared outrageously.

He dug his fingers in her ribs and reminded her, "Woman, my name is Jagger."

"And?"

She was out of her mind.

"This is the thing," he announced. "If we go the distance and have kids, we'll go to Cali to take them to Disneyland, but only so we can go to the beach too, hit a Dodgers game, do all that LA shit because Disneyland is a one-day thing. But we're also taking them to Orlando to go to Disney World so we can do all things Disney and Epcot, which is also *Disney*. And we'll probably be there for three weeks because Disney in Florida is *not* a one-day thing. We could fuckin' *move* there and not take it all in."

"If slash when," she shot back.

"What?" he asked.

"You said 'if we go the distance and have kids.' But that isn't 'if.' It's 'if slash when' and the 'if' only stands when you're being ridiculous and it's annoying me. Like now."

And suddenly, Jagger couldn't give less fucks about how wrong she was about the Disney theme park debate.

"Are you that into me, baby?" he asked softly.

"Are you really asking me that question?" she asked back, not softly. "You've got a truck, Jag. It was you who put me on the back of your bike two hours ago. For me, I know what I like and I don't have any hangups going for it. But I wouldn't hassle with going to a date's brother's house for dinner and what that might communicate unless I intended to know that date and his brother really freaking well."

"Come here," he murmured, gripping her ribs and pulling her down to him.

She put a hand on his chest and stated, "You need to understand now, I'm Beatles, not Stones."

"I don't give a fuck." He gripped her tighter. "Come here."

"Though 'Gimme Shelter' might have the best lead-in of any rock song in history."

"Baby?"

"What?"

"Shut up and *come here*."

She stared in his face.

Then she slid her hand up his chest to his neck and back into his hair.

And she came there.

* * * *

It was morning, and like the day before, Archie had woken before him.

But unlike yesterday, she didn't wake up in the mood to watch him sleep.

She woke in a very different mood.

And she made it so Jagger woke up in that same mood.

Which was why they were now face to face, she had her leg thrown over his hip, and he had two fingers knuckles-deep in her wet, tight pussy.

She went for his dick.

"Nope, hands off," he growled, shifting his hips away.

"Baby," she moaned, her hips moving with his fingers.

"The first time I come for you, I come in you."

She whimpered.

"Ride those," he ordered, then to scatter her attention with the intent to take it off his cock, he took her mouth, thrust his tongue in, and encouraged her rhythm with the hand he had at her ass and the movements of his tongue.

She did as urged and kept doing it even when she broke their mouths and shoved her face in his neck.

"Clit?" he asked.

"Yeah," she gasped.

He adjusted his hand to get his thumb where it needed to be.

"Tip your head back, baby, I wanna watch your face," he told her.

She tilted her head.

Christ.

"Fuck, you're gorgeous," he murmured.

"Can I just hold your cock?" she asked.

"I'm primed, sweetheart. You touch me, I'll blow."

She moaned again, pressed into him, and her hips went overdrive.

"There you go," he murmured.

Her leg at his hip tensed and her pussy clutched his fingers.

"That's it, Archie," he whispered.

"*Jagger.*"

And he was right.

That was it.

Her eyes fluttered closed, her mouth drifted open, her tongue touched her lower lip, and the walls of her sex convulsed around his fingers as her clit contracted and released repeatedly against his thumb.

It looked great.

And it felt great.

When the tension caused by her orgasm ebbed from her body, he rolled to his back, pulling her on top, but keeping his hand between her legs, letting it glide through the wet, making her shiver and lift her knees to clamp on at his hips.

"Too much?" he asked quietly.

"No," she answered, snuggling the side of his neck with her face.

"You got plans Sunday?"

"No," she repeated.

"Early start. Take a ride. Somewhere, doesn't matter where. Vail. Breck. Estes Park. You pick. We'll have lunch. Come back. The rest of Sunday we fuck. I want you first in your bed. If you don't have time to get provisions, I'll drop them by when I pick you up for dinner Saturday. We're going out for steaks. There's something you want for our fuck-in Sunday, text it to me and I'll grab it when I go shopping. Cool?"

"Way cool."

He stopped his fingers gliding and cupped her.

She tipped her head and said against his jaw, "I don't mind you come in my mouth."

"If I can't hold out for that sweet pussy until Sunday, we can do that tonight. Or tomorrow. But we only got two days until Sunday. I can make it."

Or, at least, he hoped he could.

"Mm."

She took that as a challenge.

He grinned at his ceiling fan.

Keeping his hand in her panties, he slid it to her ass, asking, "What's today's plan?"

"My turn to cook tonight. At mine."

"Time?"

"Whenever you come over. Just hit S.I.L. We'll go up together."

"I'll text when I'm on my way."

She shifted like she was going to move away so he cupped her ass in both hands.

"Where you goin'?"

She lifted her head and looked down at him. "Sucks to say, but we gotta start our days, boyfriend."

"You don't leave my bed juicy."

Her eyebrows lifted before they lowered, her tongue came out again, the tip hit the lower, then the upper, before her teeth scored the bottom and she whispered, "What?"

"Panties off, climb on my face."

She blinked.

"I don't ask twice, Arch."

"Did you ask?"

"No."

Her eyelids lowered, she ducked to him and touched her lips to his.

Then his girl lost the panties and climbed on his face.

He was unsurprised she tasted fantastic.

He didn't have high hopes he could wait to blow for her until Sunday.

But still.

He was going to try.

* * * *

Mid-morning Jag texted her.

When it happens, how many?

How many what? she asked in reply.

Kids, he answered.

Jag was unsurprised again when her response was decisive and not delayed.

Two boys.

Two girls, he parried.

Whatever, she returned.

Yeah, he said.

She sent a single red heart emoji.

That was that.

And…

Yeah.

Chapter Nine

Effortless, Pure

Jagger

At a little after six that night, Jagger strolled into S.I.L.

The first thing he noticed was that Marley's "Stir It Up" was playing over the sound system.

And he approved.

The second was something he couldn't miss.

A petite Black woman with blonde dreads skidding to a halt sideways in front of him.

He stopped.

"Wassup?" she asked nonchalantly, even if her entrance was the opposite of that.

"Everything," he answered.

She smiled before she brazenly looked him up and down.

Inspection complete, she caught his eyes.

"I'm Joany."

"Jagger."

"I know. And seriously, it's all about Disney World, man."

Jagger busted out laughing.

He'd done that so hard, he'd closed his eyes doing it. And when he opened them again, Archie was there.

She did not come to him and give him a kiss or even say hey.

She stood next to Joany and stared at her, declaring, "You're supposed to take my back."

"Not when you're one hundred percent wrong," Joany retorted.

Archie didn't get into that.

She asked, "Was it necessary for you to race through the store to get to him first?"

Joany replied simply, "Yes."

"Why?" Archie demanded.

"I wanted an unadulterated view. If you were close, my verdict might be skewed by your loved-up vibes. I had to experience him undiluted. This, I have done. My takeaway, by the way, is he…is…*fine.*"

Archie looked to the ceiling.

As funny as this was, and as cool as it was to meet one of Archie's crew, Jag was done with it.

"We don't do this," Jagger said to Archie.

She turned her attention to him. "Do what?"

"I show and you don't come right to me and give me your mouth."

"Oh…my…God," Joany groaned. "He's a *bossy* hot biker. That's more than fine. So much more, I think I just came a little bit."

Fortunately, Jagger didn't have to respond to this since Archie walked to him, put both hands to his stomach and tipped her head back.

He dipped in and kissed her, a stroke of tongue, and that was it, seeing as she was at work and they had an audience.

"Yup, just came a little bit more," Joany declared when he lifted his head.

"I like her," Jag told Archie.

"That'll fade," Archie replied.

"Excuse me," a new voice entered the mix.

Archie moved to his side, Jag threw an arm around her shoulders, and they both saw that a customer had approached Joany.

"Do you work here?" she asked Joany.

Joany looked down at the nametag on her cropped tee.

The tee said *It's a beautiful day to leave me alone.*

Her nametag said, *Hi, my name is…*but didn't have a name, though it did have a black piece of that shiny tape you could punch letters in. There just weren't any letters.

And although the nametag declared her employment, even if it had no name, Jag read the two as Joany being someone you didn't approach to do anything but take your money at a cash register.

The customer didn't have this same bead.

She lifted up a lamp and asked, "Will you take ten dollars for this?"

"Oh shit," Archie mumbled.

But before Archie could do more, Joany reached out, nabbed the price tag on the lamp, inspected it, dropped it and asked back, "Does this look like a flea market?"

"All prices are as marked," Archie called out quickly. "Sorry, we don't barter."

"It doesn't hurt to ask," the woman said to Joany.

Joany opened her mouth.

"Joany," Archie warned.

Joany shut her mouth.

Archie relaxed.

Joany opened her mouth again and said, "Do you haggle when you're at Pottery Barn?"

"I don't shop at Pottery Barn. I only do vintage. It's about reusing. It's about the environment," the woman returned.

"Well, shit. Now I gotta like you," Joany replied.

"We can hold that lamp for you at checkout if you want to keep shopping," Archie offered.

"Cool," the woman said to Archie, then to Joany, "I want your shirt."

"Well, girl," Joany started, taking the lamp from her and extending it Archie's way without looking at her. "We happen to have these in stock. Allow me to lead the way."

Archie moved forward to grab the lamp.

Joany took off with the customer toward the clothing section.

Archie came back to Jagger.

"I would have texted, but you were already on your way. Fabe had a situation and he had to take off. I'm down an SA and I can't leave Joany alone to close. We lock the doors at seven. You cool to hang?"

"Absolutely," he replied.

She grinned at him and moved.

He followed, and they hit the checkout area that was to the left of the front door.

They walked up the two steps behind it and she set the lamp on the back counter.

He pulled his ass up on it.

She then rested her back against it close enough her body was touching his knee.

From their perch, they both studied the store.

"Any trouble with the twins?" he asked.

"No," she answered.

"Mal doing okay?"

"Far as I can tell."

"Otherwise good day?"

"Some days, I'm lucky I own the building. Other days, I rejoice I'll be able to upgrade my yurt when I go to Big Sur. Today's one of those own-the-building days."

"Sorry, baby," he muttered. Then, "Big Sur Yurt?"

"As noted, today was slow. I did some adventure research."

"Ah."

"You been to Big Sur?" she asked.

"No," he answered.

"Wanna go?"

"Will you be there?"

He looked down at her profile, watched her cheek move with her smile and she didn't push for a further response seeing as she already had the one she wanted.

"Is this before or after Iceland?" he asked.

"This is for whenever we feel like bagging on life for a few days."

"So, tomorrow."

She laughed.

Then she queried, "Your day?"

"Think we licked the rust on the Bronco. May be able to make a stab at getting that fucker running next week."

"Awesome."

"Yeah," he agreed. "You need me to go up and start dinner?"

She looked up at him. "Are you hungry?"

"Not overly, but if you are…?"

"I'm making sweet and sour shrimp. It's a shortcut recipe. It takes half an hour. Work for you?"

He nodded.

She turned back to the store.

He looked to his side, saw a turntable with a record spinning, then up on the wall above it, a Plexiglas shelf on which was the *Catch a Fire* album sleeve with the Zippo lighter on it.

"Can I pick the next album?" he requested.

She twisted her neck and tipped her head back again, and he saw her lips turned up.

"Sure."

"Can I have a cherry Coke?"

The lip curve turned into a big smile.

"Sure," she repeated.

Jag bent and kissed her before he hopped off the counter and headed to the album section.

* * * *

"So, there was a lot of baggage there," Archie was saying.

They were both sitting on stools at the bar to her kitchen, their dirty dishes shoved away, and there were a bunch of those old square photographs scattered in front of them.

"And it never left," she went on. "Mom was never tight with her grandparents. It wasn't just Grandma's white parents, it was also Granddad's Black ones. No one ever came to terms with them being together. Sign of the times, I guess. It still was fucked up."

He didn't have to agree to the indisputable.

Because it was totally fucked up.

Jag took in the handsome Black man and the pretty white woman—Archie's grandparents on her mother's side—and he saw hints of both in Archie.

But it was the more recent photos that were mingled with the rest where he saw a lot of his girl.

In the pictures of her mother.

"And making this weirder still, Granddad was not a big fan of Dad," she continued. "He saw Mom being with a white guy as her rejection of him as a Black man. Though, eventually, he got over it."

"They didn't kick in when your mom passed?" Jag asked.

She shrugged. "We were all rocked, obviously. But Mom was an only child. I remember thinking they seemed to age twenty years from the last time I saw them before she died, to the time after." She turned her head and looked at Jagger. "They never recovered. Neither of them were *old*-old when they died. After she was gone, I think they just gave up and did their time until they were gone too."

This info made Jag both pissed and sad.

"Sorry, sweetheart," he murmured. "It would have been good one adult in your life took your back."

Slowly, she turned her attention back to the photos, reaching out a hand and scooting them around.

"I've taken some time with this, and I don't blame them. I don't hold any anger," she said softly.

She shifted her gaze to him again and kept talking.

"They fell in love. That's one of the simplest, most beautiful things people can do. Of course, life makes it complicated, but the emotion isn't complicated. It's effortless, pure. But they couldn't have that. They had to fight for their love. They had to explain it. They had to defend it. They couldn't go out together without getting looks, assholes saying shit. But your family is supposed to be about no conditions, and they couldn't even be in love and be around the people who were supposed to love them. That's gotta wear a soul down. They were together fifty years. That's a success story. Something to celebrate. But they were forced to lose important things to gain each other. Then they lost their only baby. So no," she shook her head, glancing again at the photographs, "I don't blame them. Enough does tend to be enough."

Jag reached out, caught her at the back of the neck, and squeezed.

She turned to him and started, "Sometimes, bikers have a reputation—"

He knew what she was saying.

There were MCs that were racist, some implicitly, others explicitly.

"Chaos is not about that. I can't say we're poster children for diversity, because I think my mom's Apache blood is the only diversity we got. But you will not feel shit like that with my family."

She nodded and then asked, "I'm living, breathing proof it works, Jag. Why don't people get that?"

"If I had that answer, baby, I'd win a Nobel Prize."

"One of the issues, and they are numerous, is that it's a Black thing with Elijah. Along with other garbage, he's putting that between him and Dad."

Well, fuck.

"Maybe because there's nothing else to put there and he's reaching?" Jagger suggested.

"Dad's new wife is white."

"Well, fuck," Jag muttered out loud this time.

"Unh-hunh," she agreed.

Jagger didn't let her go when he looked down at one of the photos, then back to Archie.

"She was gorgeous, Arch," he said.

"I know," she whispered.

"I was too young to remember my dad," he told her.

Her eyes brightened with interest.

And again…

Fuck.

He quickly carried on, and not about that.

"But I know for certain I'd lose my shit if something happened to my mom. Honest to God, I don't know if I'd survive that."

"You would," she said quietly.

"Maybe day to day, but an important part of me would be jacked until the day I died."

"I get that, Jagger, obviously I do."

He pulled her closer. "I know you do, and I don't know what it's like for girls, daughters. I'm absolutely not downplaying what you deal with every day. I just know there's a time when a son stops being a son and he starts being a protector. And it holds no logic, we don't control every part of our worlds, there are things we cannot change. Still, if something hurt her, my mom, it would be there. There would be a feeling of responsibility. Of failure. Regardless of how ridiculous it is to feel that way, unless something happens to my ma twenty, thirty years down the line, and it's about life cycles and age, I'll feel it's somehow on me."

He could see her working on that behind her eyes.

"Never met your brother," he pointed out. "That's just where I'd be."

She nodded.

And he pulled her even closer.

"Loved seeing these pictures, baby," he murmured. "Wondered what she looked like, figured she was gorgeous. I was right."

She smiled and her next words were cautious.

"Do you have pictures of your dad?"

He let her go and sat back.

Her eyes flickered with disappointment.

Even so, Jag didn't get into that.

He just said, "Somewhere."

"Okay," she murmured. "You want dessert?"

"You have dessert?"

"I have French vanilla ice cream and I have chunky peanut butter."

That sounded promising.

"Like, you mix them together?" he asked.

"No, you plop a wad of peanut butter on a huge bowl of ice cream and eat it."

Correct.

Promising.

"You dish up, I'll clean up," he ordered.

That got him another smile and, "Deal."

* * * *

Deep in the night, in Archie's bed, Jag jerked awake, and when he did, he was breathing funny.

Archie roused at his side.

"Hey," she called softly.

"Sorry," he muttered. "Just...weird dream."

She said nothing but pushed up, draped herself mostly on him and stuffed her face in his throat.

"I'm okay," he lied, moving his hands on her.

"This happen a lot?"

Shit, shit, shit.

"Sometimes," he admitted.

She was silent, waiting for him to say more.

When he didn't, she said, "I'm giving you this, baby, but repeating the caveat you're eventually gonna have to open up for me."

"I need to get a lock on it myself first."

"It doesn't work that way."

Shit, shit, shit.

"Just...a little more time, okay?" he requested.

She kissed his throat, slid off a bit, settling into his side, head on his shoulder.

"Okay," she granted.

He rolled into her and gathered her closer.

She snuggled.

Jagger focused on trying to ease the tension in his neck without moving and disturbing Archie.

It didn't work until Archie relaxed into him in sleep.

Then he lost focus because he fell back to sleep too.

* * * *

Late the next afternoon, while Archie was at work, Jag sat on his couch, ass to the edge of the seat, slumped forward, elbows to knees, but head tipped back and his eyes on his TV.

He had his remote in hand and was fast forwarding.

He knew the exact spot and started the playback at that spot.

But once he got precisely where he needed to be, he stopped.

He was playing *Blood, Guts and Brotherhood.*

And on his screen was a pic of his dad and his mom.

They were outside the Chaos Compound, walking to his father's bike.

Jag's bike.

All he could see of his ma was her back. Her long, straight, shining black hair. She was wearing a tight red cami. Tighter faded jeans.

They had their arms around each other.

She was facing forward.

His dad was looking over his shoulder at the camera.

Smiling.

Jag stared at Graham Black's face.

Dutch got Graham. Dutch looked a lot like their dad.

Jagger got parts of him, his hair, his height, but he looked more like his mom.

Dutch even got more of their dad in that.

Even more of him.

Jag hit play and the narration started with a voiceover on the picture, then faded to a talking head of Tack.

"Can't know. It didn't happen that way," Tack was saying. *"They were one by then. Keely and Black. Made the boys by then. So it was bad, we lost him, because he was Black. He was our touchstone. Our example. Every brother's best friend. You lose that kind of equilibrium, the world ceases to make sense. But it was worse, they lost him. Because he was a man built to be a husband and father. He was the stake in the ground to which his woman was attached. Dutch was touched by that, but Jagger never knew it in any tangible way. His father would only ever be stories to Jagger. So Black's loss was a death of a part of us all. His loss to Keely and Dutch was a heartache. But his loss to Jagger was torture."*

He stopped the documentary, turned off the TV.

Then, before he could make up a reason not to, he picked up his phone and went to texts.

You got some time next week to talk? he texted his ma.

He headed to his bedroom to change so he could go to the park and work out, then get a good stretch in before he had to shower, get dressed, hit the store to stock up for their Sunday, and then go get Archie to take her out to dinner.

He didn't even get to his bedroom before his mother replied.

Hear there's a girl.
He didn't blame Hound for sharing.
In a healthy marriage, a husband and wife talked.
And any dad shared shit about their kids with the mom.
Especially if it was important.
Yeah, he replied.
Always have time for you, honey. Just tell me when, I'll be there.
Thanks, Ma.
You bet. Love you.
Love you.
Jag then changed into workout gear.
But before he headed out, and again, before he made excuses not to do it, he sent another text.
He got the reply before he hit the park.
You call it, I'm there, Tack replied.
Jag drew breath into his nose.
Then he sent a day, time and place to Tack.
He started his workout and he really went at it, ending it in a five-mile run and a thorough full-body stretch session in order to sort himself out so he'd be chill and loose.
And maybe, that night, he wouldn't dream of going out to pick up a pizza and heading back to his truck.
Only to get jumped and have his throat slit.
And leave his mom, Hound, Dutch, Wilder and Archie without him forever.

* * * *

"I knew you were the shit since, like, the instant I looked at you," Archie declared. "But Bastien's? This is next level, boyfriend."
After saying that, she pressed into his side where she sat next to him in a booth at Bastien's, her face in his neck, and she didn't kiss him or touch his skin with her tongue.
She purred.
His dick stirred.
"Stop it," he ordered. "I got less than a day to wait."
She pulled her face out of his neck.
"You mean *we* have less than a day to wait."
"I got you off this morning and I'll get you off tonight."
"It's not the same," she muttered, turning to her cocktail that had some kind of spicy, tabasco salt on the rim.
"Are you complaining?" he asked.
She took a sip of her cocktail then returned her attention to him.

"You got long, strong fingers, baby, but a girl needs some dick."

Jagger roared with laughter.

When he was done, she wasn't laughing.

She wasn't smiling.

She was pressed, her front to his arm, and reaching a hand to his face.

She ran a finger along his jaw to the corner of his mouth and along his lower lip.

Her eyes watched these movements.

When her hand fell to rest on his chest and her gaze lifted to catch his, he felt it bore deep.

All amusement fled.

"Archie," he whispered.

She retreated from her visual invasion, pushed in, touched her mouth to his, and after she pulled away an inch, she said, "Thanks for supporting the 'hood with your steak place choice."

"It's about that. It's about the retro here, which is fucking cool. It's about arguably the best steaks in Denver. It's about making you happy, since I knew you'd dig this. But, just sayin', even if your crib is blocks away, we're still spending the night at my place."

"Your turn," she noted.

"Yeah," he replied.

She gave him an eye twinkle and her focus shifted to the table because their Devils Riding Bareback were being served.

And Jagger released his breath.

Because she didn't push, she didn't demand, she didn't make him talk about what he knew she saw in his eyes, but he wasn't ready to explore. Definitely not share.

She let it go.

So yeah.

There was relief.

But underlying it was something else.

Because he knew it was only a reprieve.

* * * *

Jag came back to the bed after going to the bathroom to splash his face and rinse off.

He had Archie all over him since he'd finished her off going down on her.

She was on her side in his bed, cradling his sheet between her legs, bare hip and leg exposed, she still had on her black bra.

He slid in behind her and touched the strap of the bra.

"Want this off?" he murmured.

"Mm," she hummed, shifting enough he knew to reach in front of her and unhook the clasp between her tits.

He did that, slid the bra off and tossed it aside, seeing another one of Archie's tats.

He bent in to look closer at the small writing that went across her side, where the band of her bra had covered the skin.

It said, *The Girl Across the Way.*

He palmed it and growled, "Baby."

"Bet you wish you didn't just make me come hard, boyfriend, and bought me too many cocktails," she whispered, gazing smugly and sleepily at him.

He dropped his head and kissed the tat.

Then he pushed up and kissed her.

She near to Christ fell asleep on him while he was doing it.

"Too good with your mouth," she mumbled when he broke the kiss.

Which meant he was grinning when he turned out the lights.

He settled in behind her in a spoon, top arm wrapped around her chest.

The arm he shoved under her was wrapped around her ribs.

And his hand was on *The Girl Across the Way.*

Chapter Ten

Unhurt. Unstruck. Unbeaten.

Jagger

Sunday morning, early, his alarm went.

Jag opened his eyes, reached out, and came up empty.

He pushed up to a hand in the bed and looked around the room.

Thrown on the chair in the corner was the black outfit Archie wore to dinner the night before that was essentially a collared shirt that was clingy and almost mini-dress long, the bottom of it hugging a fitted pair of black short-shorts. She'd worn this with black knee boots with silver rivets over the toes.

Definitely testing his ability not to give in and let her at least suck him off.

Her beat-up backpack was lying on the floor next to the chair and it'd exploded since Jag dropped it there the night before.

As far as he knew, she'd slept good after he fed her, got her tipsy, brought her home and took his time eating her out.

But now she was…

Where?

He got out of bed and noted the bathroom was dark, but he looked there anyway.

She wasn't there.

He then headed out.

His search didn't last long.

He found her perched on the felt of his pool table, cross legged, wearing panties and a tank, the backs of her wrists on her knees.

Her eyes were closed.

And, okay…

There was only ever going to be one woman's ass on the back of his bike.

But he didn't expect there would only ever be one woman's ass on his felt.

Feeling his lips twitch, he retraced his steps, did his bathroom business including brushing and flossing, yanked on the jeans he wore the night before, leaving his chest bare. He headed back out, went to his kitchen and started coffee.

By the time he returned his attention to her, she hadn't moved, but her eyes were open and on him.

"Please come here," she requested.

Apparently, meditation-on-a-pool-table time was over.

This chick was something else.

No hesitation, he went right there.

He stopped, standing in front of her.

She reached out with one hand and touched the tattoo over his heart.

"OG," she said.

"Yeah," he muttered, taking her in up close, hearing the vibe of her voice, not certain what her mood was.

"Where do you go from there?" she asked.

He understood her question immediately.

She wanted to know where she would be.

Their kids.

"Where do you go from there, Jagger?" she pushed.

Her voice was soft, sweet, reflective.

She got it.

OG.

Always there.

Right at the heart.

It would always be them.

His mom. Dutch. Hound. Wilder.

His dad.

OG.

He wanted to answer her question, because he had an answer, but all of a sudden, his throat had shut down.

His throat had shut down.

She took his hand, moved it to her inner right arm, and wrapped his fingers around the three symbols inked there.

Even with his hand covering them, he knew what they were. In the last few days, he'd spent some time taking in her tats.

Those were detailed, intricate, even if not a one of them was bigger than his thumbnail.

Two Hamsa hands protecting a Chakra Third Eye.

Yeah.

With that tat, with the easy way she talked about shit, shared it, Jag knew she was there.

She knew herself or was capable of digging deep if something reared that needed contemplation.

He was not.

"Where do you go from there, Jagger?" she whispered.

He wanted to give it to her but he couldn't.

Instead, he closed his eyes, dropped his head, and felt the tight muscles pull hard in his neck.

She left his hand where it was on her arm and swept hers over his hair.

She caught it at the back in a gentle fist.

"This is mine, okay?" she stated, tugging lightly. "From now on, you don't cut it unless I say it's cool. Yeah?"

At her words, that tug, his dick started to get hard and his hand moved in a way it didn't feel like he was moving it. With a mind of its own, it went to hers and took control.

He positioned it, wrapping it around his throat.

Then he lifted his head and locked eyes with her.

"Here," he forced out.

That syllable was guttural.

"You'll be here," he said.

She held his gaze and hers was penetrating.

Deep.

"I'm gonna fuck you now," he told her.

"Yes," she agreed instantly.

"Come in you, no glove."

"Yes," she repeated.

"You clean?"

She nodded.

"Yeah," he answered a question she didn't ask that he was too. "Protected?" he went on.

Another nod.

With that, he moved.

Fast.

He jerked her legs out, yanked her panties down.

She gasped.

He felt that in his dick too.

He dragged her ass to the edge of the pool table, and when he got her there, she lay back, lifted her arms over her head and watched as he unbuttoned his jeans and pulled his cock out.

On sight of his dick, her eyes grew dark and she licked her lips.

Oh yeah.

That went right through his cock too.

He spread her legs, moved in, dick in his hand, positioning.

He dropped to a hand on the table at her side, slid the head of his cock through her slick, and finally pressed in half an inch, all while watching her face.

"Baby," she whimpered.

He pulled away, then pressed in a little further, slid back out, in, not far, and out.

"Ready?" he asked between his teeth, because he was ready.

He was ready at the Taste of Colorado years ago.

He sure as fuck was ready right now.

Ready to take her.

Ready to make her his.

"God yes," she answered.

No hesitation, smooth and quick, he stroked in to his balls.

She closed around him, fitted and silky.

Oh yeah.

Fuck *yes*.

She was everything.

Perfect.

Her back left the table, her knees slid up his sides, and she clamped on.

"Calves around the back, Archie, you're gonna be rode rough," he warned, voice thick, balls heavy and aching.

She moved instantly to comply.

And Jagger started fucking her.

Hard.

So hard, with each stroke, he grunted with the effort.

Archie tensed her legs and cocked her elbows. She planted her hands in the felt above her head and pushed down as he thrust in, holding himself above her, watching her take his fucking. Her tits bouncing. Her body swaying. He slid his free hand up her belly, over the tank between her tits, and wrapped it around her throat.

She righted her head and they locked eyes.

He fucked her harder.

Immediately, her pussy rippled around his dick and she gasped, "Jagger, baby, I'm gonna—"

She didn't finish.

Because she was finishing.

Lips parted, head falling to the side, she soared for him, her cunt clutching and seizing, milking his dick as she came.

He pulled out, tugged her legs from around him, yanking one up. He stepped away, pulled her legs back down, then whipped her to her belly. Her feet fell to the floor, and he went back in, bending over her, pressing her to the table, his chest to her back, her soft ass in his groin, his face in her neck.

He wrapped an arm around her hip, part to protect her pelvis from thumping into the table, part to go after her clit.

"*Oh my God*, fuck, Jag. *Yes*," she panted, bouncing back into him as he drove his cock into her.

He went after her throat again with his free hand, using it to push her head back so it pressed into his shoulder as he sucked the skin under his lips.

"Baby," she whimpered and her clit convulsed, her pussy spasmed, she was coming again, so Jagger finally let himself go.

Cupping her between her legs, he jacked into her until his world wiped clean of everything but his cock and her cunt, that perfect union, his dick jetting, his balls draining, her pussy clenching.

When he came down, he felt her wet tightness holding him, and his first thought was this was the first time he'd fucked that pussy, and it'd be the last pussy he ever fucked.

Other thoughts were on Archie's mind.

She was prying his hand from her throat, and he worried he'd hurt her, or scared her, but before he could ask, she was positioning his thumb, pressing it deep into the center of her palm.

And she was talking.

"Anahata. Unhurt. Unstruck. Unbeaten. The heart chakra. You. And what I'll give to you. Tatted forever in the palm of my hand," she whispered.

Christ.

Fuck.

Christ.

He shifted so he could rest his forehead against the back of her neck.

She shifted too.

So her thumb was pressed dead center in his palm.

"Our life can be at your throat, but I wanna be here, Jagger," she said. "In the palm of your hand."

Now he was getting why she kept touching his palm.

"Then you'll be there," he told her back.

"When the time comes, you pick my symbol."

"Okay."

"Like when the time comes, you give me what you need to let go. I won't ask again. I've come to terms. I'll wait a day. I'll wait four decades. Unhurt. Unstruck. Unbeaten. That's mine to give to you always. You tell me when you trust I can take your hurt and leave you with peace. Not before. In your time. On your terms."

Christ.

Fuck.

Christ.

He dug his head into her back.

She gave him long moments.

Then she said, "You fuck like a goddamn animal."

This was not a complaint.

He let out a big breath.

Then he grinned.

Now only semi-hard, he slid out, turned her again, scooting her up for comfort, and bent over her.

She curled her legs around his hips and combed her fingers through his hair, her eyes roaming his face.

His did the same to hers.

She looked sexy, sated, all good.

That had been deep. It had rocked both their worlds.

And there he was, in her arms, and they were both all good.

"Ready for the second-best ride you're gonna get today?" he asked, referring to putting her on the back of his bike and taking off into the mountains.

"Absolutely," she answered. "But first, I need a shower, you need to pour me coffee, and also get me off your table or you're gonna have a cum stain on your felt."

They would own that table until he died and he would never forget fucking his woman for the first time on it.

But he had the memory.

He didn't need a physical reminder.

So he lifted her up and she held on with all four limbs as he hitched up his jeans.

Keeping her where she was, he walked her to the bathroom.

He dropped her feet to the tile, took her head in his hands on either side and bent to touch his mouth to hers.

When he was done, he said, "Be back with your joe."

He did another mouth touch, let her go, turned away, but she caught him by the back waistband of his jeans.

He looked to her.

"Hurry, I need a sip in before we shower."

We.

Excellent.

"On it, sweetheart."

She smiled at him.

Then in a tank, no panties, she turned to the extra sink that had been free and mostly unused since he bought the place, and reached for the toothbrush she left behind the first time she spent the night.

She had some redness at her throat where he'd gripped her and a hickey on the side of her neck.

The marks he'd left made his cock jump in his jeans.

"Hurry."

His gaze went from her neck to her eyes in the mirror.

Hers were on him.

Okay, maybe the second-best ride she was going to get that day would happen in the shower.

She shoved the toothbrush in her mouth.

He moved out of the room to pour them coffee.

And he didn't fuck around in doing it.

* * * *

Archie was curled up in his lap on her couch.

She had on a short, pale yellow silk robe that was tied at the waist, but now gaping open.

She'd put it on to make them a plate of crackers and cheese.

The crackers and cheese were gone.

Now she was squirming as she let him play with her.

He'd been taking his time with his hand between her legs for the last half hour, at least.

So she was soaked.

And his dick was throbbing, so he was done playing.

"Climb on," he growled.

She didn't hesitate.

She shifted to straddle him, took control of his dick, got in position then ground down on it.

"Fuck yeah," he grunted, his head falling back to the couch.

She caught his neck in both hands and rode him.

He lifted his head, went in, and sucked her nipple in his mouth.

She made a low noise and went faster.

He switched nipples but cupped her free breast and pinched the slick bud in rhythm with her bounces.

He held the pinch and rolled as he popped her nipple out of his mouth, tipped his head back and ordered, "Faster."

"Baby," she whispered, but didn't adjust speed.

He spanked her ass.

She went faster.

Jag slid a hand up her spine, into her hair, pulling it back, arching her in front of him.

Her pussy clamped hard simultaneously with her gasp.

Jag's balls drew up.

Her tits bounced, nipples dark and peaked.

He looked down and saw his cock swallowed again and again by her trimmed bush.

Fuck.

Hot.

Too hot.

Her work was done.

He surged up, filling her, twisted, fell down with her on her back on the couch, and he took over.

She wrapped her legs around his thighs, grabbed his ass, and slid her finger to the first knuckle inside him.

Fuck.

Hot.

He grunted, reached between them and pinched her clit.

That did it.

She cried out and blew.

Then he blew, bucking deep and spewing a big load even if it was the fifth time he'd come that day, the third time that evening.

He came down and rode her gentle.

She circled her finger slowly inside him and tongued the skin of his neck and ear as she did, and when he pulled out, she did too.

He rolled so his back was to the back of the couch.

She kissed his collarbone, raked her teeth over his nipple, and slid off the couch.

He watched the silk of her robe dance along her round ass as she walked to her bathroom.

Jag repositioned to lying on his back and raked his fingers in his hair from his forehead back.

And he kept them there.

He stayed that way even after Archie came back and stretched out on top of him.

"Seems fucking you produces unending amounts of my jizz."

Her body rocked with her laughter.

He shoved a hand between them until he found the tie on her robe. He tugged it then pushed the fabric aside so they were full-length skin against skin and his hands had unfettered access to the rest of her.

Then he took advantage of that unfettered access.

"So we did Vail today, you wanna do Estes Park next weekend?" he asked.

"Can we ride up Saturday and spend the night somewhere?" she asked back.

"Does it have to be in a yurt?"

Her body shook with her humor again and she answered, "No." She lifted her head and pushed up so they were face to face. "Doesn't my boy rough it?"

"There are things I'll sacrifice at a rally when most the time I'm drunk as fuck and the rest of the time I'm hungover so I don't give a shit. If the end of the road means time spent between your legs, I want privacy and a shower nearby that I'm not sharing with other people."

"I've never been to a bike rally."

"We'll get on remedying that."

"Cool," she murmured, grinning down at him.

Using both hands, Jag pulled her thick hair behind her ears and noted, "Good call on wait-for-it, just-us, nothing-pressing-in first fuck session, baby.

Today has been the best."

"Totally the best," she agreed, dipping in to touch lips. "I'll never forget it."

"Me either."

"I have a confession to make," she announced.

"I've got ears," he told her.

She grinned bigger and stated, "I've never fucked in a yurt."

He started laughing while he wrapped both arms around her and switched their positions.

When he was on top, he looked into her eyes and promised, "We'll remedy that too."

She slid her fingers across his cheek then lifted her head, tilting it, in order to kiss him.

Jag angled his and kissed her back.

And yeah, he'd find—three more times—fucking her produced unending amounts of his cum.

So when they eventually passed out, on some pillows and blankets they'd dragged onto the floor, Jag had no tension in his neck or anywhere.

And he slept like a baby.

Chapter Eleven

I Kinda Dig You

Jagger

Even though he wasn't expecting her, Jag knew she was there before he saw her.

This was because, across the three huge bays of the garage, the vibe shifted from men at work direct to the heavy air of a slew of dudes who were on the make.

Adding to that, Joker, who was bent over an engine with him, said slow, "Well...shit."

Jag looked to his right, at Joker, who was looking through the opening at the side of the hood.

Jag then pulled out from under the hood, doing this in unison with Joker, and saw Archie strolling toward him.

She was wearing a pair of camo short-shorts with a denim-blue tube top and a white gauzy duster drifting off her shoulders that fell to the backs of her knees. She had a tangle of delicate gold necklaces trailing down her front and Adidas Superstars that had neon pink stripes on her feet.

And as she went, not a man was working in that garage—and they employed five mechanics, with two apprentices (and all of them were on shift), not to mention the Chaos brothers who worked in the garage when the spirit moved them (and that day, Shy and Dog were in the building).

Everyone was watching Archie walk to him, the duster floating behind her, one of those smiles on her face that was just that hint shy of smug (rather than her full-on smug one), which Jagger found a total turn-on (then again, he found the full-on one the same).

And the eleven men in that garage did too.

"Hey, boyfriend," she called when she was ten feet away.

At her words, he felt he'd grown a foot taller.

"Hey, baby," he replied, moving to her.

He made it and she curled the fingers of both hands in his tee and pulled him down, doing this only to make him touch his mouth to hers.

She pulled her head away but did not release his tee.

"I want lunch with my guy," she declared.

He grinned at her and replied, "I'm at your service."

She smiled up at him.

They heard a throat cleared.

Archie unfurled her fingers, so Jag moved to her side to claim her, tossing an arm around her shoulders.

She caught him through the back beltloop of his jeans.

And as they positioned, they saw Joker, Shy and Dog standing in a line.

Shy and Dog were assessing Archie.

Joker was staring at Jag.

"Well?" he prompted.

Swallowing his chuckle, Jag launched in. "Arch, these are my brothers, Joker, Shy and Dog. Men, this is my girl, Archie Harmon."

Her response was to him.

"You totally lied about them all being ugly. Like...*totally*."

He heard chuckles, ignored them and replied, "Thanks for outing me like that, baby."

She smiled up at him and that one was full-on smug.

She then turned her attention back to his brothers.

Shy came forward first, hand raised. "Yo, Archie."

She took his hand, squeezed, and then got much the same from Dog and Joke.

"I'm going to lunch," Jagger announced when Joker stepped back.

"I could do lunch," Shy said.

Shit.

"Feelin' peckish myself," Dog stated.

Great.

"Been jonesin' for a po'boy at Lincoln's," Joker put in.

Fantastic.

"Perfect," Dog declared and looked right at Jag. "Meet you two there."

Before Jagger could say a word, the men sauntered away.

Jag and Archie shifted to watch them go.

"Guess we're eating lunch with your boys," Archie observed.

"We don't have to meet them and can go wherever we want," Jagger told her.

"I love Lincoln's jambalaya," she replied, sharing in her way that she not only didn't mind, she wanted to hang with his brothers.

And he wanted her to get to know his brothers.

"Then Lincoln's it is," he said.

They started toward his bike and Arch did what Jag had learned she liked to do. As they walked, she angled her body so she was tucked under his arm, close to him and brushing against him as they went.

If she could have it, she was maximum contact all the time and she somehow pulled that off without seeming clingy and needy.

He was one with this, because if she wasn't maximum contact, he would be.

These were his thoughts when his phone went with a text.

Not losing touch with Archie, he pulled it out, read the text and quickly clicked the phone off, shoving it back in his rear jeans pocket.

Archie couldn't miss this, but she didn't say anything.

The text was from his ma.

Am I going to see you soon?

It was the Thursday after his first weekend with Archie.

He'd been blowing his mother off.

Just like he'd done to Tack, canceling the meeting he'd set with his brother and finding another space to be in when Tack looked like he was coming into Jag's.

He was telling himself this was about being with Archie, something he was as much as he could be, when he wasn't at the garage and she at the store.

They'd torn the lid off, not only with sex—and they fucked all the time— but with everything.

In the last three days, he'd spent a good bit of time out on her fire escape, and they'd played a lot of pool at his pad.

He's also eaten her for lunch in her office the day before.

And she'd met him at his place for a mid-afternoon blowjob the day before that.

It was not lost on him this uber-togetherness was what Dutch and Georgie did (in the beginning...and now).

It was also not lost on him this was what Hound and his ma did (ditto with beginning and now).

Last, it wasn't lost on him that this was what he'd heard his dad and mom did.

He didn't think about this either.

He thought about Archie. Getting to know Archie. Doing things to Archie and letting her do things to him.

The rest, he'd think about when it was time to think about it.

Or not at all.

* * * *

"*So* cute. And bruh, *so* cool of you," Archie said to Dog as she handed Dog's phone back to him after looking at pictures of Dog's kids, all three of whom were fostered, before Dog and Sheila adopted them.

Arch looked between his girl and his brothers.

This lunch had been a surprise, and not the part of it where Archie showed out of the blue and his brothers horned in, determined to get to know her.

If he'd had to guess, he would have expected it would be about his brothers giving him shit by telling Archie every embarrassing little kid or clueless teenage boy-man anecdote they had.

And they had a lot of those in their arsenal.

It was not about that.

In fact, it didn't even come close to that.

And something in that made Jag feel weird.

He couldn't figure out if it was a good weird, or a bad weird.

What he knew was, it was official.

He wasn't that little kid growing up in Chaos anymore.

You did that shit with a prospect's girl. You did that shit to harass a boy in a way you're teaching him to take it like a man.

You didn't do it when he's already a man and the woman he's with was the one you were bringing into the family fold.

"Would take away what they had to go through to get to us," Dog muttered to Archie, talking about his kids as he pushed his cell back into his pocket. "Even if it meant they wouldn't be with us. But that wasn't the way it happened. And now we got 'em."

"And they have you," Archie said softly.

Dog and Arch looked across each other at the round, high bar table they were occupying and shared a moment.

She was again wedged up to him, her stool close, their hips and thighs pressed together, and she was leaning against his side.

"Family is family, no matter how it came about," Archie went on, tossing a hand toward the table to indicate the men. "You boys know that better than anybody."

"Yeah," Dog grunted.

Shy grinned at his bottle of beer.

Joker stared hard at Jag.

This was not Joke's silent way of saying something about Archie, something Jag might not like.

Joker was intense. Joker's backstory was worse than most. Joker didn't have a family until he met Chaos and then made one of his own.

And Joker liked, even if Archie did have all of that, that she understood what Chaos meant.

"How impossible are you all going to make the task of me buying lunch for you guys?" Archie asked.

That got Joker's attention.

His heavy brows shifted tight over eyes that shot to Archie and he rumbled, "The fuck?"

Shy's head had come up and he asked, "You crazy?"

And over all that, Dog said, "Next time," which was a total lie as there'd be a next lunch or dinner, but Dog wouldn't let Archie pay for it.

Jagger, sure.

Archie, never.

Archie turned to Jagger. "I see the patriarchy is strong with this bunch."

"Babe," was all he said in reply.

She gave him a grin and reached out to nab her beer.

Lunch didn't last much longer, and Jag rode back to work with Archie tucked close, her arms around his middle, her chin on his shoulder.

And...

Yeah.

He again felt a foot taller, even sitting his bike.

Before she left, they made out in the forecourt next to her car.

And she lowered the hammer she'd come there to lower and didn't get the chance to do it since his boys commandeered their time.

"Told Dad we finally hooked up, and he wants you over to dinner. His choice, that dinner would take place yesterday. I renegotiated that."

Fuck.

Okay.

Right.

There was one thing about being "Arby's Guy," sensing she needed someone to help her navigate grief because he'd lived his life with the people he was closest to navigating grief.

It was another thing, that guy being a biker.

And yet another one, him belonging to an MC.

Chaos was not unknown in Denver, even before an award-winning documentary was seen in theaters before it was made accessible on Netflix.

What was unknown was how Archie's dad would feel about that.

Archie gave him a squeeze. "He wants me to be happy."

He looked down at her beautiful face.

Another squeeze. "And, boyfriend, you make me happy."

He drew in a deep breath.

Let it out.

Then he did the only thing he could do after she said something that dope.

He kissed her again.

When he lifted his head, she asked, "So, since this weekend we're riding, is next Tuesday good for you?"

Fuck.

"Sure," he lied.

She smiled at him. There came another squeeze.

Then she got up on the toes of her Adidas and they were making out again.

Eventually, she had to get back to work.

And so did he.

But before she folded into her car, she caught sight of the Bronco that was sitting out in the forecourt. It was running, they'd sent it off to be painted earlier that week, it looked shiny and new and shit-hot, and they were going to list it on their website for sale soon.

Studying it, she said, "You're so freaking right. That Bronco is boss. Maybe tomorrow I'll come by and take it for a test drive? Would that be cool?"

It was then, already knowing he was falling for this woman, it cemented that he was falling for this woman.

"You bet," he replied.

Part of their getting-to-know-you time had been learning she got by with the store and wasn't destitute, but most anything she wanted (usually vacations and getaways), she had to save for. Whereas, his ma socking money away for him and Dutch, and both of them getting their brother's cut of what came in from Ride, these things meant Jag was comfortable (and then some).

So he knew she couldn't afford the price tag on that truck.

But he could.

In other words, maybe they wouldn't be listing it on their website soon.

She folded in her car, which was nothing exciting. She'd stuck with Honda, and it was a solid ride, probably got great gas mileage. But it was seriously not Archie.

She'd kill it in that Bronco.

She blew him a kiss as she drove away.

This meant he was smiling when he got a chin jerk from Dog as he headed back into the garage.

Approval.

He already knew that.

He got a shit-eating grin from Shy.

Again, approval.

And again, he knew that.

He joined Joker at the car they were now working on.

Joker said nothing.

"So?" Jagger pushed.

Joke looked to him. "You already know she's the shit, you don't need me to confirm it."

Jag tilted his head to stretch his neck and felt something pop.

Joke heard it.

"Your mom's gonna dig her, man," Joker went on.

He focused on his friend.

"I got—" He cut himself off.

"You got what?" Joker prompted when Jagger didn't say more.

Jag coughed when he didn't need to and said, "Nothin'. She wants to test drive the Bronco. Tomorrow."

"Yeah," Joker said, bending back over the engine, nodding distractedly, head back in the engine. "She's the shit."

They got about an hour's worth of work done before Jagger got a string of texts.

The first from his mom.

The last one was not, and that was the one that spurred him to action.

The ones from his mom started with, *So, you're blowing your mother off but your girl has lunch with your brothers?*

He suspected it was Dog's big mouth that caused that. No doubt Dog told Sheila, and then Sheila got right on with his mom.

Even if he meant to reply, which he didn't, not until he figured out what to say, she shot off another text before he could.

Tack's been in touch.

Shit.

Tack told her Jag had reached out, then canceled.

His mother wasn't stupid. They were close. Even not being around him, she'd sense something was up.

The next was, *I get when it's new and you want it all to yourself.*

Okay, that was a good excuse, and maybe actually part of why he was hoarding time with Archie.

Then came the next, *But I sense that isn't it. Word is, you've known this girl over a decade.*

Not exactly.

But still…

I don't know what's happening with you. The next began. And went on with, *What I hope you know is the path is always clear to me.*

He was about to text back, *I know* and then some words about how she could chill (even though he knew she'd never chill, at least he could try) when he got a text from Archie.

Shit is real, baby. Mal came in and he's being a little dick. Something has gone down. He won't talk. I think I need you.

He had no idea why she would need him.

He just saw that she needed him.

So to that, he texted back.

Be there in twenty.

Then he got on his bike.

* * * *

Jag parked at the back of S.I.L., hoofed it around the side of the building and went in, almost immediately hearing a whistle.

He looked right, saw Joany up behind the cash register, ringing someone up.

She jerked her head toward the bookshelves.

Jag nodded, even though he didn't know if she was directing him to Archie or Mal, and scanning for either, he moved that way.

He didn't have to find Archie, she found him, coming quickly out of the homewares section with Fabe at her side.

Jag had met Fabe. A very tall, skinny Black dude with a fade at the sides of his head, twists at the top, a bent toward electronic music and a vibe that Jag couldn't quite put his finger on.

Björk was playing, and Jag wouldn't put it past Archie to throw that on. Joany, no way in fuck. Fabe, definitely.

Fabe seemed like a pretty laidback guy, usually.

Now he looked pissed.

Shit.

"Hey, honey," Jag greeted Archie. Then to Fabe, "Yo, dude."

"Yo," Fabe bit off.

Archie gave Fabe an *I'm sorry* look then turned to Jag.

"Okay, well, we've had a bit of a name-calling incident." Archie explained Fabe's attitude and the *I'm sorry* look.

"I'm getting smoothies. Do you want a smoothie?" Fabe asked Archie a question Jag didn't understand since they had a soda fountain stocked with ice cream, so who in their right mind would go and get a smoothie when they could be sucking back a malt?

She shook her head.

Fabe looked to Jag and arched a brow.

Jag shook his head.

Fabe stormed off.

Jag turned to Archie. "What happened?"

"Fabe was trying to do a man-to-man with Mal to get him to talk and Mal called him a poof."

"Poof" was better than some things Mal could have called him.

Regardless, he shouldn't be saying shit like that at all.

Jag shouldn't be, but he was curious.

"Is Fabe, uh…?"

Archie rolled her eyes and told him, "He's pan."

"He's what?"

"He does chicks. He does dudes. He does dudes and chicks together. He does trans. He fucks whoever he thinks is pretty. And he thinks a lot of people are pretty."

Well, that answered a question that hadn't been burning in Jag, but he had it.

"The fact remains it's uncool to call people names," Archie went on. "Especially people who have been awesome with you."

"Yeah," Jag agreed.

"I think Mal looks up to you," she told him. "He asked me the other day when you were coming around again."

That surprised Jag.

"No shit?" Jagger asked.

She shook her head. "No shit."

"Is he in the library?"

"The what?"

"The library, your book section."

She smiled at him. "I dig you call it that."

"I dig you dig that, baby. But can you answer the question?"

She nodded. "Yeah. Last I saw of him, he headed in there. He reads. This is another reason I know something is up. When he gets into his head, he gets into it with a book. Problem with that is, we have homework time right after school and he starts reading and doesn't do his homework. Which is how this all began. I asked him about his homework, he wasn't cool with me. Fabe waded in. And it went south from there."

Jag drew in a breath to gain some cool at the thought that Mal gave her shit, then he bent, touched his lips to her forehead, and made his way to the library.

He found Mal in that mini-maze of shelves, sitting in an old armchair, nose in a book.

He didn't miss Jag showing, his eyes flicking Jag's way, then he made a point of ignoring him, shifting in the chair to send a shoulder Jag's way.

Jag tamped down his annoyance and evened out his voice when he said, "Soda fountain, bud. Now."

"I don't want nothin'," Mal mumbled, not meeting Jag's eyes.

"I didn't ask," Jagger replied. "Let's go."

There was more belligerence in it when Mal turned fully to him and snapped, "I told you, don't want nothin'."

"Ass to a stool, I'm making you a malt."

"I don't got money for a malt," Mal retorted.

"I'm buying," Jag offered.

"That'd be awesome, if I wanted something. But...I...do...not."

"So sit with me while I have a cherry Coke."

With that, Mal lost it.

"Why can't you just fuck off?" he bit.

And Jag immediately leaned over him, it was threatening, and he meant it to be, but it was the wrong call.

Mal lurched back into the seat, his eyes widening in fear.

Okay, where did that response come from?

Jag eased back an inch physically as well as with his attitude and again modulated his voice when he said, "I give a shit. I was at work, Arch texted, and I jumped on my bike to listen to what you might have to say. You don't have anything to say, all right. But I'm havin' a cherry Coke and I'm makin' you a malt or whatever you want and we're gonna just be. But we're doing it together. You with a guy who cares and me there to listen if you decide to talk. So, will you go to the soda fountain with me?"

Mal took a minute with that before he nodded.

Jagger straightened, and Mal slithered out of the chair.

They walked together to the fountain, or Jagger walked, Mal slunk.

He didn't miss Archie watching them, Joany standing beside her.

Archie looked worried. Joany looked irritated (and worried).

They were part of Mal's village.

And so was Fabe.

Mal just needed to get that.

That and the fact that you didn't shit in your village.

"Hop up," he muttered when they got to the fountain.

Mal hoisted himself up on a stool.

Jagger went behind the counter. "What do you want?"

"Chocolate shake, made with syrup, not chocolate ice cream."

That was specific for a kid who didn't want anything.

Jag didn't comment on that.

He put his hands to his hips and stared at the stuff behind the counter, primarily the old-fashioned three-rod shake machine, then he looked at Mal. "Do you know how to work any of this shit?"

Mal stared at him open mouthed a second, then he cracked a smile.

Okay, the smile was good.

But Jag didn't comment on that either.

Out of nowhere, Archie ordered, "Sit down, you goof, I'll make your stuff."

Jag watched Mal clam up completely in the face of Archie.

He then gave her a look.

She mouthed, "I'll hurry."

Jag rounded the counter, sliding a finger across her hip as he did, then rested his ass on a stool by Mal's.

She didn't lie. She hurried.

Mal avoided watching her.

It wasn't that long ago Jag had been Mal's age so he knew what was going on with this.

He was crushing, huge.

So much, whatever was fucking with his head had come out in an ugly way, a way that he'd disappointed her, and now he was embarrassed he'd acted like a dick.

When Jag had his cherry Coke, Mal had his shake, and Arch had taken off, he let Mal have a couple of swallows before he admitted, "All right, kid, I lied."

Mal looked up at him.

"You're gonna get a lecture, a short one, but an important one," Jag went on.

Mal's face started screwing up.

Jag was quick about saying what he had to say before the boy said something he'd regret.

"Fabe's a cool guy. We both know that. What is *not* cool is you talking trash to him. And I'll just say that's *to* him or *about* him if he's not around. He is who he is and how he is and that's none of your business, outside how he treats you. And I know he's cool with you. So there's not one single reason for you not to be cool with him. Are we on the same page with that?"

Mal looked guilty and hid it by turning away and slurping up more ice cream.

"I'll take that as a yes," Jag said, lifting the glass and taking a sip (and Archie had bona-fide Coca-Cola glasses, with the bulbous top and the narrow base).

Shit.

Fountain cherry Coke made with two syrups and seltzer just couldn't be beat.

They sat in silence.

They sat in silence longer.

Mal made those slurping noises that meant his shake was gone.

And they sat in silence after that.

Jag had hoped the kid would open up, but it seemed he wasn't going to.

He still gave him more time before he got off his stool, grabbed both their glasses and headed behind the counter to put them in the bus bin.

He then positioned himself opposite Mal at the counter and leaned into his forearms to get eye-to-eye with the boy.

When they locked gazes, Jag spoke.

"Right, I gotta get back to work, Mal. It'd be groovy you worked on your homework a little. And when Fabe gets back with his smoothie, it'd be cool you said words to make amends. That's up to you. But from here on in, your day fucks with your head, you need someone to sit with and just be, you tell Arch to call me. I'll be here."

He then reached out, rapped his knuckles on the counter in front of Mal for no reason at all, just to punctuate his point, and he started to make his way to wherever Archie was.

"You really came right here when Archie texted?"

Mal's question made him stop and look back at the kid.

"I'm standing here, aren't I?" Jag noted. Then joked, "I mean, as much as your joyous company lights my day and gives the promise of a million better tomorrows, I do gotta work to pay my mortgage."

His joke made Mal crack another smile.

That smile did not have a long life.

"I…" Mal seemed like he was going to say something, but Jag figured what came out of his mouth next was not what Mal intended to say. "I'll say sorry to Fabe."

"Awesome," Jag said.

"And I'll get on my homework," Mal continued.

"Great, kid."

Mal pulled his lips in and nodded.

Then he slid off his stool and crept through the store to the back, where Archie had storage, a break room, the bathroom, and a setup for the kids to watch TV, play videogames, and sit at a table and do homework.

And again with the creeping.

He couldn't say he knew Mal all that well. That was the longest period of time he'd spent with the kid and they'd done it barely speaking.

But he always seemed full of something, himself, swagger, whatever.

Now he seemed…

Beaten.

Archie was at his side before Mal made it to the door to the back.

Joany was with her.

Joany spoke first.

"What was up his ass?"

"He didn't share," Jag told her as Archie slid an arm around his waist simultaneous with him curving an arm around her shoulders.

Joany gave them an up and down and stated, "I hate to be the one to inform you of this, but it's impossible for you two to physically fuse."

"You are very wrong about that," Archie returned. "Do we have to have a convo about the birds and bees?"

Joany made a face. "Don't gross me out. You're my girl. You're asexual." She jerked her head at Jag. "He's not, of course. He's *very* sexual. But you have Barbie parts."

Jagger started chuckling.

"Learn early, Jag, don't encourage her," Archie advised, not taking her eyes off Joany.

Jag didn't quit chuckling.

"And *again*," Archie said this to Joany, "stop perving on my boyfriend."

"If you date a hot guy, you give up the right to ask friends and acquaintances not to perv on said hot guy," Joany shot back.

"That is not true," Archie retorted.

"Sis, if I was dating a hot guy, I'd *so totally* let you perv on him. It'd be my civic duty."

Jag started laughing.

Fabe showed, his lips wrapped around a straw stuck into a smoothie.

He handed another one to Joany, stopped sucking, and asked Jag, "Are they having the perving-on-you discussion again?"

"Again?" Jag asked.

Fabe nodded.

"They used to fight regularly about if Prince should have gone back to Prince after he assumed the symbol, since the symbol, everyone has to agree, was kick-freaking-ass," Fabe declared. "Now they fight about perving on you. And by the way, I'm on Joany's side of that argument. You're seriously perv-worthy and it's just selfish not to let that happen."

Jag looked down at his girl. "Where do you stand on Prince and his symbol?"

"Symbol, dude," Archie replied.

He gave her a squeeze and murmured, "Good girl."

"Are you *high*?" Joany demanded to know. "Prince is the single coolest name in the history of rock. And onward from that, it's the single coolest *single* name in the history of celebrity."

"Does anyone know who I'm named after?" Jag asked the three of them.

Archie petted his chest and murmured placatingly, "Baby, ol' Mick is cool..." long pause, "*ish*."

Jesus.

"Is Mal straightened out?" Fabe asked, thankfully taking them out of this discussion.

Jag looked to him. "He'll probably apologize when he sees you again."

"Not big on the 'probably' part but...okay," Fabe mumbled.

Joany slurped, did it huge, then moaned, "Oh shit, ice cream headache."

She had both eyes looking down at her nose.

Jag was back to chuckling.

Man, Archie's people were seriously the shit.

After he was done doing that, he said to Archie, "I gotta go. Walk me to my bike?"

She gave him a look he wasn't surprised to receive seeing as he'd never asked her to walk him to his bike when he hit her store.

"'Kay," she replied, and on this short answer, his phone chimed.

He pulled it out, saw another text from his mom, and put the phone back into his pocket without viewing it.

Archie again ignored this, and Jag didn't feel good about it.

He could not miss a point punctuated by her letting him fuck her for the first time on his pool table that she was going to allow Jag to be Jag however that came about.

She wasn't going to push, nag or wheedle.

But this meant he was avoiding giving her the deep.

And he didn't feel right about that.

They knew financial deets about each other. She sat down with his brothers and broke bread. He knew the musical preferences of her shop assistants, people who were also her friends.

But this, whatever it was, he was holding to himself.

Not giving it to his mom.

Not Dutch.

Not Hound.

Not Tack.

Not Archie.

And that was not just because he didn't know what "it" was.

This was in his head as they walked with arms around each other to his bike. They took the way through the store, rather than going around it, exiting out the back door.

But when they got to his bike, and Jag curled Archie to his front, he didn't get into his mom texting or why he might be avoiding that or any of the other shit that he was avoiding thinking about.

He informed her, "I played the wrong card at first with Mal, got in his face physically, and he reared like he thought I was gonna follow through with that."

She was watching him closely as she said, "I see you think that's important for me to know, but if anyone gets in your shit, you're gonna retreat. Am I wrong?"

He shook his head. "Maybe not, but it didn't feel that way. I didn't lift a hand, not even to point in his face. It was threatening, but in no way a threat. Do you know what I mean?"

"I think so."

"Do you think the Harris brothers would take bullying to the next level?"

The point he was making dawned on her.

He knew this when she whispered, "Oh shit."

"Fuck," he whispered back. Then asked, "How do the kids get to your store?"

"They walk from school. It's a hike, but it's good exercise."

"Together?"

"I…" She shook her head. "No. They have cliques. They bond in store, mostly. But out of the store, from the way they filter in, my guess, not so much."

"And Mal shows alone," he deduced.

She nodded.

"I don't know where to go from here, baby. If we can't get him to talk, we can't go to his parents about what's going down. I can't show at his school and escort him here, that's creepy. I'd like to put the lean on the Harris brothers, but that's creepy too. And since Mal isn't saying anything, I don't know if there's anything to lean on."

"We need Mal to open up," she remarked.

"Yeah," he agreed.

"Did you feel he might get there with you?"

No, he did not.

"I'll swing 'round tomorrow," he told her.

She smiled up at him as she arched into him and said, "I kinda dig you, Jagger Black."

He grinned down at her and tightened his arms around her, replying, "Good, seein' as after we scarf down the order from DoorDash you're gonna text me about in an hour or so, I'm gonna spend the rest of the night inside you.

It'd be awkward that happens and you weren't into me."

She started laughing.

He kissed her in the middle of it.

Then they let go, he waited until she went in the back door before he took off.

About an hour later, he got her DoorDash order, ordered it and what he wanted, so it arrived at his place twenty minutes after she did.

They scarfed it down, then spent the rest of the evening fucking, and after, they passed out.

And in all that, Jag did not reply to his mother's texts.

He did not reach back out to Tack.

He didn't connect with Hound or Dutch.

And yeah, that was about being with Archie.

It was also…

Not.

Chapter Twelve

Sleeping Dragon

Archie

They'd made a tent of some sheets and were tangled in each other and a mess of pillows on a rug on her floor.

It was Sunday afternoon. Jagger was snoozing. On his back. Naked.

Archie was at his side, not snoozing, but also naked.

They'd spent the night before in a B&B in Estes Park.

Now they were home.

And Archie was down with how into each other they were. How much time they were spending together.

They were meant to be, after all.

However…

Lying on her side, up on an elbow, tucked close to him, she studied Jagger's handsome face through the fading sunlight coming through the light sheet.

He was beautiful.

But he looked conflicted, even in sleep.

She trailed her hand up his flat belly to his pec where she absently rubbed a thumb across his nipple.

He stirred, turning to her, wrapping both arms around her and pulling her tight, front to front.

"Baby," he murmured into the top of her hair, "I'm all for another round. Just give me five more minutes."

This had not been her intent.

But she didn't need to explain that because she felt him settle into her and back into sleep.

Archie held him like a lover, and she held him like a friend.

She held him light, but she held him loving.

And as she did, she thought of their conversation that morning over breakfast at the Notchtop Café in Estes.

Primarily the part where she'd alluded to Elijah being an issue when it came to co-owning the building.

And specifically the part where Jagger visibly struggled with pushing her to talk about it.

She let him off the hook, giving it to him without him having to ask.

"He's a pain because he demands half the rents on the apartments and for me to pay him rent on the space for the shop. I get this, he's half-owner. Money is made off that space. He's entitled to his share. Absolutely. Where the issues are is around utilities and maintenance. He did not pony up on the improvements and I keep a handyman on retainer because issues crop up and I'm no plumber or electrician, but they need to get fixed and fast. The shop has a security system that I pay for, I pay all the utilities on that space, and I pay the maintenance contract on the security for the apartment entrance. He wants half without any deductions, says I made the decisions to have that other stuff, so they're on me."

Jag said nothing and it was not lost on Archie that his silence was heavy.

Then again, this subject was heavy.

And it was one she'd broached because she wanted to discuss it with him, not talk at him with him just listening.

She'd done enough of that in her own head.

Though mostly, she could tell he was pissed on her behalf.

He just wasn't saying anything.

"I feel it isn't on me," she pointed out in order to spur on a conversation. "The security on the store, as the owner of the business, I get. At a stretch. But as the owner of the building, you want security for that space, and I feel it's something you'd offer a tenant, even if that tenant is me. You definitely want to provide it for your apartment residents. And we did have the discussion, we just didn't agree. Mostly because Elijah thinks we should jack up rent to pay for the handyman and the security and point-blank feels he shares no responsibility for the shop space at all."

When she stopped speaking, Jag still said nothing.

So she informed him, "You're allowed to have an opinion, Jagger."

"You know I'm gonna side with you," he told her.

"You don't have to," she replied. "I'm open to alternate viewpoints. We can have a discussion about this."

"Babe, I have no experience with rental properties, either commercial or residential. Though, I don't think it's out of bounds to increase rents in order to offer better services to your renters. That said, my guess is, you both own this building outright. If you don't have a mortgage on it, that just means extra money for him, so it seems greedy to demand more when he's not shelling out anything to have that asset in the first place. Were inheritance taxes a big hit?"

"Grandmoms and Pops had no other grandchildren, we got everything, and they'd planned well for retirement, so yes. The government took its share and that share was hefty. But we still had more than we had before they passed, so you're right. It's just greedy."

She left that a beat.

Then declared, "Greedy and lazy."

She had him in the zone, she knew it when, this time, he didn't hesitate to demand, "Give me more on that."

Relieved he was finally engaging, Archie didn't hesitate to offer it.

"It wasn't my job to take care of them when Mom died, Jagger. And I'm not going to make the blanket statement that men are incapable of coping when shit gets real. I suspect there are men who are. It's just that those two weren't those men. They both fell apart when we lost Mom and I held us together. I was fourteen and I stepped into her shoes. Cooking. Cleaning. Making grocery lists and asking Dad to take me to the store. I'm writing shit on the family calendar and riding Elijah's ass about being prepared to go to practice after school and studying for a test. We're family. You do what you gotta do. Honestly, as much as it sucked, it was what it was, and I was taking care of people I love."

When she stopped talking and it was clear she had more to say, Jagger prompted, "But..."

"But, now, when it's me who deals with the rental payments, collecting them then giving him his cut. When I get their calls if something's wrong in a unit and I coordinate the handyman. When I sweep and mop the hallways and stairs twice a month to keep the space nice. And he demands half of what we make with incidentals taken out of my half, I get crotchety about days of yore when he leaned on me to keep his shit tight, to keep his family together, to keep his home."

Jag's voice was quiet when he asked, "Are we talking about Elijah now, honey, or your dad?"

She shook her head.

"Dad copped to it. It took him a while, and that while happened when my stepmom entered the picture, with my stepsisters, and he clued in and was confronted with how much I did. The first time I came home from school, he sat me down and we chatted. He got emotional, it overwhelmed him how much he laid on me and he didn't even realize it. He then went on a stint of trying to make up for it, which did not go down great with Elijah."

"Well, shit," Jagger muttered.

"Yeah, you're seeing how this feeds into itself. The thing is, you gotta be pretty fucking selfish not to see *why* it does."

"Yeah," Jag agreed.

"And, you know, I'm in retail. There are going to be fat times, there are going to be lean times. The shop isn't that old. I'm just getting my mojo with that and learning which is which. Christmas is big, obvs. Summer, sales pick up. And I'm learning how to stretch the good times to cover the bad. But anyone can use more bank. I sacrificed for him then and I'm sacrificing for him now because Elijah's so…" Archie shook her head, shrugged and said, "*Elijah*. It's easier just to suck it up and to put up with his shit."

Jag had fallen silent again.

"You don't agree?" she pushed.

"I will repeat, I'm gonna side with you."

That was unhelpful to say the least.

Thus, Archie nabbed her coffee mug, sat back from her Irish Benedict and looked to the floor.

"Babe," Jag called.

She looked back to him.

"What I'm gonna say is gonna suck," he told her.

"What are you gonna say?" she asked.

"You haven't had it easy with all of this, but you sucking it up is gonna keep fucking you. No one likes to get fucked. Not that way. You are the single chillest chick I know. But right now, your voice is wrong when you talk about your brother. You're hurt and you're angry and you're enabling that. If you want it not to get out of control, you can't do what's easy. You gotta face it."

You gotta face it.

Archie said nothing but she was finding that Jagger Black was not one of those oblivious dudes who was incapable of inner reflection (he just didn't seem real hip on sharing those reflections).

And she knew that comment triggered that he needed to be doing some reflection.

But when she saw the pain shadow his eyes, something that was too damned familiar (and it was that and they hadn't even been together two weeks) she did what she'd been conditioned to do with the men in her life.

She set about making things easy on him.

This time, by sidestepping that completely.

"So, you think I should…" She let that trail for him to pick it up.

"First, did you use some of your inheritance on improvements?"

She nodded.

"And your brother did not kick in on any of that?"

She shook her head.

The air got heavier, which meant Jagger was getting more pissed.

But he got a handle on it and continued.

"Okay, what I think is that you should deduct half of what it's inarguable he should pay for. If you want, I could go over all of it with you to offer feedback but definitely anything to do with the rental units and maintenance of them. Cleaners don't come cheap. Not sure how long it takes you to clean the common areas, but that's part of maintenance and I'd deduct an hourly rate for that too."

He took a breath, and when she nodded that she got what he was saying, he went on.

"Personally, I'd make a list of what it cost to do the improvements, provide him with that list, and make a schedule of deductions for it until he's paid his half, but he still gets a monthly payment so he isn't totally out that income."

Archie sucked in a quick breath at the thought of that.

"It's only fair, baby," he said softly. "If he agreed or not, he's reaping the bennies of your investment. He wants to be a slum lord, owning a property he doesn't care for, he can buy you out."

Jagger was right.

He really was.

Damn.

"And if he has an issue with it," Jag carried on, "he either sits down and has a rational conversation with you about it or he pushes it to ugly."

She didn't have a good feeling about any of that.

Especially the last part.

"Ugly?"

"He could sue you, Arch, but I think it'd take a miracle to get a judge to agree that he's not responsible at least for standard upkeep of a property."

"Or I could buy *him* out."

His head ticked. "Is that an option?"

"I'd either have to dig into the rainy-day nest egg I have that's what's left of what I inherited from my grandparents and still, probably have to make payments. But the thing is, Elijah is such a pill, I'd rather he just be out of it and not have to deal with him at all."

Jagger got a look on his face that Archie did not like.

So she asked, "What, baby?"

"I told you about Dutch and Georgie looking into that murder and Dutch not telling me or Hound about him getting involved in that."

He did do that, so she said, "Yeah."

"The only thing in my life that hurt worse was when we found out Hound was lookin' after this old lady in his building, and I mean, they were really tight, and he never introduced us to her. We never knew anything about her, until after she died."

It was Archie who was quiet then.

"What I'm sayin' is," Jagger continued, "I've never met Elijah. And warning, I'm making this about me, but I'll tell you truth, baby. If Dutch ever said his life would be better without me in it in any way, that would cut so deep into the bone, I'd never stop feeling that hurt."

He reached across the table and Archie stopped cradling her coffee cup to give him her hand.

"Maybe if you gave that info to Elijah, he'd have an epiphany, feel the same way and do something about being such a drag on you and your family," he finished.

She sensed someone was having an epiphany, and it wasn't Elijah and not because he wasn't there.

She sidestepped that too.

"I'll have a conversation with him," she said.

Jag nodded, letting her go and returning to his Colorado Burrito.

Conversationally, they moved on before they went back to their B&B, packed up, got on Jagger's bike and locationally moved on.

But this didn't mean Archie didn't see the issue that lay like a sleeping dragon between them.

Her man was troubled. She didn't know why. She wondered if he knew why.

She had come to terms with that, deciding to let that be his and only hers if he offered it.

The thing was, she did that for him because she sensed he needed time with whatever it was. To face it himself without pressure. She couldn't see how it would help to push him to focus on something he clearly wasn't ready to tackle.

But now, she was wondering if that was the right call.

Though, she didn't have to wonder who to ask if it was.

And who that was wasn't Jagger.

* * * *

"Hold the phone!" her dad, Andy Harmon shouted when he opened the door to Archie. "A double dose of my daughter in a week? Starting on a Monday? What did I do to earn this awesomeness?"

He didn't let her answer.

He yanked her into a bear hug.

Archie's father was a big guy. Not as tall as Jagger, but tall, and brawny. He'd never let himself go, even now after he'd cranked into his 50s.

But he had a bit of a gut.

This was due to Haley, the stepmom, who loved to cook, and was a proud curvy girl, from the moment she met Archie's dad to that day. She was this to the point the woman was deep into the double digits size-wise and wore a bikini.

And looked cute in it.

That was something Archie had always respected her for, and not just the cute part.

Archie hugged him back, mumbling, "Stop being a dork, Dad."

"Oh my goodness, oh my goodness, thank God we're having spaghetti," Archie heard her stepmom cry. "I can make more pasta and throw a couple more pieces of Texas toast on the cookie sheet."

Archie broke from her dad, came in the house more fully as her father shut the door, and assured Haley, "I'm not staying for dinner. Sorry. I'm meeting Jag for a movie. I just…uh, wanted to talk to Dad a second."

Andy and Haley exchanged glances about what Archie would want to talk to her father about that she couldn't call or text about, and Archie knew they were coming to the same conclusion, just the wrong one.

"It's about Jag," she said.

Not Elijah, she did not say. *At least not now, maybe later*, she went on not to say.

Haley looked relieved.

Her dad's gaze grew sharp on her.

"Is everything okay with him?" Andy asked.

"It's fantastic. He's the greatest. I can't wait for you to meet him. Totes looking forward to tomorrow night."

Andy and Haley exchanged another glance.

Then Haley did what Haley was prone to do.

Waded in when her dad was being clueless.

"Andy, honey, she's meeting her guy for a movie. She can't stand around forever. Get her a drink and have your chat. I'm gonna go stir the sauce."

She shot Archie her sweet, somewhat goofy, sadly still-nervous-after-all-these-years smile and she headed to the kitchen (and Elijah was responsible for those nerves—being such a dick, it eked into how Haley thought Archie felt about her).

"You want a drink, honey?" Andy offered.

"No, Dad, just…"

How did she even start this?

Especially when she needed to be at the theater in forty-five minutes.

But all the together time with Jagger meant she didn't have a lot of windows to do something like this.

And right now, she needed to do this.

"Archie, what's up?"

The concern in her father's voice got to her and she laid it out.

Quickly.

No nitty gritty, but her father knew who Jagger was. That Jagger had lost a parent. And that he'd been someone to Archie before he was someone to Archie. So she went over that part fast.

"The thing is, like I said, he's great. We're great," she started to sum up. "Everything's going great. Joany likes him, and Joany makes everyone earn a like."

"That's big stuff, Joany liking him," he agreed.

"I just…there's something…off."

As was his wont, Daddy Bear reared up instantly, and Andy declared, "Archie, if you're feeling at all strange in your gut about this guy—"

Before he went too far down that path, Archie pulled him back to the right one. "He's lost."

Andy's head jerked back in surprise. "Sorry? Lost?"

"I think it's about his dad."

Her father closed his mouth.

"And I know there's something there," she carried on. "I even have this feeling I might have triggered it. At first, I warned him we'd have to get into it. Because, you know, I'm giving him all there is about me. And that should go both ways. Then I decided that was wrong. I should let him be. I should give him space to come to me when he's ready about this, or about anything, really."

Andy grunted, which was no help at all.

"But, the thing is, I think I can find out without him telling me," she announced.

She then watched her father's jaws bulge, an indication he was clenching his teeth.

In other words, proverbially biting his tongue.

"Dad," she prompted.

He unclenched to say (still unhelpfully), "I want to guide you, sweetheart, but I haven't even met this guy."

"Okay, but this is my guy, and I think you get how deep he's my guy, and I want to be there for him. Am I there for him by just being there? Am I there for him by pressing him in a gentle way to face whatever's troubling him? Or am I there for him by going around him to find out what's troubling him so I can be there for him from a place of knowledge and he doesn't have to give me that knowledge or maybe even know I have it?"

Her father looked perplexed.

"How would you do that last?" he asked.

"There's a movie about his Club. I didn't watch, but I read about it. His father is mentioned in the blurb. Like, really predominantly."

Andy grunted again.

For shit's sake.

"Dad!" Archie snapped.

"Okay, honey, I'm not in a place of knowledge to be able to advise what to do about this."

"Well, you're a guy, aren't you?" she threw out the rhetorical. "How would you feel if I watched a movie about your life and your history and your dead dad without you knowing I did that?"

"I…Archie, I really want to help—"

Jagger was right.

She was usually very chill.

Starting with her mom, Archie had learned this.

Bryn Harmon was chill. She was not only a catch-more-flies-with-honey person, she didn't allow herself to get worked up about things.

They'd never gotten to the zone where Bryn could explain her sorcery in this matter, but either by nature, or nurture, Archie had inherited it.

And after losing her mom, there was so much to get hyped up about, she'd have exhausted herself if she'd broken the seal on that and let that all hang out.

So she didn't.

But further, it was like paying homage to her mom that she also didn't give in to the drama.

She just got on with things.

That said, right now, with her dad being clueless again, she wanted to scream.

She didn't.

Haley did.

Not scream, exactly, but she lost patience and she did this also exposing she was totally eavesdropping.

"Oh, honestly, Andy," she snapped, coming out of the kitchen and glaring at her husband with exasperation.

She then looked to Archie and spilled the beans.

"We saw him, a while ago, riding his motorcycle with some of his buddies. Andy told me who he was to you. Your father was worried, him being in one of those gangs—"

"Clubs," Archie corrected quietly.

"Right, they made a point of that in the movie," Haley stated, bobbing her head. "And yes, that means we've seen that movie. I'd noticed it trending on Netflix and I knew that...uh, *Club* was in Denver and I mentioned to Andy maybe we should watch. Well, we sure did when we saw your guy wearing that patch."

Archie felt her heart speed up a little.

"And?" she asked.

"And, I'm sure your father will disagree, but I'm proud I have a man who was not afraid to shed a few tears when he learned all your guy has lost."

Archie had not yet taken a seat.

After hearing that, she found a chair and sank into it.

Andy watched his daughter do this, biting impatiently, "Haley."

But Haley kept her gaze steady on Archie.

And she kept her shoulders squared.

Last, she kept talking.

"I'm never, ever, *ever* going to say you're lucky you had the time you had with your mother. Andy talks about her and there is no question why he loved her so very deeply. I love your father like crazy. I still wish she was here for all of you. But I will say, after watching that film, I had some concerns about you hooking up with that young man. Because you two are not on equal footing with something essential to life. You had something he didn't have and he's in a position where all he lost is surrounding him all the time. He can't get away from it. But he also can't understand it. Not in the way everyone around him does. And that has to be...well, it has to be torture. To be of something so good and pure, and never having known the touch of it. Except as a phantom. A ghost. A story someone tells that is integral to who you are, but to you, it will only ever be just a story."

Oh God.

Archie thought about her mom.

All the amazing things about her mom.

The way she'd smile at her dad.

The way she did voices when she read stories to them when they were little.

The time she sat in bed with Archie when Archie's first crush decided he liked some other girl and she told her story about how her first crush went through the entire second grade, starting with Bryn. So she had to watch as he went through the rest of them, and that was so much worse than Archie's story, Archie felt better. But how her mom told it, by the end of it, they were both laughing.

How, every time they went to the grocery store, she made a game of them picking a treat, and made a point of teaching them how to share that love, because they each got to pick a candy bar or a bag of chips, but they also had to pick something to take home to their dad. And they couldn't pick something *they* wanted, they had to think hard and pick something their father would like.

And the totally bonkers and insanely loud way she'd shout and cheer at one of Elijah's games that was *so* embarrassing when Archie was thirteen, but looking back, Archie saw the love and pride in it, how open her mother was in sharing it and how beautiful that was.

The thought of not having those memories…

Having her dad or her grandparents share things about her mother, but never knowing them herself.

God.

Unthinkable.

She knew that Jagger didn't have this, but until that moment, it never really sunk in just how much he'd never had.

"Haley," her father bit again when he watched Archie's eyes fill with tears.

And again, Haley ignored him.

"Watch that movie," she advised firmly.

"Haley!" Andy clipped.

Haley was not to be denied.

"Watch it, doll. And I will never advise anyone to keep something from someone they love, especially not a partner. So tell him you intend to watch it. But watch it. You need to. For him. For you. And," she cocked her head, trying to take the intensity out of what she was saying, "because it's a really good movie."

"Mom would say that."

Haley grew still at Archie's words.

Andy went solid.

"She would advise me to be strong. She would expect it," Archie said.

Neither Haley nor Andy replied.

Archie got up from her seat and went to her stepmom.

She then hugged her and said in her ear, "Thank you."

At first, Haley seemed surprised, and until that moment, Archie hadn't realized she hadn't been ugly or mean, but she might have been standoffish.

This meant Haley was stiff, until Archie spoke those words into her ear.

She then curved Archie in her arms and relaxed in her hold.

And damn, being held in Haley's arms felt nice.

Shit.

Maybe the still-nervous-after-all-these-years wasn't just about Elijah.

But about her too.

Archie kept hold but she shifted her head so she could catch Haley's eyes and she shared, "I asked him if he minded if I watched. He said he didn't. But he was weird about it when we talked about it, so I think he would."

"Then you two need to have a conversation about why that would be. Because there is a good deal of history behind that Club that's concerning, but they're beyond that. So unless he thinks you'll be judgy." She kept Archie in her arms even as she shrugged and concluded, "And I know you two are new, but the one thing he has to know about you is the last thing you are is judgy."

That was such a nice thing to say.

"Thank you for telling it like it is," Archie said.

Haley looked cute and kind of embarrassed when she replied, "My pleasure."

Their hug couldn't have been different than one from her mom—and make no mistake, Archie did not forget an iota of what a hug from her mom felt like.

But her mom was tall and thin, not average height and rounded.

Her mom wore Tom Ford perfume.

Haley wore Chloe.

But dang, how did Archie miss that, when her dad found someone to love, he'd given the same thing to Archie?

"I can't wait for you to meet him, I think you're really gonna like him," Archie told her.

And Haley looked her dead in the eye when she replied, "If he's anything like his father, I know I will."

Yeah, she had to watch that movie.

This meant ditching the shop so she could watch during the day because Jagger had her nights.

She gave Haley a squeeze, Haley squeezed back, and when they let go of each other and turned to Andy, they saw his eyes were bright with tears.

"Such a lovable lug," Haley said softly.

She was so right.

Archie went to her dad, kissed his cheek, got another hug, and felt like a loser bitch that she'd made him wait this long to witness his two girls connecting.

She'd make amends later, starting tomorrow night.

Now she had to get to the theater.

She'd already blown off a pickup from Jagger, who wanted them to go to the movie together.

And by the time she hit the Chez Artiste theater, she was cutting it close to the movie starting, and was five minutes late for when they agreed to meet.

Jag was waiting for her with the concessions he'd already bought.

And Archie felt that sleeping dragon shift when Jag saw her, and she knew he wanted to ask why he couldn't pick her up and why she'd barely made the screening time.

Giving him permission not to share, she'd somehow taken away his ability to ask.

She didn't push about something important, and he was returning the favor—with everything.

But she hadn't asked for that favor.

More, she didn't want it.

After giving him a greeting kiss, she grabbed her drink and the nachos, he had the popcorn and his own drink with the Milk Dud box poking out of the back pocket of his jeans, and they hit the theater.

They were seated and settled before she leaned to him and shared, "I had to pop by my dad's. I needed to talk to him about something and it ended in me bonding with Haley. Also realizing I've never really bonded with Haley. That's a longer story I'll tell you after the movie."

"Cool, cool," he muttered, grabbing a chip loaded with ridiculously yellow cheese and more jalapeños than she'd be able to deal with, and she liked it spicy, and shoving it in his mouth.

"Baby," she called.

He looked to her.

"You know you can ask me anything, right?" she queried.

"Yeah," he said, going back to the chips and turning again to face the screen as he chewed.

She caught his jaw and brought him to face her again.

"I'm serious, Jag."

"I didn't think you weren't."

The lights dimmed, and since they couldn't get deep into this during a film (not to mention, she was a trailer girl), she let his jaw go and went after her own chip.

But she couldn't focus on the trailers.

Because somehow, she'd messed up.

Now she needed to figure out how to fix it and evidence was suggesting going right to the source, that being Jagger, wasn't the way she could do that.

It was clear he was a get and give kind of guy.

She gave him headspace, and he was determined to return it no matter that she didn't need it.

And that was all kinds of sweet.

But that didn't negate the fact she didn't need it.

So she needed to find another fix.

Archie had the feeling she'd find the path to that fix watching a documentary she really, seriously wanted to see.

And she was completely dreading watching.

Chapter Thirteen

Boys Like You

Jagger

Outside the school, Jagger sat on his bike next to Dutch, who was also sitting his.

They'd found a place just around the corner where they could see the entrance to the school, but you'd have to be looking to see them watching.

They were this way because they didn't need anyone getting up in their shit about what they were doing.

It was bordering on creeping.

But Jagger wanted answers.

Since that sitch with Mal the week before, Jagger had made a point to hang at the store, mostly just to be around, be visible.

Be available.

For Mal.

Mal hadn't taken him up on this in the way Jagger wanted, sharing what might be going down at school (or after it) that continued to drag his mood down.

That didn't mean Mal didn't respond to Jagger being around.

They connected.

It was surface, but definitely Mal got something out of Jagger giving a shit.

Could be it elevated his position in the kid gang at the store, having Jagger's attention, Jagger being Archie's, Archie being so fucking awesome.

Could be he just needed a consistent man in his life since his dad was temporarily out of the picture, and Fabe didn't play favorites, but he was also at work, and his work wasn't hanging with the kids, so he didn't have the time.

"What's the gig with his dad again?" Dutch asked, bringing Jagger out of his thoughts and into the now.

His convo with Archie that weekend got him to thinking.

It also prodded him to reach out to his brother, share what Archie did for her community and get into what was going on with Mal.

He finished this with sharing with Dutch that he thought it was time for some sleuthing, and asked him if he wanted to join in.

First, Dutch thought it was the shit that Archie stepped up for her people that way (and he was right).

Second, Dutch hadn't hesitated when Jagger asked if he wanted in.

And there they were.

Jag felt good about this.

It was right. Two brothers hanging together, working something important. It was how it should be.

And maybe he should go to his ma and Hound, share about Archie, her kids and Mal and get their take on it.

One thing Keely and Hound Ironside knew was raising boys.

But for now…

"The dad's in the military. He was transferred. He's now stationed in one of the Carolinas, and he's currently deployed," he answered Dutch's question. "But I get the sense from Archie that the dad isn't an issue."

"But the kid doesn't talk about it?" Dutch asked.

"Nope," Jagger answered, thinking this said a lot, just not certain what it said.

Dutch didn't ask about the mom. Or the sick grandma.

He asked about the dad, like the dad might be an issue, when in this case, the dad wasn't an issue.

But that was Dutch's first go-to.

And there it was.

It was a thing, boys and their dads.

It wasn't just Jag.

It totally was a thing.

On this thought, Mal came out of the school.

And he did it walking fast.

This heightened Jagger's attention, since Mal wasn't doing anything fast these days. He still slunk around the store like he had shoes made of concrete.

"There he is," Jagger said.

"Which one?"

"Black kid. Jeans. White tee. Gray hoodie."

"Got him."

Jag's back snapped straight when he saw what came next.

"And there are the twins. The two white fucks following him."

Watching Mal walk like he was trying to look like he wasn't running away, but was totally running away, Jag rolled his head on his shoulders.

While he did, he felt—and heard—three pops.

They were so deep, Dutch heard them too. Jag knew it when he felt

Dutch's eyes on him.

"Shit, brother," Dutch said quietly. "That's fucked up."

"It's all right."

"It isn't. Seriously, how are you that wound up when you're livin' the goodness with Archie? Is this kid under your skin that much?" Dutch asked.

Jagger had a feeling that wasn't about Mal.

Jag kept his eyes on the kids as they made their quick way down the sidewalk when he answered, "You know it happens. It always happens no matter what's going on in my life."

"You gotta get on top of that," Dutch advised.

"Right," Jagger muttered, then louder, "We don't roll, we'll lose them."

He felt Dutch's focus shift away. "Two bikes are loud. We need to give them some more—"

Dutch stopped talking when they watched Aaron Harris advance fast on Mal and shove him so hard, Mal went down to his hands and knees.

Seeing that, without a word between the riders, two bikes roared to life when Aaron didn't hesitate to draw back a foot to kick.

Jag and Dutch rolled out, and when they got close, like they had a mind meld, they both rolled up.

Dutch, straight up on the sidewalk, cutting off the Harrises' retreat, Jagger, beyond the action, cutting off an advance.

The second Harris brother, Allan, who'd been hanging back while Aaron whaled on Mal, tried to make a break for it, but was caught short by Dutch grabbing the back of his neck and pulling him around, giving him a shove to keep him pinned between the bikes.

Aaron not only saw there was no retreat, school had just let out. There were kids everywhere.

He'd waited until they were off school property, and probably out of sightline of staff, to instigate his attack.

But now he had an audience.

And he was so intent to retain his street cred, for him, retreat wasn't an option.

With Jag and Dutch in the mix, he was too young to completely hide his fear, though.

Jagger parked his bike, switched off the ignition and dismounted.

Dutch had already touched one of the kids, Jagger didn't think it wise to go there.

What he should do, he had no clue.

He had to go with his gut.

"What'd I tell you, if I found out you were fuckin' with my boy?" he demanded irately, eyes locked to Aaron, but he jerked his head down to Mal who was pulling himself up from the sidewalk.

Aaron had gotten a kick in and then some. Jag saw it before they rolled in.

"You can't—" Aaron started.

Although Jagger didn't advance, he leaned toward Aaron, and they were not close, but the way Jagger did it, Aaron still shut his trap and leaned away.

"You don't know what I can do, motherfucker," he threatened. "And I can guaran-damn-tee you, you just bought trouble. Now fuck off." When neither twin moved, he roared, "*Now!*"

Allan bolted.

Aaron had to save face, so he glared at Jagger a beat before he turned and jogged in the direction his brother took.

Jag watched him go, caught Dutch's eye, saw his brother's jaw was tight, knew he was pissed (and that would be *very* pissed), but he wasn't half as pissed as Jagger.

Jag then looked down at Mal.

"You okay?"

"Good, yeah, okay," Mal muttered.

"Bud, that piece of shit kicked you."

"I'm alright."

"You wanna ride to the shop with me on my bike?"

Mal shook his head and he did it quick, glancing around under his brow at the kids who were hanging for the show.

Jagger felt that. At Mal's age, he probably wouldn't climb on the back of some guy's bike either. And he not only grew up with bikers, he knew one day he'd be one.

It was then Jagger looked around, and he saw Martin, Colby and Dex, three of Archie's kids standing close.

What he wanted to do was ask why the fuck Mal was coming out of that school by himself when the Harris twins might think twice if he had a crew with him.

But they still had an audience, what with two bikers rolling up like that, their bikes still on the sidewalk.

So he'd get into that later.

"Walk your bud to the store, yeah?" he asked them. "Make sure he's good. Can you do that for me?"

"Sure!" Martin said readily and with some exuberance.

Right.

Maybe it wasn't that he was Archie's and they thought Archie was cool.

Maybe they just thought Jag was cool.

Colby and Dex only nodded, though Colby came forward, tagged the arm of Mal's hoodie and said, "C'mon, Mal. Let's get to S.I.L."

They started to stroll off, but Mal stopped, looked back and up, mumbled a "Thanks" Jagger almost couldn't hear, then they moved away.

Jagger watched them go and felt Dutch come up to his side.

"Okay, man, that's an issue. There's bullying and then there's shoving a kid to the ground and kicking him."

"The mom has to know," Jag said, not taking his eyes from the retreating boys.

"The mom has to know," Dutch agreed.

Jag was not liking this.

He explained why to Dutch. "I'll never get to him if I rat to his mom."

"Maybe not," Dutch replied.

Jagger turned to him.

"Okay, probably not," Dutch allowed.

"They can do him damage, and it's smart not to hit him in the face, Dutch."

Dutch's jaw got tight again.

"You don't just know that kind of shit. You *learn* that kind of shit. They're fuckin' twelve," Jagger carried on.

"This is not about them, Jag. It's about your kid. Mal. You gotta tell Archie. His mom has to know. The school has to know. But first, you need to call Archie. Someone has to look him over. At the very least, he's got scrapes from takin' that fall. The kid was wearing sneaks, not steel-toed boots, but a kick can break bones no matter what you got on your foot. He needs to be checked out."

"By a doc or his mom, it isn't cool Archie does it."

"Exactly."

"Fuck," Jag muttered.

"This sucks, but it's better than where you were half an hour ago, not knowing what was up with him. He might not like how you handle it, Jagger. But the bottom line is, you've found out it's something that needs to get handled, and now it'll be handled."

Jag nodded.

Then he got out his phone.

Before he made the call, he asked his brother, "You wanna check out Archie's shop?"

Dutch didn't reply verbally.

But with the way he smiled, he didn't have to.

They moved to their bikes with Jagger calling Archie.

She didn't pick up, which didn't bother him. She wasn't prone to lounging on her couch all day waiting for a call from Jagger. And on his bike, he'd probably be to the shop faster than Mal.

They backed their bikes off the sidewalk and rode side by side to the store, parking in the rear.

Since Jagger was showing more often to see to Mal, Archie'd had a key cut for him. This meant, instead of having to walk around the building, they went to the back door.

And once they were in it, Jagger had his answer as to why Archie didn't pick up his call.

Jag hadn't seen Archie's brother since Elijah was sixteen.

But there was no mistaking the tall, good-looking man who was right then openly pissed as all fuck and fully up in his woman's shit.

Like…

Physically.

He had six inches on her but there was less than an inch between their faces, and Jagger couldn't hear what he was saying, but there wasn't a centimeter of his body that did not share he was all kinds of furious.

Instinct guided Jagger's next moves, which were to get behind Archie, curl his fingers in the back of her jeans, pull her away from her brother and step between them.

"What the—?" Elijah started angrily.

"Maintain space or I won't, and you won't like how I won't," Jagger growled.

"Jagger, baby," Archie murmured, and he felt her hand fall light between his shoulder blades.

He also felt Dutch get close and watched Elijah's eyes dart to him.

And he noted something he didn't when he walked in and saw what he saw.

The storage space wasn't only taken up by the fruits of Archie's day (since he knew she was hitting some flea market as well as two auctions to bulk up stock), Joany was standing there and she was pissed as all fuck too.

"You gonna stand down?" Jagger asked and got Elijah's attention again.

"So you finally made a move," he sneered.

And he was Arby's Guy to Elijah too.

Not a surprise.

"That isn't an answer to my question," Jag noted.

"This is between Arch and me, so beat it," Elijah replied.

"And you can have a conversation with your sister. What you can't do is be up in her shit when you do."

"This is none of your business," Elijah returned.

"You're right and you're wrong. Whatever you're talking about is none of my business. But I'll repeat, you *do not* get up *in your sister's shit* when you're conversing with her. And *that* is absolutely my business."

They scowled at each other way too fucking long before Elijah took a step back, stabbed a finger at his sister and stated, "We're not done but I'm not talking about this with your dog in the room. You'll hear from me."

"Elij—"

Archie didn't get her brother's full name out.

Without looking at anyone, he stormed to the door, which had a push bar and a sturdy hinge at the top to avoid the heavy door slamming.

Elijah still put the effort into slamming it.

Jag turned to Archie.

"Let me guess, you told him he was paying his half of the handyman," he deduced.

She'd looked mildly freaked, and equally mildly put out, but when he said that she smiled that almost-smug, totally-hot smile of hers.

"And then some," she shared.

"Okay, I need some assistance here," Joany stated in Archie's direction, bellying up to them, "'Cause, see, I got hella mindfuck going on because simultaneously I don't know whether to touch my contacts to see if I can order a hit on that crazy-ass brother of yours. This along with beating back an inappropriate orgasm with the repeat goin' on in the back of my brain of your boy here sharing what is *absolutely his business* and how he did that. And last, tamping down my jubilation that his semi-twin has shown up and he's not wearing a ring."

"He's taken," Jagger informed her.

"Pity," she muttered.

"Hey, I'm Dutch, Jag's brother," Dutch introduced himself to Joany with a huge smile he knew melted panties.

Jagger sighed.

"I'm single, just, you know, in case shit goes south at home," she replied.

"I'll keep that in mind," Dutch promised, still smiling.

Joany's eyes darted between the brothers before she said, "For crap's sake, you two have the exact same voice. This will not help me fight my twin fantasies. You could blindfold me, and I wouldn't know who was doing what."

"Dear Lord," Archie mumbled.

"Do not tell me you haven't thought about it," Joany accused.

Archie had no comment to that.

Jesus Christ.

Now Dutch was grinning so big, it had to hurt his face.

"You wanna help me put an end to this?" Jag asked his brother.

"I don't mind being a pretty girl's fantasy," Dutch continued flirting, punctuating this with a wink at Joany.

For fuck's sake.

"If you don't tone it down, bruh, I'm sharing with Georgie," Jagger warned.

"Dude, Georgie flirts in front of my face. She knows she owns my dick. We both know I don't want anyone else to claim it. So it's all good."

"Do real people talk like this, or am I in a movie?" Joany asked Archie.

"You're not in a movie," Archie replied. "Though I will point out you just shared you nearly had an orgasm."

Archie was also smiling, and it was again semi-smug.

Probably because she knew she owned Jagger's dick.

"Huh, I did do that," Joany replied.

"Right, as cute as we're all being, two things," Jag began. "One, Dutch and me checked shit out at the school today, watching the kids come out, and they barely got a block off school grounds before the Harrises went after Mal. Or Aaron did. He pushed him to the ground and kicked him. We rolled in and put a stop to it, but the time is now to discuss talking to his mother."

Archie and Joany stared at him and no one was smiling.

"Two, we need to have a convo about your brother, because what we walked in on is not okay," he finished.

"Is Mal hurt?" Archie asked.

"He said he was all right, but I think he still needs to be checked out," Jag answered.

She digested that, then said, "Jag, honey, if we go to his mom, we're gonna lose him."

They probably were.

"As much as I want to, I can't shadow him everywhere he goes and hope the Harrises will see he has a bodyguard and find someone else to fuck with," Jagger told her. "And Mal's not dealing with this. He rolled out of school in a hurry, but he can't escape this. They're not gonna let him ignore it. We have no clue what's happening in school. We're not his peers, we're adults and we have to have his best interests in mind, baby. If he was my son, and anyone knew this was happening to him and didn't tell me, I'd be pissed as shit."

She didn't even need to process that, she nodded.

"You say there are cliques. But Dex, Martin and Colby are cool with him here. They play videogames together. They don't seem to dislike him," Jag remarked. "But they were there, and they didn't step up for him. Four against two is decent odds, especially when it seems only Aaron is the asshole. I'm saying this because we also need to find a way to get those boys to look after their friend. It's not on, them letting him swing in the breeze like that."

Through a grin, she replied, "Says the MC brother."

"It's you teaching them what a tribe is all about, Arch," he retorted. "They are not looking after their tribe. They need to look out for their tribe, and that includes Gina, Tracee and Mia."

She didn't take time to process that either.

Her eyes warmed and she again nodded.

"Now, Elijah," he prompted.

"I'm hearin' good things about this soda fountain," Dutch cut in. "Can you do vanilla Cokes?" he asked Joany.

"There is so much I can do, baby, it's not funny," Joany drawled. "But we'll start with a vanilla Coke." She held out a hand to Dutch. "Come to momma. We'll get you sorted out."

No hesitation, Dutch took her hand, tucked it into the crook of his arm and started to escort her to the hall that led to the door to the store.

As they went, Dutch asked, "So these contacts you can touch to set up a hit…?"

Joany looked back as they walked and rolled her eyes dramatically, also licking her lips.

So Archie was laughing softly as they walked out of sight.

Jagger was not.

"Babe," he called, his voice firm.

She looked to him.

"Okay, so I thought about it, and before I chickened out, decided on it and you were right. As I mentioned, it wasn't exactly a slum, but it wasn't great before I sorted things out. Now it's safe, it's nice. I looked up average rents in this area and we're over three hundred below that. I'm not saying we should jump up rents, but it's something to think about. And we can have a tenant meeting and talk about how a cost of living increase would affect them, and—"

"I'm interested in what you're saying, but this is not an explanation about Elijah being pissed as hell and nose to nose with you when I walked in ten minutes ago, babe," he cut her off to note.

She dipped her head side to side, probably to buy time, but when he put his hands on his hips, she went on.

"I called him. And I thought, maybe it'd work better if we entered into negotiations, instead of me just telling him how it would be. And since I want to meet in the middle, and I know Elijah, he'll want to feel like he won, I went for the gusto and told him not only was I deducting half the monthly expenses from his take, I would email him a list of the cost of improvements, and a cumulative of what I've spent so far on upkeep, adding to that fifty bucks a month for cleaning bills since I began doing that chore, and I'd be deducting an additional five hundred from his portion until he paid me back for his half of all of that."

That wasn't going for the gusto, that was seriously not fucking around.

"Jesus, baby," Jag murmured.

"I also told him he either came once a month to clean the common areas or he was paying me twenty-five dollars a month from here on out to keep them clean. It only takes an hour, but it isn't the most fun thing to do. I'll do my rotation, but he's responsible one way or another for his."

"So you called him with this, how did it get to him being here, in your space?"

"He hung up on me and was so angry, he left work in order not to delay telling me face to face that shit wasn't happening."

Jagger drew in a very long breath and held it.

He didn't let it out until Archie laid her hand on his chest.

"I also know where I'm gonna rest on this," she told him. "I'll eat the maintenance I've paid so far, and we can come to a figure he's okay with on the improvements, but I also have to be okay with it. That said, I'm not caring for this building without his help. So he either pays me to clean, he cleans, or we agree on paying someone to come in and clean. He also either pays extra for me to deal with accounting and admin, or he takes his share of handling that. If he wants nothing to do with any of this, he can buy me out. But if he reaps the rewards, he shares the burdens."

"Good," Jagger said softly.

"He's threatening to sell his half, but not to me."

Jag got quiet again.

"I'm no lawyer," she said. "I don't know if he can do that, but it's his and I suppose he can. And honestly, it might be better not to have to deal with Elijah. I told him this and that was what you walked in on."

"You called his bluff and he lost it."

She nodded. "I called his bluff and he went from ticked to out of his mind. Commence him getting up in my shit."

"And your take on that?" he asked.

"He doesn't want to sell. With half my rent on the store and the units, which, by the way, I give him money for my apartment too, he's making five grand a month."

"And maybe, he wants to be in on this with you," Jagger suggested.

She looked confused. "What?"

"This was your grandparents'. Your mom's folks. It's a building, but it's also a legacy. Maybe even a memory. And you're his sister. I just met him, and he didn't make a good first impression, but if he was an out-and-out prick who wasn't worth your time, you're the type of woman who wouldn't give him your time. So there's a bond, and my guess…it's not just business. I'm sure the same goes for you. You're his sister and he loves you. He doesn't want to lose this because he makes good bill on it, but also because he's in it with his sister."

He got another warm look after he said that, and she sidled closer.

"I'm currently in denial about the fact you met my brother like you just did. Not to mention, all I've done pretty much is bitch about him. Because he's not a dick. He can *be* a dick, but he *isn't* a dick."

Jag moved too, to hook an arm around her and pull her even closer.

He did this saying, "I get the distinction."

"You guys will get along. Though, warning, I'm not sure you'll be tight. Haley will love you. Dad will really like you. Eventually, after we get past this, Elijah will dig you, but you won't pal around. He's into sports, watching and playing, and he's putting himself through law school."

That law school bit was news.

"So he's not lazy, he's just conditioned to lean on you, and in some cases, that means taking advantage of you," Jag remarked.

She nodded.

Right then.

They needed to move this along.

"Okay, you're on with Mal's mom," he said. "But I think we should warn him that's going to happen. If he's not sharing with her, then he won't want to be blindsided by that, because she's probably gonna be all over it."

"She will be," Archie confirmed.

"And as for the group, I got an idea."

She was running her hands up his chest and when she got to his shoulders, she held on and asked, "What's your idea?"

"I think they should come to Chaos, to Ride. Meet the brothers. Field trip. Showing them another version of a tribe, how we work together, and I'll figure out how to do the lecture about looking out for your people without making it seem like a lecture between now and whenever that happens. Do we have to get their parents' permission for them to leave the store?"

"Yeah, I always tell them when we're off to do something. But we have an email group so it's easy. I can just pop a line to them. They'll all be cool with it. They dig when the kids have something fun to do."

"Great. Once you do that, I'll arrange some brothers to come for pickups."

She leaned some of her weight into him and said, "Awesome, boyfriend, now maybe we should talk about you being all alpha all over my storeroom with my brother, and incidentally, *me*."

"Babe—"

She placed her three middle fingers over his lips to stop him from speaking.

"I'm not going to say that was the wrong call. I honestly don't think I've ever seen Elijah that pissed. I don't think he would have hurt me, but I was not okay with him being in my face like that. That said—"

He pulled her fingers from his lips. "It's the guy you got."

She did a perplexed blink. "Sorry?"

"Me, that's the guy you got. I'm not gonna be okay with anyone up in your face, Archie, and I'm also not gonna hang back, let it happen and let you deal with it if I can do something about it."

"You knew he was my brother."

"I did. And as your brother and as a man, he needs to respect you." He shook his head sharply when she opened her mouth. "Nope, babe. No. He never should have been in your space like that. If you gleefully shot his dog, I'm out and he can take his anger out the way he sees fit. You're calling him on pulling shit, he doesn't like it, he takes a goddamn breath and gets some control. He does not come to your space and get into your face. No. End of discussion."

He said those last three words because it was worth a shot to say those three words.

But this was Archie.

Consequently, it was not the end of the discussion.

"I would have told him that once he calmed down," she returned.

"I believe you, but it didn't happen that way, and I'm just not that guy who is going to walk in on his woman in that sitch and not make the move I made."

They both fell silent.

Jagger broke it.

"That an issue for you?"

"It's definitely sweet, you looking out for me and being protective. But I can handle myself and my brother is never a threat."

"But you get where I'm coming from?"

It took her a second, then she nodded.

Though after she gave him that, she asked, "If you're having words with Dutch, how would you feel about me pulling you out of that and getting in Dutch's shit?"

He rolled his neck.

There was no popping, then again, he'd already popped it not long ago.

She did not miss this move, or likely what precipitated it, even without the evidence being audible, so her voice was sweet to soften the score she noted with her next words. "You get where I'm coming from, boyfriend?"

"All right, I'll take a breath next time. Though, just sayin', that happens again with Elijah, the fact of that alone, that breath might not work."

"Sometimes I think I should introduce you to my friend Joany," she joked. "She thinks boys like you are all kinds of cute."

He adjusted so he had an arm around her shoulders, and he tucked her into his side.

He then moved them in the direction of the door to the store while he said, "There's a dude out there special enough for your girl. He just is not me. I've figured out I like them chill."

"Mm…" she hummed, before, "I'm taking it our discussion is over?"

"My guess, Mal's here by now and we gotta talk to him, see how he is and give him the heads up. Then you got a call to make."

They were in the hall and she was staring at the door they were headed toward like she didn't want it to get any closer.

He then gave her the same pep talk Dutch gave him.

"It's good we know what's going down, babe. Because what's going down is *not* good and it needs to stop."

"Yeah, I just…"

She let out a heavy sigh and he stopped them at the door without going through it.

She looked up at him and finished, "Being an adult sucks sometimes."

"Yeah," he agreed.

"All right, honey, let's get this done."

"Yeah," he repeated.

"First though, just to say, you going to the school to check on Mal…" She grinned up at him. "I've figured out I like boys like you too."

On that, he realized he hadn't given her a hello kiss.

He saw to that.

He then made sure he did a thorough job with it.

When they were done, they turned to the door.

And together, they pushed through it to get things done.

* * * *

"Okay, that's sorted. But before I call her, you need to be real with me, Mal. Are you truly okay? I mean, physical-wise, where they kicked you."

They were at the soda fountain, him, Archie and Mal.

And Archie was finishing things up with Mal before she moved on to having a chat with his mom.

Dutch was somewhere with Joany, and he had a feeling she'd let him select the music, considering Buckcherry was playing.

"I'm okay, Archie," Mal replied.

"Tell it true, Mal," she urged.

Jag was sitting next to the kid, Archie on the opposite side from him.

Both Jag and Mal had cherry Cokes, Archie made them then opted out of a refreshment for herself.

"I'm telling it true, honest," Mal told her.

Jag studied the kid's profile and he'd have to be a seriously good liar to be pulling that off because he didn't look like he was bullshitting.

Jag then looked to Archie, catching her nod. She pushed from the back counter, went to Mal, laid her hand flat on the counter in front of him and said, "It's because I dig you. You mean something to me. Okay?"

"Okay," Mal replied.

She studied him.

And that was when Jagger saw in her what he felt in himself, but he couldn't pinpoint what it was until then.

Mal was not their zone anymore.

Like she said, it sucked being an adult, but it was more.

They were powerless to take care of him in certain ways because they were his tribe, but they were not his *tribe*.

He really needed to get the other kids to Ride.

Her eyes came to him, he gave her a smile he hoped made her feel better, and then she reached out and touched Mal's forearm before she murmured, "I'm off to call your mom. Be back."

With that, she took off.

Jagger lifted his Coke and sucked some back.

Dutch showed and took the position Archie had been in at the back counter.

"Belated intro, that's my brother, Dutch," Jagger introduced.

"Yo," Dutch said to Mal.

"Yo," Mal replied, then bent his head to the striped, paper straw coming out of his glass.

Jag couldn't get a bead on him.

But just to cover his bases…

"Don't be pissed at Arch. Like she said, she's sharing with your mom because she cares about you."

"You guys think it's this. It's not this. Though, Dad's ticked about this,"

Mal mumbled to his drink.

Jag shot a look to Dutch who had his arms crossed on his chest, his boots crossed at the ankles, but he didn't move after Mal spoke, except to catch Jag's look.

That was an opening and Jag wanted to jump on it and tear it wide.

But he fought against that urge, and instead proceeded carefully.

"Your dad knows about the twins?" Jag asked.

Mal sucked back more Coke.

"Mal, buddy, please tal—"

Mal let go of the straw, and still slumped over his drink, he turned only his head to Jag.

"He wants me to tell Mom. I don't want to worry her. I can handle the twins."

"No offense, bro, but it wasn't looking that way to me," Jag replied warily.

"I don't care about them."

"You kinda hid that you were racing away from them, but not totally," Jagger pointed out.

"Not wanting to put up with their shit isn't the same as caring about them."

You couldn't argue that.

"Have they done this before?" Dutch asked.

Mal looked to him and Jag didn't know whether to give Dutch the sign to shut up, or not. Jag barely knew the kid. Dutch didn't know him at all. And he was finally talking, they didn't need for him to clam up.

"The shoving, yeah. The kicking, no. The generally being a pain in the ass, all the time. But they don't matter," Mal answered Dutch.

Jag let out a relieved breath, hearing the news that today was the day it escalated, and today was the day they were making moves to put a stop to it.

Then he asked, "So your dad knows and…"

Mal looked to him. "And I told him I can hack it. I made him promise not to tell Mom. So he's ticked that the Harris brothers are being pains in my ass, and he's ticked because he thinks Mom should know. He's also ticked that school hasn't done something about it. But I told him I'm the man of the house now, so I get to make that choice. And he got me, so he stood down."

Right, well…

Shit.

"You wanna explore that?" Jagger asked.

"What? That he and Mom split?" Mal asked back. "Not really. It sucks. It happened. They fought a lot and it's better this way. I don't have to listen to them shouting at each other. And they don't have to shout at each other. But I'm her guy now, he's not anymore, and I gotta look after her. I told him it's what he taught me to do. Even if they fought a lot, he looked out for her, still does. So he knows he gave me that and it's what I gotta do."

Jag did not get where this was going, this talk of looking out for his mother when it wasn't her that was being harassed by some assholes.

So he cautiously pushed, "What does that mean?"

"It's cool you guys are named weird names."

It took a sec, but at this abrupt change in topic, Jag released the tension in his shoulders that was caused by his excitement and hope that Mal was finally opening up.

Mal had shared.

He was done sharing.

They got what they got, and Jag wasn't going to push it.

"I wish I had a weird name, like LeBron or Chadwick," Mal continued.

"Those aren't weird names," Dutch said.

Mal looked at him. "Don't fake it. White people totally think Black people have weird names."

Dutch wisely decided not to reply because Dutch, like Jag, didn't give a shit what anyone named their kid, and not only for the obvious reasons they wouldn't give a shit about something like that, but they both knew what Mal said was not wrong.

"Mal is a cool name," Jagger told him.

"It's short for Malcolm," Mal replied.

"Malcolm is a cooler name," Jag returned.

"I know. And you don't have to educate me. Mom and Dad told me. Made me read about him. I know I'm named after Malcolm X. He's theirs though. Or their parents' and he was passed down to them. But LeBron and Chadwick, they're mine," Mal stated.

You really couldn't argue that either.

"So name your kid one of those names," Dutch suggested. "That way, you can give him that and keep those names alive, at the same time give him who's a piece of you and keep Malcolm X alive."

Mal stared at Dutch a beat before he turned to Jag.

"Your brother's dope," he declared.

Jag grinned at him. "Pretty much, yeah."

Mal kept eye contact when he said, "Thanks for today. It's cool you care. And I'm really not mad at Archie. So Mom will know now. I'll deal."

"All right, Mal. But just to say, it's clear there's more, and if you need to talk, like I told you, I'm there."

Mal nodded a boy-man nod that was more man than boy. "Thanks. Though even if Dad doesn't get to call very often from where he's at, he calls. I talk to him. So I'm cool. Honest."

He wasn't cool.

But again, they got what they got that day, and it was more than Mal had been giving.

So he wasn't going to push.

"Okay, buddy," Jagger said.

Mal turned back to his drink and sucked more up.

He then said to Jag, "I never had a cherry Coke. It's pretty sick."

Jag grinned at him again. "Stick with me, Mal. I've got a lot of things to share that are awesome, and totally bad for you."

Mal grinned back, it was genuine and there didn't seem to be anything dragging on it.

A minor win, but a win.

He'd take it.

And for today at least, they'd managed to get it done.

Chapter Fourteen

The House He Built

Jagger

"I don't think I'd ever even heard of a yurt until Archie mentioned it."

"Her trip to Portugal sounded totally rad. I wanna go and stay where she stayed."

"Archie's gonna do Archie, but you won't catch me staying somewhere that I don't have my own bathroom and the room isn't cleaned every day by maids."

"You are *so boujee*."

"You say that like it's a bad thing."

"It kind of is. You're like, not enlightened at all."

"Power to the people and especially power to the ones with vaginas, and my power is going to be making scads of money and then staying at the Ritz during my bi-annual trips to Paris to go shopping."

"Ugh, gross."

"Whatever."

The comment about the yurt was Haley's.

The ensuing discussion was between Hellen and Liane, Haley's daughters, Archie's stepsisters.

Hellen was twenty, going to the University of Colorado in Boulder, studying business. She was the boujee one, and she didn't let down that side and dressed for dinner at what was still her home, considering she was a student, like she was having sushi with some real housewives somewhere.

Liane was eighteen. She was also at U of C in Boulder, her major undeclared. She was the granola one and she also represented, wearing a tee that said A WELL-READ WOMAN IS A DANGEROUS CREATURE, dark-wash jeans that, regardless of the wash, still had a number of splits and tears in the legs and Birkenstocks.

Jagger really wanted to find their conversation hilarious, because it was. They'd generally been hilarious since he and Archie arrived.

But Archie and her dad had disappeared into the kitchen with the last of the dinner dishes, with Andy telling Haley to take a load off, he and Archie were going to serve dessert.

And since dessert was cupcakes, which didn't take a lot of prep, Jag was distracted because they'd been in there a while.

He didn't get a read from her dad, or Haley, or the girls, that they didn't dig him.

There had definitely been a lot of looking him over.

But Archie was chill. He was chill.

And Jag found out straight away he had no worries about any of them having an issue with bikers.

This was because he'd discovered that fathers of daughters with dead mothers had long memories.

Jagger had won the guy over years before and Andy wasn't effusive about that, but he also didn't hide it. The rest of them fell in with that from the moment Jagger walked in the door.

So he wondered what was up with the disappearing act.

He turned his attention to Haley, who was fidgeting with the napkin in her lap.

Instinct, or more aptly, the vibe of her attitude took his attention to Hellen, who did not miss her mother's manner, which seemed suddenly anxious, and Hellen didn't like it.

Liane, the baby, didn't notice it.

Shit.

Archie had told him she'd finally begun to bond with her stepmom, and she was super happy about it. But she also told him that she'd always liked Haley.

She wouldn't want her anxious.

And she probably wouldn't keep this from her stepmom anyway, it was just likely that she didn't want to get into it and drag down what had been a good meet-the-boyfriend night.

"It's not my place to say," Jagger started.

All three women turned their eyes to him.

"But Archie has been having some issues with the way the building she co-owns with her brother is being handled," he continued. "She confronted him with that today and it didn't go too good. It's a guess, but I suspect she's sharing that with her dad right about—"

"*It's entirely unacceptable!*"

Everyone at the table jumped, including Jagger, as they heard Andy's thundered words coming from the kitchen.

"*No!*" he roared. "*You absolutely do not treat your sister like that!*" A beat then, "*Absolutely not! This is done! Your stepmother and I will buy your share!*"

Okay, well, first, he wasn't yelling at Archie.

And second, apparently Andy wasn't hip on what happened with Elijah that day either.

He also didn't hesitate to share with Elijah that he wasn't.

"Think on that!" Andy shouted, the thunder muted, but the man was still pissed so he was also still loud. "Yes, it would have been your mother's. Now it's yours. And if you don't get your goddamn head out of your ass, half of it *will* be Haley's because she's a *member of this goddamn family* and even *your grandparents treated her like that!*"

Fucking hell.

"Uh…" Haley said, hands to the arms of her chair like she wanted to get up, but she wasn't getting up.

"Go, Mom," Hellen encouraged. "It's your house, your husband and E being a douche is ruining another one of your dinners. You should know what's going on."

Haley looked to Hellen, Hellen nodded, Haley then said to Jag, "Sorry, I—"

"Go, me and the girls are good," he assured.

She looked relieved and then she took off.

"He's not even here and he's fucking things up," Hellen muttered under her breath.

"H, chill," Liane replied.

"I'm not gonna chill." Hellen was no longer mumbling. "I mean, you just heard Andy. I'm sure E is acting like the world revolves around him with whatever's up with him and Archie, because that's what he does, like, *all the time.* Then Andy mentions Mom, E's got some shit to say, it's his usual not-nice shit, and I'm tired of it. She's not a homewrecker, for God's sake. Bryn had been dead for years before Mom entered the picture."

Liane gave up on Hellen, who was getting worked up, and turned to Jag.

"Sorry," she said.

"No apologies necessary," he replied.

"We're usually not loud or crazy," Liane told him.

"No, that is completely wrong," Hellen enunciated every word carefully. "We're always loud *and* crazy when Elijah rears his head. Fortunately, he doesn't do that very often."

"He's our brother, H, stop it," Liane hissed.

"I'm tired of biting my tongue when that asshole fucks shit up. And he's not my brother, Liane. Not once has he treated me like he was my brother, or you like he was yours. He acts like Mom did him some grievous harm and us like we stole the family silver. I'm sick to death of it."

Liane's voice got quiet when she said, "Girl, cool it. Mom would toe-tah-lee *freak* if she heard you cuss like that, especially in front of company."

Hellen turned to him. "Am I offending you?"

"Nope," Jagger answered.

Hellen threw a hand his way. "See?"

"How would you offend Jagger?" Haley was back in the mix, walking into the room.

"No reason!" Liane lied brightly.

"I'm sharing it like it is about Elijah," Hellen told the truth.

"*Shh*," Liane shushed her sister.

This was because Archie and Andy were also coming into the room.

Andy looked like he was ready to murder someone, which was funny as fuck, considering he was also carrying a big tray of cupcakes that had massive froths of pink icing on top of them.

Archie had a stack of dessert plates.

"All right, so how about we think about cupcakes, and eat them, and even talk about them, and continue enjoying our night," Haley said, seating herself at the foot of the table and sounding kinda desperate.

"Love you, Mom, but…" Hellen started, she turned toward Andy, and having heard what she had to say before they joined them in the dining room, Jag shot his eyes right to Archie and gave her a look.

She bit her lip.

Hellen went for it.

"Andy, you know I love you too. You stepped up. You helped raise me and Li. All you do is love Mom when Dad has never been anything but a dick to her, and sometimes us. And Archie." She looked to Arch. "We're not close, but we're cool, and I like you loads. But this Elijah thing needs to be out of the kitchen and discussed among the family because Andy is right. He needs to get his head out of his ass."

"Hellen Katherine Moynihan, mouth, please," Haley snapped.

"Mom, seriously?" Hellen shot back. "We're having dramas and walking on eggshells *and the guy isn't even here.*"

"We'll discuss it later," Haley decreed.

"Why, because Jagger's here?" Hellen asked. "For as long as I can remember, Archie's never brought a guy to dinner. And you made me and Liane drive down from Boulder to meet him *the first time he shows for dinner.* So, it's not lost on me that's something special and he told us what's up so it's not like he's not in the know that Elijah can be…" her eyes slid to Andy and back to her mother before she finished, "*difficult.*"

Jag looked again to Archie.

She caught his gaze and tipped her head a bit to the side in unnecessary confirmation he was something special.

He felt his lips twitch.

"Hellen, sweetheart," Andy murmured.

Well…

Shit.

That did it.

Two words, and Hellen shut up.

Now he needed the story about Haley's ex because Andy didn't strike Jag as an authoritarian.

That was respect, love and possibly gratitude that closed Hellen's mouth.

"Maybe we should talk about it, Dad," Archie suggested.

"Oh boy," Liane mumbled.

"We don't have to, Li," Archie said to her quickly. "And if it's making you uncomfortable, we won't."

"I'm sorry he's being a dick to you, but—" Liane began.

"Now you with your mouth, I won't say it again." Haley was coming to the end of her rope.

"I'm sorry he's not being cool with you," Liane amended, aiming this Archie's way. "But can we have one family night when it's not all about Elijah?"

"Too late for that," Hellen pointed out the obvious.

It took a lot, but when Jagger's chest started bouncing with suppressed laughter, he was able to stop it.

Seriously, he liked Arch's stepsisters, particularly Hellen. She was the shit.

Then again, he'd always liked a woman who spoke her mind.

Archie gave him another look, that one said, *Behave.*

"You know…"

Everyone turned to look at Andy who was standing at the head of the table, still holding a big plate of cupcakes.

"In a perfect world, my son would be sitting at this table with us," he went on.

Jag didn't feel much like laughing anymore.

"He's not," Andy continued. "And this is not the first night where I've sat with my girls, my son not here, and felt light in my life, because I have all of you, at the same time felt the pain of not having my son be a part of it. And that pain never fails to cut sharp, clean through my heart."

Total silence.

But something made Jag stop looking at Andy. He turned his attention to Archie, and the second he saw her, he felt his neck muscles constrict.

And he opened his mouth immediately.

"Arch, don't."

"Fuck…*that*," she bit off.

Oh shit.

Jagger stood.

But she took the last step to the table, dumped the plates on it and was on the move, he knew, to her bag.

Jag took off after her.

Her bag was in the living room, which was off the dining room through opened double doors, so they had an audience.

He didn't think about that.

He got close as she hit the couch where she'd left her purse. By the time he got there, she'd already snatched it up and was digging in it.

"Take a breath, baby," he said quietly.

"No," she clipped toward her bag.

He wrapped a hand around the side of her neck and advised, "You don't want to say something you'll regret."

She tipped her head back, her black hair flying, and asked, "I don't?"

"Maybe you do in this moment, but you won't—"

"Tell me you would not lose your fucking mind if your mother said those words," she demanded, her arm slashing up, finger pointed toward the dining room, indicating her dad.

He couldn't, so he didn't.

"Tell me you wouldn't lose it if Hound said those words," she pushed, dropping her arm.

Jag again couldn't, so he didn't.

"Right," she snapped, engaged her phone, hit some buttons, and as she did, he realized the others had joined them.

"Archie, honey, I think—" Andy started.

"I'm not even gonna start with you," a male voice came over the speaker on Archie's phone.

Jag let her go and stepped back.

"You're on speaker, *with your entire family listening*," she announced.

"Then I'm definitely not—" Elijah tried.

"I don't care what you're not. Jagger's over here, Elijah. Jagger is sitting down to dinner with *your family*, and I bet Dad asked you to join us, and you blew him off. This man is important to me. He's mine. And tonight, *I gave him to my family*. But not you. No, when Jagger first met you, you were in my face so bad, he thought he had to protect me *from my brother*. You could have pulled that together if you'd been here tonight to show him you were a decent guy, but you're not here. You. Are. Missing. *Everything. YOU!* Because of what?"

"I'm not doing this now," Elijah said.

"You absolutely are because *I swear to fuck*, if you don't, I won't speak to you until you apologize to me, to Haley, to Hellen and Liane, and most of all to Dad for *breaking his heart over and over again*."

Elijah didn't say anything, but Jagger could see the screen, and he hadn't disconnected.

"What's your goddamn beef?" Archie demanded to know.

"I'm not going to say it again, I'm not doing this now."

"And I'm not going to say it again either, Elijah. I'm done ignoring your shit. I'm done putting up with your shit. I'm done excusing your shit. It's now or never, Elijah."

Fuck.

An ultimatum.

Not good.

"Baby," Jagger whispered.

She pinned him with a look.

Christ, he didn't think she could even get this angry.

It was lowkey glorious.

He closed his mouth.

"We'll talk when you've calmed down," Elijah stated.

"Like you took a beat and got your shit together before you accosted me at my store today? That kind of calm? Because if so, we can talk now, because I'm *that kind of calm right now, Elijah.*"

That was a score.

"I'm not putting on a show for Haley and her girls and your new beau." Elijah's voice was betraying a hint of impatience.

"Her girls? *Her girls?*" Archie's voice was rising. "You mean *our sisters?*"

"Ohmigod, how sweet," Liane whispered, but the whisper was thick.

"They are not—" Elijah began.

"*Do not fucking finish that!*" Archie screamed, loud and shrill.

Whoa.

Jag moved in again and caught her on both sides of her neck.

She looked up at him, and the second she did, two tears tracked down opposite cheeks.

His gut started burning.

"Your sister is crying," Jag declared, his voice crisp and sharp.

Nothing from Elijah but a hand came between Archie and Jag and nabbed Archie's phone.

It was Andy.

Jag pulled her into his arms.

When he got her there, her arms curved around him and got tight.

Andy spoke into the phone. "We need to end this now."

"Dad—"

"*Two* of your sisters are crying, Elijah, and so is my wife, who cares deeply for you whether you want that or not. She's given it to you from the beginning. Now, Haley started preparing this dinner last night, Elijah, because she knew how important it was. And then she spent hours in the kitchen this evening because she wanted Jagger to know that too. Something I've seen her do on countless occasions *for you.* And now that dinner is ruined, as so many of them have been before, and I need to look after my family. We'll talk later."

"Take me off speaker, Dad."

"I can't, son, I have other things I need to do right now."

And with that, Andy disconnected.

He looked to Jagger. "You have her?"

"Yes," Jag answered what he thought was unnecessarily, but he was not yet a dad.

Andy nodded and turned, "Liane, honey, come here."

Liane wandered to him, and the minute she got close, she was in his arms.

Hellen was holding Haley.

Archie sniffled into his chest.

"Welcome to the family, Jagger," Andy remarked sarcastically.

Before Jag could say something to try to defuse the situation, Archie's phone rang in his hand.

Andy looked to it and declined the call.

That hurt to witness, and it probably killed Andy to do it.

But Elijah would have to be fucked right the hell up if he didn't feel the worst of that.

Not there, by his choice. Blocked out, by his actions.

Knowing he caused pain and unable to do anything about it.

Also on him.

Which would be gutting.

At least it would be to Jagger.

Jag decided not to reply to Andy's remark. He just held Archie with one arm and caught her around the back of the neck with his other hand, giving her a reassuring squeeze.

"One thing I know right now, I need a flipping cupcake," Hellen declared.

Haley cry-laughed, so did Liane, and Archie turned her head, pressing her cheek to Jagger's chest, but she didn't let him go as she said, "I do too."

"I'm eating three of those babies," Andy announced.

"I'm so, so glad I doubled the recipe," Haley stated.

"I'm so, so glad you *always* double the recipe, Mom," Liane said.

"Well, I have to send my girls home with cupcakes." Her gaze fell on Archie and she concluded tentatively. "*All* my girls."

Archie lurched in his arms and shoved her face in his chest again.

"I'm sorry, I shouldn't—" Haley began quickly.

"You should." Archie's voice came muffled, but no one missed it.

He knew this when Haley whimpered.

So did Liane.

"Oh, for God's sake," Hellen said, holding tight to her mother even as she shuffled her mom in the direction of a box of tissue. "It's good Jagger and me are badass or this would be totally pathetic rather than just mostly pathetic. And just to note, I'm epically disappointed that Archie's turned to the dark side and become a crier. This is completely messing with my plans to have a girls' night viewing of *The Fault in Our Stars*."

He felt Archie's body start shaking with laughter in his arms and he could have kissed Hellen for it.

"What? I'm not badass?" Andy asked.

"It's impossible for Dad Units to be badass," Hellen returned.

"She better not say that around Hound," Jag whispered in Archie's ear, and her shaking got worse.

Hellen continued in her attempt to lighten the atmosphere, and she did it with a threat to Andy. "But do I have to share with the class what happened when you and me watched *Me Before You* together?"

"Please, God, don't," Andy begged.

Liane giggled.

So did Haley.

"Dad can get the weepies," Archie confided in a mumble.

"Right," Jag mumbled back.

Everyone started migrating back to the dining room as Archie pulled her face out of his chest.

"So, as you now know, I can have my not-so-chill times."

"You losing it in the face of the pain of someone you love, pain that someone else you love is causing, let me go on record as saying is all kinds of hot," he shared.

"You think everything I do is hot."

"That's because, so far, everything you do is hot."

Her mascara was totally fucked up and her eyes were already a bit swollen.

But she made even that hot.

He didn't share that.

"I'm really looking forward to meeting Hound," she said.

And shit.

He needed to get on that.

He shifted them so they were still connected but aimed at the dining room table.

He then started them that way.

"He's looking forward to that too."

She gave him a squeeze.

While he was returning it, Andy caught his eye.

And Jag knew, even if fathers of daughters with dead mothers didn't have long memories, he was still in with this family.

Because Andy Harmon cried at sad movies, loved and helped raise two girls who were not his own, adored their mother, and put up with a ton of shit from his son because he was his son and he loved him too.

So that was the house he built.

And that was the people he had in it.

And Jagger was now in that house.

So that was the way it always was going to go.

Jag made sure Archie was seated before he took his own chair.

And as Andy put cupcakes on plates and passed them around, everyone got two.

Except Andy, he took three.

And Jag, who got three too.

* * * *

Jag was on his back, Archie curled into his side, nuzzling his skin with her nose and mouth and trailing her fingers over his chest. He had his arm around her and was tracing random patterns on the skin of her shoulder.

They'd fucked, she'd cleaned up, and they were in her bed even though they'd planned to spend the night at his pad (after the emotion of the day, he wanted her to have her space).

It was dark because it was late.

But the space by the bed lit up with her phone going again.

She had it on silent.

And neither of them had to look to know who it was.

"How many is that?" he asked softly.

"Who cares?"

She did, he knew.

He said nothing.

Her brother was blowing up her phone.

She didn't block him, but she didn't pick up.

To take her mind off it, he urged, "Tell me about Haley's ex."

She drew in a breath, let it go, which he hoped was letting the shit happening with her brother go (at least for now) and gave it to him.

"I've only seen him a couple of times. Never met him. Liane played lacrosse in high school. He came to a few games. He's a workaholic. He abandoned them without officially abandoning them, if you know what I mean."

"I do," he confirmed.

He felt rather than saw her nod.

She then continued.

"Haley tried to get him to work on their marriage, not his job, he kept promising he would, but didn't. She got fed up with it, and when he was away on business, which he was a lot, she had the locks changed. Asked him for a separation. He's not big on failure and wouldn't even discuss it. He also wouldn't change his ways and spend more time in his roles as a husband and father. So she saw no way forward except to file for divorce. He's never forgiven her and he's not the kind of guy who lets things lie. That means now, even though they've been divorced since the girls were little, I think it's been maybe ten, twelve years, he still intermittently gets in her shit about 'giving up on them.'"

"What a dick."

"Yeah, and I will note, I saw him go to a few of Liane's games. And I didn't go to all of her games, but I'd say more than half of the ones I went to, he wasn't there. But Dad never missed one. And Hellen plays the flute, and she's had some concerts, and I've never seen their dad at Hellen's gigs, not once. My dad…again, always."

"Really dig your dad, baby," he murmured.

She cuddled closer. "I do too."

He grinned at the ceiling, tracing random partners on the point of her shoulder.

"We need to arrange you to meet my folks," he told her.

"I really wanna do that. Do you think they'd come here? My haul today included this pretty kickass table with these pale blue bucket chairs. I haven't put it out on the floor because it'd fit perfect up here. And I need a dining room table. They could help me christen it."

"They'd love that."

"They can name the night, boyfriend. All my nights are for you anyway."

Christ, he liked that.

So much, he rolled into her and took her in both of his arms in a way she knew how to read.

This meant she pressed into him and tipped her head back for his kiss.

When he finished with her mouth, he whispered, "I'm sorry your day sucked."

"It happens."

"Wanna fuck again?"

"Yes."

He grinned at her.

Then he kissed her.

And after that, they fucked again.

Chapter Fifteen

I Try to Be

Jagger

"Got something I've been putting off talking to you about."

It was the next morning after dinner with Archie's folks. Jag was at her bar, sipping coffee and watching Archie make breakfast (eggs, cheese, sautéed mushrooms and taco sauce in a tortilla—it looked awesome, but he'd already learned his woman could cook).

"What?" he asked.

She didn't answer his question and he had a feeling that wasn't about the fact she was folding burritos.

"Babe?"

She looked from the food to him. "I'm going to watch that movie. The one about your Club."

His gut fell like he was on a roller coaster.

"Are you still okay with that?" she asked.

"Sure," he muttered.

"I just…wanted you to know," she said, her gaze intent on him.

He nodded.

"I'll watch it during the day sometime, so you don't—"

"We can take a night off from each other."

She stopped moving and her gaze got even more intent.

"Do you want to take a night off?" she asked.

"You said you have a sales assistant who's on vacation so you're short staffed."

"To my dismay, we're never covered in customers, Jagger. Lafayette has been on vacation, he's coming back to work today, but I leave the floor all the time to Fabe and Joany. I did it yesterday to go out and search for stock."

He didn't say anything.

"Do you not want me to watch that movie?" she asked. "Tell the truth."

"You've only met a couple of the men."

"And?"

Christ.

What was his problem with this?

"I want you to meet Hound first," he blurted, he had no idea why, it just came out.

"I can do that, baby," she said softly.

"Cool," he muttered.

"Now, we've been together a lot. Do you want some space?" she asked.

"No," he said immediately, watching her closely. "Do you?"

"Not even a little bit. Been waiting a long time for you."

Thank fuck.

She put his burrito in front of him with the bottle of taco sauce and stood opposite him with hers.

Once there, she said, "There'll come a time, probably, when I'll need my zone. Joany's bitching about the fact we haven't been out in a while. But I'm digging where we're at, you and me. We're not open on Sundays, as you know, and I left the store to them last Saturday, so I think I should hang here for this one. But I'd love to go for another ride on Sunday, or just get out of town, even if it's to go to Evergreen or Morrison for lunch."

"We'll figure something out."

"Cool."

He forked into his burrito, took a bite, then poured more taco sauce on it.

"My man likes the spice," she said.

He looked at her. "Yeah."

She tipped her head to the side. "You okay?"

She was not going to watch that movie.

Not yet.

This meant he was okay, so he nodded.

"Okay," she murmured, then forked into her own burrito.

"Don't move that dining room table on your own," he ordered. "I'll get Dutch or one of the guys over and we'll move it up here for you."

She chewed her burrito, her eyes on him.

She then swallowed her bite and said to him, "You're such a guy."

"Well, yeah."

"You know I move furniture, and shelves, and boxes around all the time. It's part of my job," she shared.

Dragging shit around her store was one thing.

Carrying it up some stairs was another.

To communicate that, he repeated, "Don't move. That table. On your own. I'll get a brother and we'll move it up here for you."

And that was when she grinned at him.

They did breakfast, he helped with cleanup and they made out at the door before he moved out and headed for home.

He needed to change clothes and get to the garage.

He did the first part of that, but on his way out to his bike, he stopped and texted his ma and Hound.

You guys free to have dinner at Archie's? I want you to meet her and she said she'd like to cook for you.

He knew how much he was on his mother's mind when her reply took about two minutes to chime in.

Absolutely! When?

You pick. Neither of us have anything on. He texted back.

Thursday? Friday? His mom replied before he'd even made it out to his bike.

Like I said, you pick. Neither of us have anything on. He returned.

But is Friday night a date night for you two? Would that be cramping your style? His mom shot back right before he fired up his bike.

And before he even got his thumbs again to his screen, another came in from her.

If so, we can do Thursday.

He was about to tell her he didn't give a fuck—*neither of them had anything on*—when thankfully, Hound butted in.

Friday. And we're getting a sitter.

The man speaks. His mother texted. Then sent, *Which means the discussion is over.*

No, I'm just sick of my phone fucking beeping with you rattling on when Jag says they don't give a fuck which day we show. Hound declared.

I don't rattle. His mother retorted.

Woman, you are in another room from me in the same house right now. Why are you texting? Hound asked.

To which his mother said, *Love you, Jagger. See you Friday and can't wait to meet Archie!*

And that was the end of that.

Jagger started up his bike and headed to work.

But he did this smiling.

* * * *

The next day, in the afternoon, Jag sat at the soda fountain next to Mal.

Mal was showing him the difference between a chocolate shake made with chocolate ice cream and one made with vanilla and chocolate syrup.

Actually, he wasn't. Archie had made the shakes.

But it was Mal's idea.

So they both sat there with two full shakes in front of them because Archie didn't fuck around with halfsies.

The taste test was done, and Jag had discovered that Mal was right.

The syrup option was seriously better.

As they slurped between the two, Jag asked, "Your mom okay with all the stuff?"

From Mal: *Slurp.* "She freaked out at first." *Slurp.* "Went into the school and lost it on the principal." *Slurp.* "He stepped up surveillance of the Harris brothers." *Slurp.* "They were suspended today."

Jag turned from his shake to Mal. "They fucked with you again?"

Mal shook his head even with the straw still in his mouth.

Slurp.

He then let the straw go and looked up at Jag.

"There's a girl. She's in a special needs class. She's super pretty but she sees letters backward or something."

"Dyslexic," Jagger told him.

"Yeah. That. They mess with her too. Mostly because Aaron likes her, and she thinks he's a dick. The more she puts him off, the more Aaron pulls shit with her. They messed with her today. Since teachers were on high alert about them because Mom lost her mind, they were caught."

"Allan in on it?"

Mal put the straw between his lips, shook his head and, *slurp.*

Then he said, "No, I wasn't there. I didn't see what they did. But I figure it was a guilt by association thing."

"He ever in on it?" Jag asked.

Mal shifted the glasses in front of him while shaking his head again. "Allan's quiet. Get him away from Aaron, he's not a total asshole. But twisted props to him, he never leaves his brother hanging."

Jag didn't have any brothers who were dickheads, either of the blood or of the cut.

But he suspected, he got fucked repeatedly because of their damage, it'd eventually begin to get old.

"I should probably tell you not to cuss," Jagger noted.

Mal shot him a smile. "You probably should."

Jagger smiled back but said no more on that subject.

Instead, he said, "You walking with the store crew here after school like I told you?"

Mal got instantly serious.

"Yeah, but I don't blame them, Jagger," he said. "No one wants to be a target of those jerks."

"There's safety in numbers," Jag pointed out.

"Maybe." He shrugged. "Maybe not. But I get not wanting to take chances with that."

"I don't get that, bruh, because you look out for your own. Even if you get your ass kicked doing it, or someone dogs you, it doesn't matter. You take your brother's back."

Mal lost interest in his shakes and stared at Jagger.

"Same goes for you with them," Jag continued. "It sucks, they've been messing with you. But if their focus shifts, Mal, to one of your bros, or one of the girls, you back them. You with me?"

"You're like my dad, but white and a biker."

"Way you talk about your dad, I'm gonna take that as a compliment."

"You should."

They stared at each other.

Jag smiled first this time.

Mal returned it.

Then they went back to their shakes.

* * * *

"There's, like, one thing sexier than watching you bond with Mal."

It was late evening and they were out on Archie's fire escape.

They'd ordered in from the Ethiopian place. They'd eaten it.

And now, she'd made some cocktail with prickly pear syrup.

It was sweet as fuck, and after a double dose of chocolate shakes and a heavy dinner, he wasn't going there.

So he had a beer.

He also had his girl sitting between his bent legs, resting back against his body.

"What's sexier?" he asked.

"Your face when I suck you off."

At her words, he squeezed her hips with his thighs.

She shifted in his arms so she could look up at him.

"Have I ever told you how handsome I think you are, Jagger Black?"

Well…

Fuck.

He wasn't sure any woman had said that to him straight out.

But Archie saying it, like that, the way they were out on her fire escape, with her so goddamn pretty, right then, and all the time.

"No," he replied, his voice on that one word weird, hoarse.

"I think you're super fucking handsome, boyfriend," she whispered.

"I think I need you to suck me off right about now, baby," he whispered back.

"First, I need to know if your folks don't eat anything. I'm going to the grocery store first thing tomorrow, after you leave and before the shop opens."

"Ma isn't picky," he shared. "Hound will eat what you put in front of him, avoid what he doesn't like, but heads up. He's a meat and potatoes guy."

"Gotcha."

Jagger trailed a finger down her hairline, in front of her ear, and along her jaw.

And while he did, he felt his gut grow tighter and tighter.

Archie, who didn't miss much, didn't miss that.

"Jag?" she called.

He held her jaw in the palm of his hand and looked into her eyes.

"It's a miracle," he said.

Her black eyes warmed, her beautiful face grew soft, and she asked, "What?"

"If your mom was even one percent like you, how your dad got over losing her enough to move on."

Her eyes instantly filled with tears.

"Hey, hey, hey," he chanted quietly. "I'm sorry, baby. I shouldn't have—"

"That's the most beautiful thing anyone ever said to me."

A tear stroked down her cheek.

Jag caught it with the apple of his hand.

"I hope I'm a lot like her," she said. "I try to be."

And I hope I'm a lot like Graham Black, but I have no idea if I am, and I never will.

"Honey," she called.

When he refocused on her, he saw she was watching him closely.

"You're you, and I don't know her, but she'd have to be whacked not to think you're the best thing ever created," he told her.

Humor lit her features as she replied, "She wasn't whacked."

"Then there you go."

"You think I'm the best thing ever created?"

"Don't fish, you know I think you're the shit and have since the first minute I laid eyes on you."

That got another expression lighting her features.

"Can I go down on you now?" she asked.

"Absolutely," he answered.

She laughed and it was half chortle, half giggle. This meant it was half sexy, half cute.

While doing it, she pushed up his chest to kiss him.

And when she was done doing that, they went inside.

* * * *

He was curved over her, moving inside her, Archie on her hands and knees under him, Jag on his knees, one of his hands laced with hers in the bed, the other one between her legs, fingers toying with her clit.

She was breathing heavy.

He was listening to it and letting the sound of it ramp him up as he alternately nibbled and tasted her neck.

"Baby, faster," she breathed.

"In a minute," he murmured, stroking inside slow.

Real slow.

Christ, her wet pussy felt fucking *amazing.*

"Jag, honey, *faster*," she repeated.

"In a sec, sweetheart."

"Then lay off my clit," she ordered.

And have her amp down?

Fuck no.

Instead of doing what she said, he rolled it harder.

"*Jag*," she whimpered.

Yeah, he liked it like that.

He grinned against her skin.

She pushed up, hard, driving back her hips so he fell to his calves and both their torsos came up.

Then she bounced on his cock.

And she did it fast.

"Damn, baby," he teased.

"Shut up and back at my clit," she moaned.

He didn't backtalk and did as told.

Archie's head fell to his shoulder, and she panted, "Ohmigod, I love your fucking cock."

"No shit?"

"Aren't you close?" she asked, sounding almost desperate.

"Archie, you sucked me dry half an hour ago. I'm not a jizz machine."

She stopped and she did it full of him.

Nice.

"Jizz machine?" she asked.

"I can produce, as you've forced me to prove over and over. But every man's got his limits."

"I want you to come with me."

"Then you're gonna be riding for a while."

She twisted her neck to look more fully at him. "I need you to do it *now*."

He grinned at her. "Baby, just go. I'm good."

She pouted.

Shit, she was hot.

He resumed his work at her clit, and went after her tit, her eyes closed slowly, and she started bouncing again.

"There you go," he murmured encouragingly. "Kiss me, Arch."

She turned to him and kissed him.

It didn't last long before she was arcing into her work on his dick at the same time coming for him.

When she was evening out, she rode slow until she stopped, again full of him, and twisted her head to rest her forehead in his neck.

"What are you gonna do with that hard-on?" she asked, her voice gentle and sated.

"That's my question to you," he replied.

She chuckled quietly and said, "I told you to come with me, boyfriend. That orgasm was sweet. Now I'm about clean up and shut-eye."

"I can do that."

She lifted her head and looked at him.

He lifted her totally off him, put her on her back in the bed, then rested on top of her.

"You want me to clean you up?" he offered.

"Yeah, Jag."

He touched his mouth to hers, then to the hinge of her jaw, and he left the bed.

He came back with a washcloth, took care of business, headed back to the bathroom to dump it, then out again to Archie.

When he arrived at the bed, he found her wrapped around the sheet in a way that was her signature, and an invitation, the side of her ass, hip, thigh, the curve of her back, shoulder and arm on display, hair all over the pillows.

He accepted her invitation and went in for the spoon, tucking himself close, and curling his arms around her.

"Only boy I know who's good with giving a girl a rush then moving on, his dick still hard."

"Hmm," he hummed.

"I'mma gonna get up in a minute and brush my teeth," she mumbled.

"All right, baby," he whispered, knowing by her vibe there was no way in hell she was getting up to brush her teeth.

He was right, she was asleep in less than five minutes.

So he was careful when he moved away from her to go to the bathroom to brush his own teeth.

He had eyes to the mirror and the brush in his mouth when her words came back to him.

I hope I'm a lot like her. I try to be.

And with these words in his head, he remembered something he hadn't thought of in years.

His mom, sitting alone at the table in the kitchen, her hand wrapped around an empty bottle of beer, staring at the refrigerator like it'd open itself and spit a fresh one at her.

He also remembered the expression on her face.

And he had to stop brushing, because suddenly, he felt like he was going to hurl.

He spit.

Rinsed.

Put his brush back in Archie's holder.

And bracing his hands in the sink, he went back to staring at himself in the mirror.

"That fridge wasn't gonna spit a beer at her," he said to himself. "My father would never let his wife sit with an empty bottle without bringing her another beer."

He dropped his head and closed his eyes.

If your mom was even one percent like you, how your dad got over losing her...

After his dad died, Jag's mother had lost herself in grief for nearly twenty years before she pulled her shit together.

That was the man his father was.

That was the magnitude of her loss.

I hope I'm a lot like her. I try to be.

"Christ, *Christ*," he bit off toward the sink.

He got it then.

He knew what was eating at him.

And it was huge.

Unwieldy.

And ultimately unanswerable.

Because he was grappling with how he could give Archie all he should be if he didn't know who to be.

He wanted to give her a love that wouldn't die even with death.

The kind of love his mom had with his dad.

And the man who could give him that not only had he never met...

They had no chance in hell ever to meet.

Yeah.

What was eating him was huge.

Unwieldy.

And lost to him forever.

Chapter Sixteen

Free to Be

Jagger

"It's set for next Tuesday, yeah? The parents are gonna show at the Compound for dinner?" Jagger asked.

"Yeah, baby," Archie answered.

"Right. Good," he replied. "I got the guys sorted. Dutch, Joker and Hugger are gonna swing by in their trucks to ferry the kids to Ride. We're gonna do a store tour, a garage tour and finish with the parents showing and a cookout at the Compound."

They were in her kitchen.

He'd just finished pounding some pork chops into cutlets for the schnitzel Archie was making for dinner for him and his parents. She was at a bowl that was full of broccoli, cheese, red onion and bacon she was mixing with some dressing made of mayo, sugar and vinegar.

She hadn't yet met him, and still, she was going to serve the perfect Hound Salad: mayo, bacon, cheese, sugar with a nod to something green.

"They're really gonna like this food, baby," he told her after she turned to the fridge to shove the salad in.

She shot him a smile. "Awesome." She wandered the short way to him and leaned against the counter close by his side. "Now, can we talk about how cute it is you're all in to plan this field trip?"

"Sure, but before you push me up on that pedestal, when I do good things for your kids, I get head, so it's not entirely altruistic."

She busted out laughing.

The buzzer sounded.

"I'll get it," she said, still laughing. "Can you dredge those cutlets in flour?"

"What's dredge?" he asked.

She changed her mind. "Never mind. You get the door. I'll dredge."

He nodded, kissed her cheek as he passed her and headed to the intercom.

He hit the button. "Yo."

"Let us up," Joany demanded.

Needless to say, Joany was not who he expected since his parents were due any second now.

Because of this, he turned his gaze to Archie to see how she wanted to play this.

And as he did, she was saying, "For shit's sake."

The intercom sounded again.

"Dude, buzz us up," Joany repeated her demand.

"Ask her 'who's us'?" Archie ordered.

He hit the button.

"Who's us?" he said into the speaker.

"Me and Lafayette," Joany answered.

Again, Jag looked to Archie.

The instant he caught her eyes, she queried, "How non-judgy are your folks?"

"Very."

"*Very* very?"

"*Very* very. Why?"

"*Dude! Buzz us up!*" Joany shouted through the speaker.

He hit mute and waited for Archie's explanation.

"Okay, Joany is here because Joany is an equal mixture of protective and nosy," Archie started to explain.

"I've been getting that," Jagger replied.

"And your family is coming, and I'm sure she just wants to make certain it's cool, but also, she likes Dutch, she likes you for me, and she probably wants in on the sitch to either take my pulse or take my back. That said, after she gets over being protective and nosy, she's friendly and she thinks of me as family. So I should have predicted she'd horn in on this because I've never had a boy's parents over for dinner and she knows this is big."

Never had a boy's parents over for dinner.

Nice.

He grinned at her, she did an eye roll, and he moved them along, saying, "Right."

Not on speaker, but from outside, they heard, "*Dude! Buzz. Us. UP!*"

"And Lafayette is super cool," Archie went on.

Okay then…?

"So…I don't get it," he said. "Why did you ask if my parents are judgy if he's cool and Joany is…Joany?"

"Because La-La is also La-La. Some days, he's in skirts and makeup. Other days, he's in leather. He just goes with his flow and you never know what that flow is. If he came to work in a tinfoil hat, I wouldn't blink."

This was something else to dig about her.

Her posse ran the gamut and that said seriously cool things about the woman who was Archie.

"So, essentially, anything," he remarked.

"Yes, but I've no doubt he's only with Joany right now so he can drag Joany out before she invites herself to dinner. But like I said, he could be wearing a tinfoil hat while he does it."

"My parents won't care."

And that was what she got back from him and Chaos, because they not only let people be who they were, they got in the life so they could be free to be whoever the fuck they wanted to be themselves.

"*Duuuuuuuude!*"

That came from outside.

"Sure?" she asked.

"*Your parents are here! Buzz us up!*"

Again, from outside.

"Too late now," he said.

"*Go back to the front!*" Archie shouted in the direction of the window.

"*La-La's there! The parents are parking out back. Buzz! La-La will open!*" Joany shouted back.

Jagger hit the button to let them in and asked Archie, "Do they have the interior code?"

"Yeah."

It was then he noticed Archie didn't look upset or anxious.

In fact, she hadn't been either all night and they'd been prepping dinner for at least the last half an hour.

This was because, for Archie, Joany was Joany and she was there and what would be from that would be.

Lafayette was whoever Lafayette was and what would come from that also would come.

His parents were going to like her, and either she knew that, or she knew Jag liked her so much, he didn't care if anyone else did, so she didn't have to worry about it.

And she didn't.

It was the first time he realized how much like his mother she was.

Keely Black Ironside not only gave zero fucks what anyone thought about her, she understood how cool she was and always would be.

It was just a part of who she was.

And it was a part of who Archie was.

"What's that look on your face?" she asked.

"Just thinking again about how much of the shit you are."

"I'm the shit times a thousand."

Jagger busted out laughing at that.

He also looked around her pad.

She might not care what anyone thought of her, but this night meant something to her.

Joke had come with him to bring up the dining room table, and Archie had been right. It looked great in her space.

Now it was set with plates, silverware and wineglasses, and there was a pretty bouquet of fresh flowers in the middle.

There was another small bunch of fresh flowers on the edge of her bar.

The place always looked lived-in and funky, but she'd tidied, so now it looked lived-in and funky on purpose, with style and flair.

And he'd seen the inside of the fridge. So he saw that she'd made a trifle out of passionfruit and meringues that looked like it took her three hours to put together.

Candles were burning.

She had Ray LaMontagne playing and four types of beer in the fridge.

All of this for his mom.

Hound.

Him.

He recently saw a picture of his mother and father on the night they met.

He saw the way they were looking at each other.

And Jagger felt that look.

He *was* that look.

With Archie.

She was his.

And she was his entire future.

He was so into this thought, his body jerked in surprise when there was a knock on the door.

Before he moved the short distance to answer it, quickly, Archie asked, "Jagger, baby, are you okay?"

"Yeah," he muttered, and opened the door.

Hound and who he assumed was Lafayette were standing at the back.

His ma and Joany were at the front.

Jag noted that Lafayette was mixed race, Black and maybe Asian. He was also tall. But with the women blocking him, Jag couldn't see anything else.

He and Hound were staring at the backs of the heads of the women in front of them.

"Jag, honey, hey!" his mother cried, coming forward, grabbing his shoulders, and pulling him down for a kiss on the cheek.

"Hey, Ma, come in," he said, shifting aside.

"Jag, honey, hey!" Joany echoed in order to take her shot to get a smooch, reaching up a lot higher, since she was so much shorter, to grab his shoulders and pull him down for a kiss on the cheek.

"Hey, babe," he muttered, chuckling.

Hound came next.

"Son," he said, pounding Jag on the arm.

"Hound," Jag returned.

Hound went in and Jag saw that for Lafayette, it was a T-shirt-and-calf-length-pleated-skirt day.

There was some makeup.

And the guy could grow a fierce beard.

"Hi, I'm Lafayette and I'm vowing to you now we will be here all of five minutes and then we'll vanish."

"Hey, I'm Jagger and it's okay," Jag replied.

"You're new," Lafayette returned. "You'll learn Joany Control."

Jag started chuckling again as Lafayette entered.

He shut the door and turned, seeing Archie rounding the bar and heading their way.

So he introduced, "Ma, Hound, this is my girl, Archie. Arch, this is my mom, Keely, and my stepdad, Hound."

"Or Shep," Keely said, extending a hand. "You can also call him Shep."

She could call him Shep?

No one called him Shep.

"No one calls me Shep but you, woman," Hound stated.

There you go.

"Is that a declaration or simply information?" Keely asked.

"Both," Hound answered.

"Keely, Hound," Archie butted in. "So glad you're here and I finally get to meet you."

She'd made it to Keely, and they were shaking hands in that way women do which was more like holding hands.

"She's making schnitzel," Joany announced from where she was peering over the bar to the kitchen counter.

"Upon learning this knowledge, my night is complete," Lafayette proclaimed. "Can we leave these good people alone now?"

Yep.

Archie had read that right.

Lafayette was there solely to keep Joany in hand.

"I'm pretty sure Archie wants us to stay for a cocktail," Joany told Lafayette.

"I'm pretty sure I can buy you a cocktail down the street and it will heighten the odds that you'll still have your best friend *and* your job in the morning if I do," Lafayette retorted.

"You're back from vacation, we need to celebrate that," Joany shot back.

Lafayette turned to Keely and Hound. "For your information, I do not require a welcome home celebration after I spent two weeks alternating between a lounger at a pool and a treatment table in a spa."

Keely started laughing quietly.

But although Jag thought Lafayette was funny, he was watching Joany.

She had a strong personality, definitely a take-me-as-I-come person, and he dug that about her. She was also nosy. And for certain protective of Archie. Last, if she liked you, she was friendly and hilarious.

But something about this was off.

Because one thing he didn't realize until this moment she was not, was a pest.

"What's going on?" he asked.

"What?" Joany asked back.

Jesus, she was really bad at trying to pretend to be innocent.

"Is something going on?" he pushed.

"No," she totally lied.

He knew this was a lie because she was so bad at doing it, she couldn't even hold it up on one word.

It was confirmed when Archie demanded, "Joany, talk. Is something up?"

"Oh my God, did you rope me into some shenanigans?" Lafayette demanded.

"No, I just...La-La, you have a steady hand with a shaker, why don't you do some cocktails for these kind folks while I go out on the fire escape with Archie for a quick beat?"

Oh shit, Jag thought.

"Oh shit," Lafayette said.

"Unless you're sharing something personal to you that absolutely cannot wait for me to complete hosting a dinner party for my boyfriend's parents, I don't have anything to hide from Jag or his family," Archie declared.

Joany looked from Arch, to Jag, to his parents, back to Arch.

She then spilled.

"Okay, I might be wrong, but I could swear I saw Elijah casing the store."

"Casing...?" Archie asked, but the look on her face was suddenly not right.

"He drove by three times," Joany shared. "That I saw," she concluded.

"You're joking," Archie said.

"I could be wrong," Joany replied.

"If it was three times, and you know what he looks like, and what he drives, which you do, for both, how could you be wrong?" Archie asked.

"Okay, I'm probably not wrong," Joany admitted.

"Why didn't you say anything?" Archie demanded.

"I tried!" Joany returned hotly. "I've been sending texts for the last half an hour."

This was true. Her phone was binging. Archie was ignoring it because she'd been making salad.

"You weren't replying," Joany went on. "I showed to warn you. Hence," her head bounced to indicate where she was standing. "I'm here."

"Arch?" Jag asked leadingly.

She looked to him. "I got three voicemails from Elijah today."

"Well, shit," Jag murmured.

"Um…who's Elijah?" Keely queried.

Before Jagger could answer, Archie told her, "My brother. We had a to do. We're on the outs."

"You're still not picking up from him, babe?" Jagger inquired.

She shook her head to Jag. "No. Not since that scene at Dad and Haley's." She turned back to Joany. "Why would he be driving by? That's weird."

"Maybe working himself up?" Joany asked back.

"For….?" Archie trailed off on that and looked to Jagger because they probably knew for what.

"Okay, I'll get drinks for everyone and maybe you should call him," Jagger suggested.

Archie got a stubborn set to her face, "He—"

"Call him, baby, and tell him tonight is not the night and you'll hook up with him later," he instructed.

"I don't want to hook up with him later. He had his chance to talk things out the other night," she reminded him.

He made note, as laidback as his girl was, she could hold a grudge.

"We can talk about this later, for now—"

Jagger didn't finish that when there was a loud banging at the door.

He doubted it was one of the tenants, only two of which he'd met in passing in the hall, but they were even more chill than Archie.

"I'll handle it," he said.

"No, you won't, *I'll* handle it," Archie declared, stalking his way.

"How about *I* handle it," Joany said, and she sounded more ticked than Archie and Arch sounded pretty ticked.

"How about you girls stand down and I'll chat with Eli," Lafayette suggested.

Everyone was moving to the door but only Jagger got out of the way after receiving the look Archie was sending.

The pounding came back right before she opened it.

And when she opened it, Jagger didn't have time to blink before Elijah was in.

For him to be this, Archie went flying, because he barged in, shoving open the door and making her do so.

Annnnnnnnd…

Hell no.

Jag started to move and then everyone was moving.

Lafayette and Joany rushed toward Archie.

Keely got close to Jagger.

And Hound had Jag with an arm around the chest from behind and his voice in his ear.

"Cool it, son."

"What'd I tell you about this, Arch?" Jag growled, his eyes locked to Elijah, his body locked so he didn't move to punch that fuck in the throat.

Elijah was looking around and not missing fresh flowers, candles, Ray LaMontagne or the set dining room table.

"What's going on?" he asked.

"What's going on?" Archie repeated.

And Jagger didn't have to keep his body locked anymore at her tone.

It wasn't incredulous.

It wasn't wounded.

It wasn't shocked.

It was a profound mix of all three.

Elijah didn't miss that either and he went still.

"What's going on?" She said it again.

"Baby," Jagger called softly.

Hound let him go.

But Archie didn't look at Jag.

She only had eyes for her brother.

"Do you care?" she asked.

"Ar—" Elijah started.

"I spent an hour at the grocery store. Hours and hours straining passionfruit and making meringues and mixing and layering cream and mascarpone. Chopping veggies. Cleaning my place. All this because my man's parents were coming over. I met them all of five minutes ago, four of those five minutes spent talking about you. Now you have a bee in your bonnet, and you bust into *my home* and you ask *me what's going on?*"

"I could hardly know this was happening when you don't pick up my calls, Archie," Elijah pointed out.

"And so you've decided now is the time to chat, you hammer on the door and push your way in?" Archie asked.

Elijah looked embarrassed by that and was not making eye contact with anyone but Archie.

"I'm sorry my timing is off, but that does not negate the fact we need to have a conversation and we can't do that if you don't accept my calls or return my texts," Elijah shared.

"So write me a letter, send me an email, don't barge into my home when the timing suits you," Archie shot back.

Lafayette entered the discussion.

"I think now it might be good for a few of us to leave."

He took Joany's hand but looked pointedly at Elijah.

Elijah ignored Lafayette. "We need to set up a time to talk."

"And I'll get on that when I'm ready to talk," Archie stated. "Not now, when I'm having a dinner party for Jagger's parents."

Elijah appeared to be getting angry. "You can't just leave me hanging until you're ready to speak to me."

Archie shook her head. "I'm not doing this now. I have something happening. Go. I'll get in touch."

"When?" Elijah demanded.

"When I get in touch," Archie replied.

"I spent all week worried about that scene you instigated at Dad's—"

"Eli, really, you can't miss I've got something happening right—"

"And now you want me to just take off and wait until you deign to—"

All right, Jag was done.

"Listen, friend," he began, starting to move closer to Archie.

Archie looked to him and he didn't stop moving until he was at her side, but he shut his mouth.

She turned back to her brother. "Go, Elijah."

"We'll have brunch on Sunday," he decided.

"No, we won't," she refuted. "Sundays are my days with Jagger. I'll be in touch."

"Archie—" Elijah tried again.

But finally, she lost it.

"*Oh, for God's sake!*" she rapped out loudly. "Tonight is *not about you.* That scene at Dad's was not *all about you.* The entirety of everyone's lives are *not all about you.*"

She drew in a big breath.

And then she let him have it.

"Mom dying was not *all about…YOU!*"

Jag put his hand on the small of her back, but other than that—other than letting her know he was close, and she could call on him—he was powerless to do anything.

And he didn't want to, because he wanted his folks to spend time with his woman, he wanted to eat schnitzel and fruit, meringue and cream.

But she needed to do this.

Elijah looked like he'd been sucker punched. "I can't believe you just said that to me."

"I should have said it ten years ago," Archie retorted.

"Word on that," Joany muttered.

Archie shot her a look.

Joany pressed her lips tightly together.

"I lost her too," Archie said to her brother. "Dad lost her."

"He got over her pretty quickly," Elijah returned sharply.

"No, he didn't, it took years for him to find and marry Haley. And Mom's picture is still in his wallet."

Oh fuck.

At her deteriorating tone, Jag moved his hand from her back to curl his fingers around her hip.

"He just moved on with his life," she continued. "He has a great capacity to love. He has to give it to somebody. Okay, so you can have whatever it is you need, Eli, do you honestly want him to have nothing? To be alone? To grieve and pine for her until *he* dies? Is that what you want?"

Elijah said nothing.

"And what am I to you, Elijah?" she pushed. "I was your cook and your cleaner and your caretaker after she was gone. Now I'm your administrator and property manager. When do you start being the big brother and maybe think about what your little sister needs for a change? When do you kick in with this family, Eli? When does it stop being all of us tiptoeing around you and your grief? When are you gonna wake up and see we all lost her, we're all trying to move on, not because we want to, but *because we have no choice?*"

It was torture, not pulling her in his arms.

But Jag held still, close, but not invasive, and let her have what she needed.

"I don't have to be okay with my father marrying another woman, having another family, being with someone that is not my mother," Elijah bit.

"Yes you do," she fired back.

Elijah's head jerked.

"That's what love is. That's what family is," Archie stated. "Finding a way to be okay with someone you love being happy. Even if, at first, it hurts. There is absolutely nothing wrong with Haley. She loves Dad like crazy. She treats him like gold. She cares about us. He didn't *have another family*. He added *to ours*."

Elijah stood there, motionless and speechless.

Arch wasn't the latter.

"Now, honestly, if you cannot get your head out of your ass, Eli, I have to tell you, in front of company, two of those company I do not know but I very much want them to like me, but I have to say this anyway…we have an official problem," she declared. "Because I'm not playing this game for you anymore. You either figure it out, and I'll help you, or we co-own a building and that's it. And if you have some issue with how I manage it, you'll have to put it in writing, and I'll decide how I feel about your concerns. If you don't like my decision, you can let me buy you out, or you can sue me."

Elijah's eyes widened. "Are you honestly standing there reducing us to that over *Haley?*"

"No," she whispered, and Jagger's gut clenched at the pain in that one syllable. "I'm reducing us to that because I'm sick and tired of you treating me like shit."

Hearing these words, Elijah's entire upper body jerked.

"I don't treat you like shit, Arch," he said quietly.

"It's me having the feeling, Eli, and I can assure you, it feels like you treat me like shit. You break Dad's heart, over and over again, I'm powerless to do anything but watch, and it hurts witnessing it. You act like I'm your personal assistant, and I'm not. I have a life and a business and I'm falling in love."

Well.

Damn.

Keely made a noise.

Hound sounded like he'd swallowed a grunt.

There was some tittering in the area Lafayette and Joany were occupying.

And Jagger got even closer to his girl.

But Archie was focused.

"And do you know why all that hurts so bad?"

Elijah didn't say anything.

But Archie did.

"It hurts so bad because Mom would hate how you're behaving."

Elijah looked away.

Oh yeah.

There it was.

He knew that was the truth.

"And you know it," she finished.

Elijah turned back. "Maybe we should discuss this another time."

"Yes," Archie agreed. "Maybe we should."

Elijah shifted his attention Joany and Lafayette's way. "Good to see you guys."

Lafayette's eyes narrowed in annoyance and Joany's widened in fury.

"Are you for real?" Joany asked.

Lafayette murmured, "Quiet, baby girl."

Joany shut up.

Elijah looked at Jagger and said, "One day, we'll spend time and there won't be a drama."

"I fucking hope so," Jagger replied.

Elijah's jaw clenched.

He then turned to Keely and Hound.

"I'm sorry to intrude."

Neither said anything.

Finally, back to Archie. "We'll work this out."

But she wasn't backing down.

"Yes, we will, if *you* do the work."

His jaw jumped again before he dipped his chin, turned and walked out the door.

"Swear. To. *God.* If you don't get me a goddamn cocktail, right…freaking…*now*, I will *scream*," Joany declared in Lafayette's direction the minute the door latched.

Jagger pulled Archie around and into his arms, calling, "Hey," since she was looking at Joany.

She tipped her head back and gave him her gaze.

"I think cocktails are so totally in order," she announced.

She had tears in her eyes.

He dipped his face closer to hers and whispered, "Baby."

"Best memories, best memories *ever*, bar none, Jag, were when we were all together. I had mom moments with her I treasure. I think of them and they hurt at the same time they feel *so good*. But the birthdays and Christmases and going to Mile High Stadium to see fireworks on the Fourth of July all together, those were the best. Because she was at her happiest, all of us together. I did not lie. She'd hate this. She'd *hate it*."

Her nostrils were flaring with the effort it was taking to try to fight the tears, so he cupped the back of her head and pulled her face in his chest.

His phone in his back pocket rang with a call, which was probably a robocall because no one ever phoned him.

He ignored it and held Archie close.

"We're gonna skip," Lafayette said quietly, sidling close and taking Joany with him.

"Right, man," Jagger said. "Nice to meet you."

Lafayette nodded.

"She needed that," Joany told him as they passed.

"I know, babe. Go have a drink. Thanks for trying to take her back," Jagger replied.

Joany patted Archie and she pulled her face out of his chest to give Joany a weak smile as Lafayette and her moved out.

Jagger's phone had stopped ringing, but he heard Archie's that was in the kitchen start right up.

She ignored it, and even if Jagger didn't and he thought that was weird, he had to stay with her because she was turning them to his parents.

"I'm so sorry," she said.

"No need to be, darlin'," Keely replied gently. "You want us to take off? We can do this another night."

"No, no, we have tons of food and I'll rally, I promise," Archie said.

"How about we make a deal and Hound and me finish up whatever needs done in the kitchen, you and Jag chill out with a drink for a bit, and we'll reconvene over dinner. You cool with letting me in your kitchen?"

"I couldn't—" Archie started.

"I love to cook, so does Hound," Keely assured.

"I love to feed her, and my boys, I don't actually like to cook," Hound amended.

Keely sighed, but not with irritation, because she didn't miss the first part of what he said.

Jagger relaxed because Archie's lips were turning up.

But Jagger's turned down because Archie's phone stopped ringing, and Jagger's started up again.

That finally got Archie's attention, and her gaze came to his, her brows drawn.

"Just a sec," he murmured, pulled it out, and when he saw the screen, quickly took the call. "Hey, Mal, what's up?" he asked, using Mal's name so Archie would know who it was.

She no longer looked puzzled, she looked worried.

Mal's voice came in his ear.

"My grandma died, and I need you."

Jagger dropped his head, turned from everyone, and gave Mal all of his attention. "Sorry, buddy, what?"

He sounded choked when he said, "Gramma died. Mom's not good. We need to get to the hospital, and I took her keys because she's cryin' so bad, we won't be safe. I need you to drive us."

"Okay, bud, I'll be there. Does Archie know where you live?"

"I think so."

"Okay, I'll ask her. Be there as soon as I can."

"Thanks, Jagger."

"You bet, Mal. Hang tight. Be there soon."

Mal hung up.

Jagger turned to Archie. "His grandmother died. His mom is in no shape to drive to the hospital. He wants me to take them."

"I—" she began, her eyes sliding to Keely and Hound.

"You go, we'll sort out your kitchen," Keely said immediately. "Do we need a key to lock up?"

"I have an extra," Archie stated hurriedly, rushing toward the kitchen.

Jag caught Hound's eyes.

"This one of those kids Dutch told us about?" Hound asked low.

Jag nodded.

"Fuck," Hound murmured.

Archie rushed back to him with her bag in her hand.

Keely came to her and grabbed the key.

"Okay, let's go," Arch said. Her fingers locking around Jagger's, she pulled him toward the door. "Sorry. So, so sorry. We'll reschedule."

"Don't think about it for a second," Keely said.

"You be safe out there," Hound said.

"Yeah, thanks, later," Jagger called as they walked out.

"How'd he sound?" Archie asked in the hall as they moved swiftly down it.

"Like he was holding it together but was about to lose it."

"Shit," she bit out.

And they both broke into a jog when they hit the stairs.

Chapter Seventeen

Every Kind of Love

Jagger

"You cold?"

"Nah."

"It's cold out here, bruh."

"I'm fine."

Even if Mal said that, Jag shrugged off his leather cut and put it over Mal's back.

And Mal didn't hesitate to settle into it.

They were out on Mal's front stoop. Arch was inside with his mom, Shanta, and a couple of Shanta's friends. Shanta was nursing a glass of wine and a phone conversation with her sister, Arch and Shanta's girls were making calls and to-do lists.

Mal's aunt lived in Phoenix, and she was going to head up.

They'd been to the hospital and obviously had come back.

Earlier, when they first got to Mal's, Shanta had been understandably out of it. But she got it together, and that was when Arch kicked in and got the friends involved.

Mal's grandmother had been battling cancer. It wasn't looking good, but she was in treatment. However, she'd been battling that shit so long, her heart was weakened and it just…gave out.

So her life being shortened wasn't the surprise, it being that short was.

It was getting late. It was definitely cold.

They should probably leave, but he wasn't sure where Mal was at, and he didn't feel good leaving him unless he knew the kid was good being left.

And Mal was being his usual quiet, so Jag wasn't figuring that out.

"It's why I was acting like a dick," Mal suddenly said.

"Sorry?" Jag asked.

"At S.I.L., to Archie. When I got kicked out of group. It wasn't the bullying or just acting out. It was Grams. I didn't…" He cleared his throat. "I wasn't…I guess I just wanted to be seen."

"That tracks," Jag said quietly.

Jag felt Mal's gaze, so he looked at the kid when Mal kept talking.

"This is why the Harris brothers don't matter. Their damage, it's stupid. It doesn't mean anything. Mom is…uh, *was* real tight with Grams. We were…we were all, uh, *real tight*. And this hurt her. Watching Grams go through this. It hurt her and I didn't…I didn't…"

Mal trailed off.

Jag didn't say anything.

Mal kept going, and when he did, it was the first time since Jagger met him that he sounded like a little kid.

"There wasn't anything I could do to make things better. She's my mom, Jag, and she hurt, and I didn't know how to make things better."

Christ, he felt those words.

He felt them deep.

"I get that, buddy," Jagger said quietly.

Mal shook his head, turned away, and there was a thread of disgust in his voice when he said, "You can't get it. No one—"

"My dad died when I was three."

Mal's head whipped back around so he could look at Jagger.

"I don't remember him, not at all," Jagger told him. "But my mom loved him, brother. I mean, like, *for real*. Like, once-in-a-lifetime, lost-forever love. All my life, she was in pain. Every day of it. And I had to see that and couldn't do dick about it. So when I say I get it, Mal, I'm not handing you a line of bullshit. I really get it."

Mal just stared at him.

Jag held his gaze.

Then Mal turned away again, but after several long beats, he fell into Jag's side.

Jag slid an arm around his shoulders.

"I'm sorry about your mom," Mal mumbled.

"She's good now, happy. Found another love, and it's once-in-a-lifetime too. And just to say, we're lucky, because that's what every kind of love is. You just gotta open yourself to it."

"Yeah," Mal said.

They were quiet.

Mal broke it.

"Sorry about your dad."

Jag swallowed.

Nodded.

Realized Mal couldn't see him nod.

So he said, "Yeah. And goes without saying, but I'll say it, sorry about your gramma, bud. Losing someone you love sucks. And that's just all there is to it."

It took a sec, but eventually, Mal replied, "Yeah."

After that, they sat together on the stoop, in the cold, until Archie came out and said it was time to get Mal inside, warm and with his mom, and then it was time to leave.

So they took care of Mal, gave hugs to his mom.

And they left.

* * * *

It was under his seriously watchful eye that he and Archie walked into her apartment after leaving Mal and Shanta.

Now, you could be the most mellow person in the world, and a night that intense was going to fuck with you.

In other words, this night had to have fucked with his woman.

But this was one of those times.

One of those times like she gave him, so it was one he had to give her.

A time for space.

A time for her to share with him when she was ready, if at all.

And like usual, it was fucking with him.

Because she just got in her brother's face about his rampant grief running roughshod over their family, grief that was hers too and she didn't get to wallow in it and let others take care of her like her brother did.

And for the last three hours, they'd been neck deep in the fresh grief of Mal and Shanta.

Archie had to be feeling it.

Now, she was wandering into her kitchen while Jagger turned on lights and watched her.

When she got into the kitchen, she looked at something on the counter, then she lifted her head, caught sight of him, but gazed around before she came back to him.

She raised a piece of paper and shook it.

A note from his parents.

"Your folks made the schnitzel. We have plates if you're hungry."

He could eat a whole roast pig.

"You hungry?" he asked.

She shook her head.

"I'm good too," he lied.

She nodded at that, and pointed out, "They also cleared the table. Cleaned the kitchen. You're gonna have to give me your mom's number so I can text her to thank her."

"Will do, baby, but maybe now we should go to bed."

She stood there, watching him across the apartment, and it felt like it was as

208 / Kristen Ashley

closely as he was watching her.

He dropped his cut down his shoulders, tossed it on her couch, and asked, "You wanna go to bed?"

Not taking her eyes from him, she moved his way.

She stopped close, and still didn't take her eyes from his as she touched him.

Putting her hands on his chest, she slid them up to the sides of his neck.

He put his hands on her hips.

She squeezed his neck. "You good?"

"I'm good, uh...*you* good?"

She didn't answer his question.

Her gaze bored into his and she said softly, "Jagger, baby, you hungry?"

"I'm okay, Arch. You tired?"

She didn't answer him again.

She urged, "Talk to me."

He wanted it the other way around.

He wanted her to talk to him, tell him how it felt to lay it out for Elijah. How it felt to be around Shanta when her grief was so fresh and raw.

About anything.

He wanted her to give whatever she needed to him so he could take it from her.

He just didn't think he should ask.

"Jagger, baby," she shifted one hand to wrap it around the back of his neck, the other she moved to wrap around his throat, "*talk to* me."

He heard the words, but he didn't *hear them*.

Because it seemed like all the blood in his body all of a sudden had rushed to his head, his vision had blurred, and his mind had blanked of everything.

Except her hand at his throat.

His voice didn't even sound like him, it was jagged and harsh, when he demanded, "Take your hand off my fucking throat."

She did this immediately.

But he was lost.

Gone.

Blind, he couldn't even fucking see.

Couldn't think.

What the fuck?

What the fuck?

Christ, he had to get out of there.

He had *to go*.

He moved.

She got in front of him, hands to his chest, saying sharply, "Jagger!"

"I'm takin' a walk, be back," he forced out.

He moved to the side, losing her.

She got in his way again, hands flat on his chest, but this time she put weight into them. "Jagger, what's happening?"

He tried to lose her, failed.

God.

Fuck.

God.

He shook his head hard.

What the fuck?

What the fuck was happening to him?

She was pushing him back. "Jagger, honey, look at me."

There wasn't anything I could do to make things better.

He was moving backward, and he heard Archie demand, "Jagger! Look at me!"

I have a life and a business and I'm falling in love.

He went down.

Vaguely, he understood he was sitting on the couch because she'd pushed him there.

He felt her crawl in, straddle his lap.

She had his head in her hands and was gently shaking it.

"Come back to me, Jagger, baby. Come back. Look at me, baby. Please," she begged, sounding freaked.

Freaked and distressed and even panicked.

"I don't know…how to…love you," he forced out.

"Okay." She kissed his forehead. "Okay." She kissed his cheek. "Okay, baby." She kissed his lips. "Give me more. What do you mean by that?"

"I will be the best father to our kids, Hound taught me that. But I don't know how to love you."

"You do."

"He got his throat slit. Dad. They slit his throat."

He heard it, the hiss of breath, the sting of pain.

He felt it knifing through him as it cut through her.

Christ, it hurt.

Always…

The hurt.

Then she was kissing his face all over, in between whispering a tortured, "God. God. God."

"He died before he taught me how to love," he told her.

She wrapped her arms around his head and held it tight to her chest.

"He loved her so much. She loved him so much. *He loved her so much.* So much, losing his love *broke her.* I don't know how to love you like that. I don't know how to take care of you. He died before he taught me."

Her body bucked, her sob filled the room, and she held on tight.

"He died before he taught me," Jagger repeated. "I don't remember…" He swallowed. Hard. "I don't have any of him. I don't remember his love at all."

Archie was rocking him, he felt her lips at his hair, she was humming nothing, just a sweet sound from her throat, as her body pulsed with her weeping.

"I don't know how to love you," he whispered, the words ragged. "I don't know how to take care of you."

"Baby, what are you talking about? You've been taking care of me from the second you laid eyes on me," she replied. "I felt your love all the way across a cemetery and you didn't even know my name."

A noise came out of him, low and animalistic, and his arms went around her.

He knew by the sound she made when he latched on that he was holding her too hard.

He just couldn't stop.

"I needed nothing, until I lost her," she said into the top of his hair. "And then I saw you, and I got what I needed."

He made that sound again.

She held his head so tight against her chest, she was probably giving herself a bruise.

"Everyone loves him so much," he pushed out. "And I have no fucking clue who he is."

"Oh, baby," she whispered, kissing his hair, rocking his body, holding on tight. "He's you."

That was when it happened, it broke, coming hard and fast and hot, it poured into her shirt.

At the end of it, they were lying on her couch, Archie wrapped around him, Jagger with his cheek resting on her chest, his arms curled around her body, his mind a fog, his body exhausted.

"I shouldn't have kept away. I shouldn't have nursed my fucking pride. I should have come to you sooner," he muttered to the back of the couch. "I should have been there to help you deal with Elijah's bullshit. I should have been there for you. I should have had you."

"The trigger," she whispered.

"What?" he asked.

"Nothing, honey. Shh," she shushed.

"He would have had you. He wouldn't have waited."

He was talking about his dad.

Graham Black.

His father wouldn't have kept his mother hanging.

Jagger didn't do the same.

He'd failed the woman he loved.

"Jag, honey, it didn't happen that way. It happened this way. And for us this was the way it needed to happen. I'm not angry. I'm not hurt. I have you now. I've got what's mine. I'm good. So good, baby. So, so good."

He took in a deep breath, let it go.

And another.

And then, "All my life, she grieved for him. I had to watch, loving her and not being able to help her."

Archie stroked his hair.

"I didn't get it, until I saw you. And I was scared as fuck how I felt about you. Because love for me was mixed up in loss. In pain. In void."

Arch stayed silent and stroked his hair.

He dropped his head back, and she tucked her chin in her neck to look down at him.

And he said, "I love him and have no memory of him. I miss him and I never knew him. He's everywhere and he's never been there. All that shit is whacked. It makes no sense."

She cradled his cheek in her hand and replied, "It makes perfect sense to me, because he's right here and I'm so, so, *so* glad he is."

He's right here.

Jag pushed up and took her mouth, rolling on top of her.

Archie rounded him with her arms and kissed him back.

He ended it and shoved his face in her neck.

She returned to stroking his hair but added his neck, shoulders and back.

"I wanna watch that movie with you," he said into her skin.

"Right now?"

"No. I don't know when. But soon. Though, tomorrow during the day I'm hanging in the shop with you."

"Okay, we'll go to your place after we close."

"No, here. When we watch it, I need to watch it here." He lifted his head and looked down at her. "I need to be in your space when I see it again."

She nodded, swiping her hands over his forehead, his cheeks, pushing back his hair, touching him constantly.

"I have to talk to my mom," he admitted.

"Yeah, you do," she said gently.

"Will you be there with me?"

"At your side, baby."

At his side.

He bent and touched his mouth to hers.

He lifted away and told her, "I also need to sit down with Tack. They were best friends. I need to know my father. I need to feel what he feels when he says the words. I need to look at his face as he's saying them."

She nodded. "You want me there for that too?"

"I don't know. Can we see?"

"We can do anything, honey."

We can do anything.

They could.
They were alive.
Breathing.
They had time.
She was right there.
Right there.
And she was his.
"You okay after all that happened tonight?" he asked.
"I am now."
He felt a rueful grin hit his lips. "Not sure how that can be, me losing it on you."
"Because you gave that to me, and it's precious, I needed it and you needed to let it go."
"Well, if you say it like that," he joked.
Her mouth got soft, letting them have that moment of humor, before she kept talking.
"There's also more. Because you asked me if I was okay and I need that too, Jag. We'll work this out, with time, getting to know each other better. And you've gotta tell me if I'm wrong, but I sense you need space to sort your head out. The thing is, I don't. I need *you*. I've needed you since that day I first saw you. I need you to ask. I need to talk things through with you. I need to lay shit on you. And you can't hold back, thinking I need space. Thinking I need what you need. I've been shouldering everyone else's shit for a long time, honey. I don't want that. I want someone with me to help me carry the load."
Shit, he'd fucked up.
"That's me, Archie. I'm that someone. I hear you and I won't hold back again."
"If you mean with me and the burdens I'm carrying, okay. If you mean with you, you do what you need to do too. If you need to hold on to what you're feeling until you're ready to give it, you do what you have to do. Am I making sense?"
He nodded.
Something changed in her face and he braced at the sight of it.
She didn't make him wait.
"The thing with your throat...I won't touch it again."
He settled some extra weight on her, not much, just hopefully enough to show her he was relaxing and take her to that place with him.
"With your mouth, I'm good. Not your hand apparently, okay?" he shared.
"Okay, boyfriend, but just to say, you put my hand there when we were talking about tats."
"I was in control of that, tonight—"
She cut him off, nodding. "Yeah, I get it. And I'll steer clear."
He touched his mouth to hers.

Lifting away, he realized he still felt foggy, tired.

But also relieved.

Jesus, he'd been holding that so deep and so long, he didn't even know it was there.

And it was weird, the hold it had on him was so strong, how dazed and fatigued he felt in letting it go.

Still, if felt fucking great to let it go.

"Now, tell it true, are you hungry?" she pushed.

He looked at her beautiful face, her eyes warm on him, the relief she also felt openly visible.

And he said, "I could eat my weight in schnitzel and I'm not even bothering with bowls when we tackle that trifle."

That was when Archie smiled.

* * * *

Archie moved on him until Jagger was done watching her move on him.

Then he curled up just enough to reach out and catch her by the back of the neck.

He lay back, bringing her down with him, keeping his hand curved around her neck as he stroked inside her mouth with his tongue, and she stroked his cock with her cunt.

She got there before him, because that was her way, and because he was in a constant state of sated considering how much cum she coaxed out of him by any means necessary.

So when she came, he swallowed her noises. Then she got focused and gave it to him, and she consumed his groan.

It had been slow.

It had been lazy.

And as usual, it had been awesome.

After, he curled his arms around her and she tucked her face under his jaw, in his neck, but she did not lose his cock.

It was the morning after their big night.

She needed to get ready to go to the store.

He needed to run home to grab some stuff since he was staying the weekend at her place.

He also needed to check on Mal.

Neither of them moved.

Eventually, biology took over, and they lost their connection.

They still didn't move.

But Jagger ended the silence.

"I think I'm going to Tack first. Outside of drawing Ma out, getting her to talk about him more, which she's been doing lately anyway, I don't know if I want her to know where my head's been at. I don't want her to think she should have hidden her pain, which would have hidden how much she loved him, and that was important for me and Dutch to know. I don't want her to regret anything."

"I think that's a good decision, honey," she murmured.

"I'll call him today."

"Okay."

"Gonna pack a bag, stay here with you for a while. Groovy?"

"One hundred percent."

Good.

He needed her space, her smell, her shit around him.

They'd move in together at his place, eventually, mostly because it was bigger.

When marriage and kids came, they'd find their own place.

But now, this was all her and he wanted nothing but that.

"I'll text Mal, see if he wants a visit," Jag carried on. "But be back to take you out to lunch. You pick. Though I might have him, if he wants to get away. If I do, it's his pick."

She snuggled closer and said, "Sounds like a plan."

They both fell silent.

Archie's phone ringing ended it.

She shifted, turned her head, reached out and nabbed her phone, all without really moving, and definitely not losing any contact with Jag.

"It's Elijah," she announced.

"You ready for that?" he asked.

She lifted her head and looked down at him. "Maybe the time is nigh."

Her phone stopped ringing.

"Do you agree?" she queried.

She needed Jagger to help her work through things.

And he was there to do that with her.

"I do," he said. "It goes without saying, I'm about you. But he was not down with losing contact with you. He didn't go about it right, but he was pretty messed up you weren't available to him. And I don't think that's about him needing you to deal with his shit however that comes. I think he loves his sister. He might not show it, but he probably loves your dad. That scene with that phone call at your dad's house was serious, and he was on the outside of that. His doing. But being shut out after he hurt you that bad clearly ate at him."

"Yeah, it clearly did that," she agreed.

"I hate that it's your job, but outside is where he put himself, with you, your dad, Haley and the girls, and he needs someone to show him the way in."

"Yeah," she muttered.

"But if you decide to do that, you should do it only when you're ready," he added.

"Mm," she hummed, looked to her phone, hit some buttons, and when he heard it ringing, she put her finger to her lips.

He grinned at her.

Apparently, she was ready.

"Thanks for returning my call," was her brother's greeting.

"Please don't make me regret it," Archie replied.

A beat then, "What I did last night was messed up. It was completely out of line."

Even through the phone, it sounded like that was painful for him to say.

Which gave Jag more insight into Elijah because the pride was definitely strong with this one.

"It was," Archie agreed.

"I'm sorry about that," Elijah said tightly.

"Apology accepted."

"I think...I need...to take some time...to take stock," Elijah admitted like he was being tortured for those words.

"Mm-hmm," was all Archie gave him.

Elijah came to his end.

"Jesus, I just miss her, Arch," he spat.

"I do too, Eli," she said gently. "So does Dad. You can't think just because he has Haley that he doesn't. He loved Mom. He's just not one of those guys who can be alone. He likes company. He likes taking care of people. He's loving and social. He'd be miserable if he spent his life all by himself, honoring their marriage when half of that marriage is no longer of this world."

Elijah was quiet.

Archie kept going.

"You've hurt Haley. Also Hellen and Liane."

"I—"

"You can't deny it and you can't excuse it. I've seen it," she cut in quickly. "She's great. Those girls are great. We can never have Mom back, but they aren't chump change, Eli."

"Like I said, I need to take stock," Elijah reiterated.

"Right," Archie said.

"And I can't lose you while I'm doing it."

There it was.

Archie locked eyes with him.

"Right," she repeated, but this time it was softer.

"I don't...all I can say is I'll be working on it. All of it. Just...give me some patience," Elijah not-quite asked.

"I'm going to point out you've already had a lot of that, Eli, but I'll give you more because I love you, because you're family and because that's what Mom would want me to do."

Utter quiet from Elijah after that.

Archie moved on.

"I'm not managing this building without your help, Eli. So you either pay me to manage it or you help."

"You were right about all of that. I was just being a dick. No clue why."

Jagger had a clue.

Like Mal, or anyone who felt lost to their pain, Elijah needed to be seen.

The thing was, in Elijah's case, he'd been seen so much, Archie, and probably Andy too, had put up with his shit so long, he was addicted to it and he didn't know how to operate any other way.

"Deduct what you need to deduct for me to pay you back and for you to do what you have to do to keep things good," Elijah went on. "I can't help right now, with school and work, I can't add on. We're preparing a brief at work and I'm working eighty-hour weeks and still have to hit class and study. I'm barely sleeping, and shit is intense."

"You could have told me that, Eli."

He sounded impatient when he replied, "I guess I'm not a great communicator, Archie."

"Trust me, take stock on that too, brother," she advised. "Not just for me, Dad, our family, but anyone in your life. You acting like an asshole to get your way is going to get old real fast with people who are not bound to you. You with me?"

"I'll take stock."

That sounded like it was gritted through his teeth.

Archie grinned at Jag.

And that was a little sister who liked to make her big brother squirm.

Jag smiled back.

"Though, your big takeaway from this is that I love you," she said. "I'm done putting up with your shit, but I'll never be done loving you. You dig?"

"Dig?"

"You hardly need me to define that slang, bro."

"You're such a hippie," Elijah muttered.

"I'm not a hippie. I'm not anything. Why do people need to label? It's gross."

"Okay, I have thirty minutes to write a five-thousand-word paper before I have to haul my ass back into the office, so I don't have time for this. Your takeaway is, I love you too. And you've been heard. It's time I try to be the son my mother raised."

"Your father too," Arch pushed.

It took a second before he said, "My father too."

"All right, go get at that paper. Love you, bro."

"Love you too, you goof."

Hearing that, Jag let out a breath.

Archie also relaxed on top of him.

"Later," she said into the phone.

"'Bye, Arch."

They disconnected, she tossed her phone to the floor at the side of the bed and smiled huge at him.

He gave her a squeeze. "Happy?"

"So happy, I'm give-my-guy-a-blowjob happy."

For fuck's sake.

"Baby, I just came not twenty minutes ago."

"Bet I can make you come again."

He wouldn't take that bet because he'd bet she was right.

He also was never gonna stand in the way of a blowjob.

Twenty minutes later, she proved they were both right.

Chapter Eighteen

That Is Everything

Tack

Thirty years before…

The lights of Denver lay out before them.

"She's the one."

"You haven't hid that, brother."

"I can't go on."

A beat.

Two.

Three.

All loaded.

Then the response…

"Nope."

"Gonna fill her up with babies, and I'm not giving them this, Tack. I'm not givin' them the Club like it is. They're not inheriting this block of pure shit from me."

They'd rode together, side by side, up to Lookout Mountain so they could see this view.

It was Black's idea.

He'd met Keely.

The fall had been hard and swift.

But they both already knew where their path led as brothers.

Keely just solidified it for Black.

"Getting the Club right needs patience," Tack told him. "This is gonna be slow, Black. We can't make any sudden moves. Every step planned out, purposeful."

"You need to cut Naomi loose."

That made Tack look to his left.

To his brother.

To Graham Black.

"Brother—"

Black looked right, their gazes caught and hung.

"She's draining you and you know it," he said. "And we need your shit sharp."

He was not wrong. If Tack had ever loved his wife—and those days, he asked himself frequently if he ever had, and came up short every time—he'd fallen out of that as hard and swift as Black had recently fallen in.

"A man in love wants that to be contagious," Tack noted.

"No, a man finds love, he wants the men he loves to have that bounty. She looks at me, brother, and the world takes flight in her eyes. All I wanna do is follow, and I couldn't give that first fuck where it goes, as long as it's never lost to me."

"Always a poet," Tack muttered.

"I'm not fucking around with you, Tack," Black bit. "Life is too goddamned short to waste it on leeches like Naomi and you know that better than me."

Tack clenched his teeth.

"Cut her loose," Black advised.

"First, she's the mother of my kids, and second, Black, we got some important matters at hand, brother, and Naomi is not one of them," Tack pointed out.

Black held his eyes and sighed.

He then looked to the lights.

Tack did too.

"The babies you two will make will be beautiful," Tack told him, and it was no lie.

Black was a good-looking man.

Keely was amazing.

"Oh yeah, they will. Boys. We're gonna have a crew of boys," Black declared. "She pops one out, fill her with another one."

Tack felt one side of his lips hitch up. "Not sure you can make that call."

"Keely is so on board with that, it isn't funny."

"I meant about them all being boys," Tack shared.

"I'll take girls, love 'em with all I got. That baby is her mixed with me, love every cell in their bodies with everything that makes me."

"Good you got that attitude, 'cause far as I can tell, chances are fifty-fifty."

"We can have five girls and we'll go until we got at least two boys."

Tack looked at his brother again. "Why?"

Black looked at him too. "You gotta ask that?"

"I did, didn't I?"

"Okay then, a man needs a brother."

Tack had a brother.

He was a piece of shit.

He found others.

Some of those were pieces of shit too.

But not the one at his side.

No, absolutely not him.

So Tack understood where he was at.

"I wanna watch 'em grow up," Black said. "Teach 'em how to set up a tent. Show 'em the glory of sitting in the quiet, under the stars. Take 'em for a ride. Show 'em the thrill of wind in their faces. Teach 'em how to change oil. Get 'em dirt bikes. Knock their heads together when they pull shit so they won't be assholes. Watch them find a woman and do the work beforehand so they'll know how to treat her. Then, when they find the one, know in my soul a goodness complete, because I know they got what I found in their mother. And then spoil their babies so bad, they end up hating me. That's gonna be my life, brother. That's what's gonna make Keely and me. That's a great life right there. That is everything."

Tack had a son and a daughter.

Their mother was one thing.

His Rush and Tabby...

Another.

So Tack knew that Black, like Black had an annoying tendency to be, was right.

That was everything.

* * * *

"Been waiting a long fucking time for today."

Jagger Black took his gaze from the stars blanketing Tack's house in the mountains and gave it to Tack.

"Twenty-four years. A long time, sitting on it, until you were ready to hear that story," Tack continued.

Jag said nothing.

Tack did.

"You were his everything, Jagger. Everything."

He watched the man swallow.

Then Jag turned his attention back to the stars and whispered, "Wind in their faces."

"Wild wind, that was your dad. His edges have been smoothed with memory. Everyone remembers Keely being the crazy one, always up for a good time. Even, I think, your mom remembers it like that. But she didn't know him before her. Before her, he dragged life around like it was his pet. Had a hold on that leash and owned it. Then he found her, and shit settled down fast, because he had to be her anchor so she could fly free."

Tack let that sink in a second.

And then he gave him the rest of it.

"You remind me of him, Jag, a lot more than Dutch. Black was responsible when he had something to be responsible for. Dutch was responsible because he never had a time when he didn't have to be."

It was a blow, Tack knew. For a variety of reasons.

He watched it land, the flinch.

But then Jagger's face eased almost to the point it looked serene.

He'd never seen Jagger look like that.

And seeing it, Tack felt a roughness in the back of his throat because finally, after waiting decades, he'd been able to do right by his friend.

And what would be more important to Black, do right by his son.

Tack watched Jag look over his shoulder.

So Tack looked over his.

The woman Tack had met half an hour before was standing in the kitchen with Tack's wife, Tyra.

Tyra was bent over, pounding a hand on the kitchen counter, and he could see in her profile, she was laughing.

And Tack suspected he looked serene, seeing his wife like that.

Laughing.

Then again, even if he didn't show it (mostly so he could give her shit, because they both got off on it), Tack had that feeling a lot, because his wife laughed all the time.

A cool customer, Archie was watching her, a shit-eating grin on her face.

"Would he like her?" Jag asked.

He looked back to his brother. "You love her?"

Jag looked at him. "That's happening, yeah."

"She make you happy?"

"Yeah, but it's more. It's like," Jag shook his head, "I know it sounds crazy, but it's like I was put on this earth for her."

"Then no, Jag, Black wouldn't like her."

Jag stared at him.

So Tack finished it.

"He'd love her with everything that made him."

A beat passed.

Two.

Three.

All loaded.

And then…

"I really remind you of him?"
Tack Allen nodded once.
And answered, "Absolutely."
And yeah.
That look on Jagger Black's face?
No other word for it.
But serene.

Chapter Nineteen

Brotherhood

Archie

"Babe, it's kinda hard for me to do you when you're sitting on my ass."

"Shush, Jag."

It was that next Tuesday.

First thing in the morning.

And it was going to be an important day and both of them had to be ready for it.

To be that, Archie reached over and found the bottle she'd set by the bed last night.

She tipped some oil in her palm, twisted the cap back on, coated her hands in slick and then put them to Jag's back.

"Babe," he murmured.

"You're tense, it's a heavy day, we need to release some of that, so just go with it," she murmured back, using the apples of her palms to press and stroke upward on each side of his spine until she got to his broad shoulders, where she spread the pressure out.

Jag was quiet as she kept this up, Archie seated on his ass, putting her weight into it when needed. Her hands were heated by his skin and the oil that not only offered ease to her ministrations, but warmth to his muscles.

"You good?" she asked after a bit, digging her thumbs in where his neck met his shoulders, a place she found was often super tight.

"Yeah, baby," he said quietly. "You have that oil, or did you buy it for me?"

"I bought it for you."

A beat then, "Don't relax me too much I can't fuck you."

Archie grinned and kept massaging.

And replied, "Don't worry. I'd never do that."

* * * *

They weren't going to be able to carry out their plan to take the kids to Jagger's motorcycle club hangout that afternoon.

This was because that afternoon, they were sitting in a church, listening to people sharing what a lovely woman Danielle Middleton, Mal's grandmother, was.

It was a nice service. The flowers were very pretty. And Jagger looked incredibly handsome in his dark suit.

They were in a pew with Joany, Fabe and Lafayette (they'd closed the store) mid-way back on Mal and Shanta's side. There were a lot of people there (more testimony Danielle was an awesome lady).

But when it was done, Mal didn't miss catching first Archie's, then Jagger's eyes and giving them a boy-man chin lift as he walked out with his mom and aunt.

They waited their turn as folks left the church, and as they headed down the aisle, Archie looked up at her man and asked, "Do you want to go to the gravesite with the procession, or head out?"

Jagger didn't look at her, his eyes were aimed to the exit, and she knew where his head was at even before he answered, "We're there all the way for Mal."

"Okay, honey," she murmured, glanced behind them, and got a nod from Fabe, which meant he heard, and they were in too.

When they exited the church, the first thing she saw was Mal, who was standing at the bottom of the steps looking off in the distance and seeming frozen in place.

It was then she noticed a lot of people were staring in the same direction.

Archie looked that way.

And she saw, around the entrance to the parking lot of the church, there was a slew of men on motorcycles. They were wearing black, long-sleeved, button-down shirts, jeans, and had sunglasses over their eyes to shield them against the bright Denver sun.

When she turned her gaze to Jagger, he was looking at Mal.

He also headed to Mal, and since he had her hand tucked into his elbow, Archie went with him.

"Sorry," he said when they arrived, and Shanta moved her gaze from Jagger's brothers to Jag. "I didn't know. But I should have guessed because Mal claimed me, and since I'm his, they weren't gonna let this pass. So they're here to provide an honor guard escort for your mom. I can tell them to go if it's—"

He shut up because Shanta ducked her face and turned it away, lifting a hand with a hanky in it to touch under the sunglasses she was wearing.

"Don't tell them to go," Mal decided for his family.

Shanta cleared her throat, turned again to Jagger, and her voice came soft when she added, "Please, don't. Momma could be theatrical."

The sister snorted and said under her breath, "To say the least."

"She'd love a biker honor guard," Shanta finished.

Jagger nodded and started to move them away, but Mal tagged the sleeve of his suit jacket, so he stopped.

"You do that too?" he asked.

Jag and Archie looked where Mal tipped his head and they saw Gina, Martin, Colby, Dex, Tracee and Mia standing off to the side with a couple of the parents who were obviously their rides.

She hadn't noticed them in the church.

But there they were.

Archie's head came back around when she heard Jag answer, "Yeah."

She didn't know he did this.

Then again, he'd asked to use her laptop on Sunday, so she didn't have to play super-sleuth to figure it out.

She didn't wonder why he didn't tell her.

Her man was not wrong when he said Mal had claimed him and Jagger was his. They now had an even bigger thing than they'd been growing before, and that was not about Archie.

It was theirs.

And Archie had no issue whatsoever sitting back and letting them have it.

Mal's gaze wandered through his friends from group and Jagger's brothers before it came back to Jag.

"So that's brotherhood? Showing at some lady's funeral you don't know?" he asked Jag.

"It's brotherhood, it's *community*, that on one of the worst days you'll have in your life, or any day of your life, they do things that state clear in a way you can't mistake that you matter."

Mal took that in.

He then cracked a smile. "Thinking now it's pretty awesome that I stole that gamer thing."

"You did *what?*" Shanta asked, her last word rising several octaves.

Archie watched Jagger smile back.

They let Mal deal with his mother's reaction to his remark and Jagger took her to his truck.

But along the way, she made certain to wave in the general direction of the Chaos brotherhood.

She got some all-man chin lifts and only one wave, which was mostly a flick of a hand.

That was Dutch.

Jag helped her in his truck and shut her door for her, rounded the hood and got in himself.

"Boyfriend," she called.

"Right here," he said, sliding his glasses on his nose.

He then commenced scanning the area, undoubtedly watching for the convoy to start to take them to the cemetery.

"Don't freak out."

At her words, he turned those sunglasses to her.

"What?" he asked.

"Don't freak out," she repeated.

"About what?"

"About the fact that I'm telling you right now that I'm really, stupidly, crazily, totally head over heels in love with you."

Jag said nothing.

Not a word. Not a sound.

He didn't move.

He just stared at her through his kickass KD sunglasses.

Then he grunted, "Same."

She couldn't stop her grin.

Or pushing across the cab to kiss him.

Both she did.

The first big.

The second...

Hard.

* * * *

It was hours later.

She was in the Chaos Compound watching another reason why she was in love with Jagger Black happen at the pool table.

Fabe and Lafayette were playing pool with Dutch and Joker while Joany, Georgie and Joker's wife Carissa looked on (but mostly, the women were giving them shit and trying to make them mess up shots, though this was not succeeding very well).

Another reason why she was in love with Jagger was that he was not there.

He'd gotten a text from Mal that said, *Can you come get me?*

She'd watched Jagger text back, *You okay?*

To which, Mal replied, *Yeah, I just have to get out of here. Mom says it's OK. Be there soon.*

And with that, Jag asked her if she wanted to come with him, or hang. She'd told him she wanted to hang (so she could give him time with Mal and give the same to Mal).

He'd kissed her quickly and left.

But when they'd arrived, Jag had told her the gang was all there, and like Jag and Archie, a lot of them had changed out of their funeral clothes.

Since their arrival, she'd met Snapper and Rosalie, Hopper and Lanie, Tack and Tyra, Shy's wife Tabby, Dog's woman Sheila, Carissa, Rush and Rebel, High and Millie, Boz, Arlo, Hugger, Grizz, Karma, Saddle, the list went on.

Jagger had a huge family.

She liked that.

She was nursing a beer and considering going over to the pool table when Hound slid up on the stool beside her.

"Hey," she greeted.

"Hey, girl," he replied.

"Thanks for today," she said. "Mal's been leaning on Jag a lot lately. His dad couldn't come home, communication is spotty, and it seems to give him something, having a dude to hang with. So I think it meant a lot to Mal, you guys showing. Also to his mom," she told him.

"Yeah," he grunted.

"And again, sorry about the other night."

He'd jerked up his chin when he'd settled, and then had been watching Saddle behind the bar go and get a beer for him (Saddle was a man Jagger called a "prospect," or someone who was putting the work in to become a member of the Club).

But Hound looked to her when she said that.

"Don't know why you're apologizin'. It's understandable."

She nodded. "I'm glad you sat down. Wanted a moment to say thanks."

"You already did."

"Not for that."

"For what?"

"For Jagger."

He shook his head, dipped his chin sharply to Saddle when the beer was set in front of him, and looked back at Archie.

"Not my doing," he said.

"Oh yes it is."

Hound stared at her hard.

Then his voice dropped low when he asked, "He okay?"

Hers went low too when she answered, "He's working through things, but yes."

"Don't wanna put you on the spot. You don't have to say dick. But you probably could guess this anyway. His momma is worried," he muttered.

On first appearances, Hound seemed pretty rough, weathered, definitely had some life under his belt.

But there were things no one could hide.

So she knew, Jag's dad was feeling the same.

"He might reach out to her," she told him.

"You don't have to say anything."

"I do if it makes you feel better. He wants to watch that Chaos movie with me. I think he needs to share Club history with me. His dad. You. I think he'll feel a lot better when I know. But it's hard for him to express."

"I get that," he muttered, and turned to his beer.

She took that as what it was, he was letting her off the hook with that at the same time he got what he needed to feel better about it.

And she was grateful for it.

Moving on.

"My mother would lose her mind, the thought of her daughter sitting in a biker club hangout, drinking a beer, surrounded by bikers," Archie remarked.

Hound returned his attention to her and his tone was wary when he asked, "Yeah?"

"She was kind of proper." She smiled at him. "She'd come around though."

"She as pretty as you?"

"Prettier."

"Not sure I believe that, but okay," he said.

Aw, that was sweet.

So sweet, Archie listed to the side and bumped her shoulder against his.

Hound grunted and raised his beer to his lips.

"She loved family," she whispered when he put his beer back to the bar.

Hound again caught her gaze and his expression was no longer worried.

That was when he listed to the side and bumped her with his shoulder.

Archie took that as her invitation to lean into him…and just stay.

So she did.

Which was where she was five minutes later, shooting the breeze with Hound Ironside, when Jagger strolled in with Mal.

Mal's attention went right to…well, *everything*. Suffice it to say, a biker hangout that looked like a seedy bar, and proud of it, was new and fascinating terrain for Mal.

Jagger's attention came right to her with his dad.

And one could say, when he saw them together, his expression was no longer worried either.

* * * *

It was later.

Days later.

Or, precisely, the morning after the night where she and Jag watched the documentary *Blood, Guts and Brotherhood*.

She went first to her mom just to say hi.

Then, as she usually did, she wandered the quiet space and stood in front of the black marble marker that had a weathered tequila bottle sitting at the base of it, a bottle that was mostly full.

And as she usually did, she wondered how that bottle hadn't been nicked.

She then looked at the stone.

"Life is all kinds of fucked up," she said quietly to Jagger's father. "If you weren't gone, I wouldn't have him. And if she wasn't gone, he wouldn't have me."

There was no sound, no breeze, no wind through the trees, nothing.

Just quiet and peace.

"I don't know what to do with that," she admitted.

There was no rustle of leaves.

There was nothing.

"I guess the only thing I can do with it is think that you gave me him, and she gave him me."

The sun shone down on Archie and black marble, it warned her skin, it glinted the stone.

"You were a good man, Graham Black," she uttered an understatement.

Archie reached out and touched stone that was cold, even under the sun.

"Thank you."

Still, nothing.

But peace.

And with that, Archie walked away.

Epilogue

Thrill of the Wind

Jagger

One month later...

When Jagger walked into his mom and Hound's kitchen, Dutch was already sprawled at the table.

There was no Georgie.

Which made Jag feel better since he'd been ordered to come to breakfast and Archie was not invited.

But only a little bit better because this was weird.

"What's going on?" he asked.

"Well, hello to you too," his mother said by way of answer, turning from a counter that had some food prep stuff on it.

Jag didn't let up.

"Where's Hound and Wilder?"

"They're out to breakfast," she told him.

Say what?

"I thought we were here *for* breakfast," Jag noted. "Why are they somewhere else?"

"Okay, getting you caught up," Dutch put in. "It's official that this is weird on top of weird because I asked this too, as well as why Georgie was expressly left out of this get-together. Ma didn't have a lot of answers. And like I'm sensing the same from you, I'm not a fan of the mystery."

"I heard there was a drama at Ride yesterday," Keely cut in to remark.

Well.

Shit.

"It wasn't a drama...as such," Jagger lied.

Keely stared at him.

Dutch didn't sound annoyed or impatient anymore when he said, "It was totally a drama, brother."

Jagger sighed before he explained.

"Okay, so Archie decided she wanted to buy the Bronco Joker and I restored. She came around to work things out with Tyra. Someone told me she was on Chaos, I went in and Tyra was trying to hold the fort considering she knew what was going down, since she took my check for the Bronco, and Archie was making it clear she didn't understand what was going down. So I was forced to tell Arch I'd already bought it for her, and was waiting for the perfect time to give it to her. She was a little miffed that I did that."

"Miffed and *loud*," Dutch added.

Now the asshole was grinning.

"As you both know, she tends to be chill," Jag reminded them. "It's just on certain occasions when she's just...*not*. And like she doesn't hesitate to communicate anything, she doesn't hesitate to communicate when she's not."

"You do know that women are capable of purchasing their own modes of transport," his mother pointed out.

"If you think you have anything to say that Archie hasn't already shared, you'd be wrong," Jag told Keely.

"I further heard she drove away in that Bronco," Keely drawled.

That was when Jagger smiled.

His ma shook her head, came to him and took his left hand in hers.

She brought it to her and opened it, palm up.

Jag didn't pull away or make any attempt to hide what he knew someone else had shared with her.

He'd grown up with this. His family was huge, and his friends were his family. Therefore, it was practically impossible to have anything to yourself.

Not that he'd hide what was in his palm.

A new-ish tat.

The infinity symbol.

One continuous stroke that said *The girl across the way* as well as *The guy across the way.*

He had another new tattoo, it was even smaller, and it was in a place that she couldn't right then see.

A small *A.* had been added at the beginning of the tat on his chest.

His mom pressed the pad of her thumb to the side of the still-healing mark.

She then lifted her gaze to him and said softly, "I'm so glad I raised a son who would buy his girl a kickass truck."

"Ma," he whispered, reading her vibe.

She glanced over her shoulder at Dutch then back to Jag. "And I'm even more glad I raised two sons with exceptionally good taste."

He already knew his mom dug Arch.

But this...

Jagger swallowed.

Keely let him go abruptly and turned back to where she'd been standing at the counter.

Jag looked to Dutch whose long body was still sprawled at the table, but the feel of him was no longer "Hanging at Ma's."

It was "Keeping an Eye on Ma."

Feeling Jag's attention, Dutch shifted his to his brother.

They shared a look they'd shared often over the years, and this look happened anytime they felt they needed to keep their eye on their ma.

"When we moved, I found this," their mother told the counter, and both men's focus returned to her. "I honestly didn't remember it existed until we moved. He'd made them so often, he didn't need it anymore. It was in a cookbook I hadn't opened in ages."

She turned and was holding a piece of yellow-ruled paper.

"I've been holding on to it for the right time. Now is the right time. I made a copy, you get that," she said that last part to Dutch. Then to Jag, "You get the original."

"What is it?" Jagger asked.

"Your father's recipe for peanut butter and chocolate chip pancakes."

Jagger reached out a hand because suddenly, he was reeling.

"Jag?"

On his tongue, he tasted butter and syrup and peanuts and chocolate.

And in his mind's eye, misty and unclear, sitting at the table he was sitting at, a dark-haired man was smiling at him.

What was not misty and unclear was what was in that smile.

And what was in it was everything.

"Jag!"

He came back into his mother's kitchen and saw Keely close, Dutch too, and Dutch had his fingers wrapped tight around the back of Jagger's neck.

But he gave his attention to his ma.

"Dad made those for us," he said.

"Every Sunday," she replied quietly.

Every Sunday.

Dutch took his hand from his brother.

"And now, you can make them for your women, and when they arrive, for your babies," she went on. "And I can promise you, your father would love that."

They heard a crinkle noise and both men looked down to the paper Keely was still holding.

There were stains and some of the ink had run.

But in bold blue strokes, Graham Black had listed ingredients and measurements and minimal instructions to guide his way in making the Sunday morning pancakes he made his family.

And at the bottom there were some squiggly marks that looked like big blobs with some points.

"You were trying to draw hearts," Keely said. "To tell your dad how much you loved his pancakes. That's probably why he kept it when he didn't need it anymore. Those hearts."

Both men looked up, but her gaze was on Jagger.

"Me?" he asked, feeling his heart pound.

"Yeah," she said then she turned to Dutch. "That's why he gets it, honey. It's him and his dad on that piece of paper. Do you understand?"

"Yeah, Ma," Dutch replied. "Totally."

Jag was staring down at the paper with his father's writing and Jag's "hearts."

No one said anything for long beats.

Their mom moved them along.

"So, do you boys wanna make pancakes?" she asked.

"Yeah, Ma."

Both Black Brothers said it in unison that time.

"Yeah," Keely whispered.

Her eyes were bright.

Her hands came up and she cupped both their jaws.

Her smile was wobbly.

Then she let them go and ordered, "Dutch, honey, get the griddle. Jagger, baby, grab a bowl. Let's get cracking."

She shifted away.

The Black Brothers looked at each other.

Then, as they'd done time and again over the years, they moved to do as their mother told them.

And not long after, the three remaining Black OGs sat at the kitchen table and ate pancakes.

But the one who was missing still was there.

Like he always was.

And he always would be.

* * * *

Some time later…

Jag walked into S.I.L. through the back door of the store and was immediately confronted by four people.

The only reason this was okay was because Archie was one of them.

"We need to talk to you," Joany proclaimed.

"How did you even know I was here?" Jag asked.

"Dude, you wanna be stealthy, you gotta lose the bike," Joany shared.

Oh yeah.

Right.

"We're at a stalemate and we've agreed you're the deciding vote," Archie told him.

He wasn't sure that was a good thing.

He didn't start with that.

"First, do I show anywhere, and you don't say 'hey' with a kiss?" he asked her.

Archie grinned the grin he liked so much, came to him and pressed close with her body and then her lips.

"Okay, La-La, we're screwed," Joany declared while Archie did this. "And also, if I don't find a man who claims my mouth like that upon sight, I'm gonna search for a convent."

"You'd last two hours in a convent," Lafayette replied.

"Why? I love God and Jesus is my jam," Joany retorted.

"I'm not sure nuns are allowed to wear makeup and fake nails," Fabe shared.

"Okay, I'm out," Joany decided.

He really liked Archie's friends.

But he had plans with his woman, his brother, and his brother's woman, and this wasn't part of them.

So Jag tucked Archie to his side and told the crew, "We got shit to do and places to go so what's going on?"

"Who wants to start?" Joany asked.

Lafayette did and Jag knew that because he waded in.

"Well, we've learned lots has been going down at Casa de la Harris Family," he announced.

Fantastic.

Jag looked down at Archie.

"Things to know," she started. "Both of Aaron and Allan's parents have recently been incarcerated. Not county lockup. The big house. And neither of them are coming back anytime soon. Apparently, they've been in trouble with the law a lot. The mom's folks gave up on them ages ago. The dad's mom has been posting bail and paying for counsel and such, but she's recently gotten fed up and washed her hands of them. So now they're in the pokey."

Jag's lips twitched when his woman used the word "pokey."

But his mind was on the Harris brothers.

Mal had had no issues with them for some time, for two reasons.

One, his posse finally posse'd up and took his back, and Jag had been right. Bullies shied away from bad odds.

Two, having bikers ride to your aid and then give your gramma an honor guard escort at her funeral carried some weight in the middle-school world. Mal and the S.I.L. crew had earned reputations as badasses, or at least were known to be badass-adjacent, which worked.

And on these thoughts, Jag wasn't sure if he cared what was up with the

Harrises.

Therefore, he shared the honesty.

"This is only mildly interesting to me."

Archie's smile got more smug.

She enjoyed being badass-adjacent too.

"Well, Momma Harris took in the boys and she isn't feeling the love all around for when they mess up," Joany pitched in. "And obviously, Aaron broke the record for messing up after he moved in with Granny. Unlike his folks, who had no fucks to give about their kids, Granny thinks a stint in juvie might help him see the error of his ways. And according to the kids, Allan is o-v-e-r *over* his brother's damage and getting clipped along with him for shit he A, isn't a fan of doing, and B, half the time doesn't even do. So he's on the straight and narrow at Granny's house and Aaron is awaiting a judge telling him how long this lesson he's gonna learn is gonna last."

And again, Jag was right about how far brotherhood went when only one brother was acting like a brother.

Interesting to know.

He still had no idea why they were sharing this info with him.

"And I've been ambushed when I show at the store for this…why?"

"Mrs. Harris came to S.I.L. We have a rep and it's a good one. So she wants Allan back in group," Fabe shared.

Oh fuck.

"Now, here's the real sitch, 'cause me and La-La say no," Joany told him. "He was never the ringleader, but who knows how long Aaron will be gone, who else is in their crew that might come around and cause a ruckus, and generally, this family is bad news. Sure, three quarters of them are now doing time, but even though that takes them out of the picture for right now, it also proves my point."

"Let me guess," Jag began, looking down at Archie. "You think he should be allowed to come back."

"Me and Fabe, yeah," she said.

Of course she did.

"I don't think he should have to pay for his brother's mistakes," Archie told him. "They were only in group a month or so, and I didn't get to know Allan very well. The most insidious bullying Aaron did was overshadowing his brother like he did. I think he'd benefit from group. I think it'd be good for him to learn what community really is."

Shit.

She wasn't wrong about that.

Likely realizing she was losing ground, Joany belatedly laid out the rules for Jag's engagement.

"Important note, you can't vote with her just because she's giving you the goodness."

"You are very wrong about that," Jag contradicted.

Archie chuckled.

Joany did an eye roll.

"All right, Allan was never a problem," Lafayette (who, incidentally, today was dressed like Jim Morrison on the bottom with tight black leather pants, but up top he was John Lennon with a "New York City" T-shirt, though his was cropped and showed his stomach). "But it isn't about Allan. It's about the other kids. The group is tight. They've bonded. And no shade on Allan, but we have to think of his influences and what he'll bring to the other kids."

"Have you asked the kids what they think?" Jagger queried.

This appeared to flummox them.

All of them.

He was surprised and again looked down at Arch. "You haven't?"

"It's our responsibility to make these decisions for them," she said. "And that's a responsibility we took on for them, and the trust their parents give us."

"They aren't five, Arch," he replied. "Pretty soon, they're gonna have to be making a lot harder decisions. You gotta guide them now, so when they get there, they make the right ones. Hell, Mal considers himself the man of the house already and he isn't even close to having his first shave."

After he finished talking, Arch smiled up at him then turned to the team.

"Powwow with the kids next week. We'll get their input and decide from there."

The crew nodded their approval to this plan.

"Just to say, I don't want to be the tie-breaker with you guys," Jagger put in.

"Too bad and too late," Joany declared. "You are. Next up is a discussion about the kickass couch Archie found. Fabe and I want to rearrange the front of the store into a pseudo-living room that you see the minute you walk in. Archie and La-La want to rearrange the entire book section so the shelves surround the couch that's, again, set up in a pseudo-living-room-style scenario. What's your vote or do you need to see the couch?"

Weirdly, Jag kinda wanted to see the couch.

But wisely, he said, "I'm not weighing in on this."

"And I'm not lugging a ton of books around to rearrange the book space," Joany returned. She then stated the obvious, "So I need you to vote with me."

"We can make it a project, and next week, the kids can help us do it," Archie suggested.

"If we put it up front, it has a bigger impact," Fabe stated. "It shares immediately what you'll find in this store and it'll do that in a good way. And anyway, we need some *fresh* around here."

"Agreed, we need some *fresh*, totally. I'm tired of lookin' at this baby this way," Lafayette said, throwing out an arm to indicate the entirety of the space. "So I say we do a full-store overhaul. Plan it out, even close down a couple of days to get it done."

If they couldn't agree on where to put a couch, Jagger didn't want to be anywhere near when they discussed a full-store overhaul.

"Uh…" Joany cut in. "This is new to the debate, but I will add at this juncture you can't overhaul a store without breaking a nail. So, if that's the vote, I'm sitting that work out as a conscientious objector."

"That's not what a conscientious objector is, Jo," Fabe told her.

"It is so," she shot back. "I am *very* conscientious about my nails."

"Can someone either kill me or let me and Archie go so we can get the fuck out of here and start our weekend?" Jagger asked.

"We'll decide what we're doing with the store on Monday," Archie decreed. "And we'll talk to the kids on Monday too."

"Maybe we should poll the kids about the couch," Lafayette suggested.

"That's actually a good idea," Fabe agreed.

"Have fun doing something I would not be caught dead doing for two whole days and two whole nights," Joany bid to Jag and Arch. She finished with, "Or one whole night for that matter."

"You don't know what you're missing," Archie told her.

"I also don't care," Joany said.

She gave them a finger wave, a wink, and with the two guys, she wandered away.

Thank fuck that was done.

He looked down at Arch and gave her a shake against his body.

"You ready?" he asked.

"Am I dreaming, or is my man really going camping with me?" she asked back.

"My father loved camping."

That bought him warm eyes, a soft look and her melting into his side.

Then she said, "I just gotta grab my bag. I brought it down. It's in the office."

"I'll text Dutch and let him know we're on our way."

She smiled up at him, curled into him, rolled up on her toes and tipped her head way back.

Jag didn't need any more of an invitation.

He gave her a proper hello kiss.

And then they headed through her store to get to her office in order to grab her stuff and get on the road.

Halfway there, he stopped them.

Archie looked up at him curiously.

Jag sighed.

Then he asked, "Where's this couch?"

She started laughing, her black eyes alight, her expression gentle and happy and ridiculously beautiful.

Then she tagged his hand and they made a detour to look at a couch.

* * * *

The fire crackled as the velvet dark of night with its pinprick stars blanketed two dark-haired men who still had the thrill of the wind on their faces.

They sat on and laid against thick throws covering dirt and boulders in the Colorado mountains, the women they loved between their legs, using their chests as cushions.

One of the women had a certain kind of ring on her left ring finger, and soon, another would be joining it.

The other woman would have those same kinds of rings, just...later.

Not far away, two bikes sat side by side, glinting in the moonlight.

One was new.

One was old and had two lipstick kisses sealed to its tank—the kiss of the love of the man who bought that bike, and the kiss of the love of the man who'd inherited it.

Two small tents had been erected across from each other, away from the fire.

The cooler for their beer was a hitch in the side of the river that ran close to the site.

Dinner had been hotdogs and s'mores.

The bottle of whisky they were passing between them was now only half full of amber liquid.

There were no words.

No conversation.

Eyes were aimed at the fire or at the stars.

It was peaceful.

It was easy.

It was everything.

The End

Stories of the Chaos MC will continue to be told
as part of the Wild West MC series.

* * * *

Also from 1001 Dark Nights and Kristen Ashley, discover Wild Fire, Quiet Man, Rough Ride, and Rock Chick Reawakening.

Sign up for the 1001 Dark Nights Newsletter
and be entered to win a Tiffany Key necklace.

There's a contest every month!

Go to www.1001DarkNights.com to subscribe.

As a bonus, all subscribers can download
FIVE FREE exclusive books!

Discover 1001 Dark Nights Collection Eight

DRAGON REVEALED by Donna Grant
A Dragon Kings Novella

CAPTURED IN INK by Carrie Ann Ryan
A Montgomery Ink: Boulder Novella

SECURING JANE by Susan Stoker
A SEAL of Protection: Legacy Series Novella

WILD WIND by Kristen Ashley
A Chaos Novella

DARE TO TEASE by Carly Phillips
A Dare Nation Novella

VAMPIRE by Rebecca Zanetti
A Dark Protectors/Rebels Novella

MAFIA KING by Rachel Van Dyken
A Mafia Royals Novella

THE GRAVEDIGGER'S SON by Darynda Jones
A Charley Davidson Novella

FINALE by Skye Warren
A North Security Novella

MEMORIES OF YOU by J. Kenner
A Stark Securities Novella

SLAYED BY DARKNESS by Alexandra Ivy
A Guardians of Eternity Novella

TREASURED by Lexi Blake
A Masters and Mercenaries Novella

THE DAREDEVIL by Dylan Allen
A Rivers Wilde Novella

BOND OF DESTINY by Larissa Ione
A Demonica Novella

THE CLOSE-UP by Kennedy Ryan
A Hollywood Renaissance Novella

MORE THAN POSSESS YOU by Shayla Black
A More Than Words Novella

HAUNTED HOUSE by Heather Graham
A Krewe of Hunters Novella

MAN FOR ME by Laurelin Paige
A Man In Charge Novella

THE RHYTHM METHOD by Kylie Scott
A Stage Dive Novella

JONAH BENNETT by Tijan
A Bennett Mafia Novella

CHANGE WITH ME by Kristen Proby
A With Me In Seattle Novella

THE DARKEST DESTINY by Gena Showalter
A Lords of the Underworld Novella

Also from Blue Box Press

THE LAST TIARA by M.J. Rose

THE CROWN OF GILDED BONES by Jennifer L. Armentrout
A Blood and Ash Novel

THE MISSING SISTER by Lucinda Riley

Discover More Kristen Ashley

Wild Fire: A Chaos Novella
By Kristen Ashley

"You know you can't keep a good brother down."

The Chaos Motorcycle Club has won its war. But not every brother rode into the sunset with his woman on the back of his bike.

Chaos returns with the story of Dutch Black, a man whose father was the moral compass of the Club, until he was murdered. And the man who raised Dutch protected the Club at all costs. That combination is the man Dutch is intent on becoming.

It's also the man that Dutch is going to go all out to give to his woman.

Every 1001 Dark Nights novella is a standalone story. For new readers, it's an introduction to an author's world. And for fans, it's a bonus book in the author's series. We hope you'll enjoy each one as much as we do.

* * * *

Quiet Man: A Dream Man Novella
By Kristen Ashley

Charlotte "Lottie" McAlister is in the zone. She's ready to take on the next chapter of her life, and since she doesn't have a man, she'll do what she's done all along. She'll take care of business on her own. Even if that business means starting a family.

The problem is, Lottie has a stalker. The really bad kind. The kind that means she needs a bodyguard.

Enter Mo Morrison.

Enormous. Scary.

Quiet.

Mo doesn't say much, and Lottie's used to getting attention. And she wants Mo's attention. Badly.

But Mo has a strict rule. If he's guarding your body, that's all he's doing with it.

However, the longer Mo has to keep Lottie safe, the faster he falls for the beautiful blonde who has it so together, she might even be able to tackle the demons he's got in his head that just won't die.

But in the end, Lottie and Mo don't only have to find some way to keep hands off until the threat is over, they have to negotiate the overprotective Hot Bunch, Lottie's crazy stepdad, Tex, Mo's crew of frat-boy commandos, not to mention his nutty sisters.

All before Lottie finally gets her Dream Man.

And Mo can lay claim to his Dream Girl.

* * * *

Rough Ride: A Chaos Novella
By Kristen Ashley

Rosalie Holloway put it all on the line for the Chaos Motorcycle Club.

Informing to Chaos on their rival club—her man's club, Bounty—Rosalie knows the stakes. And she pays them when her man, who she was hoping to scare straight, finds out she's betrayed him and he delivers her to his brothers to mete out their form of justice.

But really, Rosie has long been denying that, as she drifted away from her Bounty, she's been falling in love with Everett "Snapper" Kavanagh, a Chaos brother. Snap is the biker-boy-next door with the snowy blue eyes, quiet confidence and sweet disposition who was supposed to keep her safe...and fell down on that job.

For Snapper, it's always been Rosalie, from the first time he saw her at the Chaos Compound. He's just been waiting for a clear shot. But he didn't want to get it after his Rosie was left bleeding, beat down and broken by Bounty on a cement warehouse floor.

With Rosalie a casualty of an ongoing war, Snapper has to guide her to trust him, take a shot with him, build a them...

And fold his woman firmly in the family that is Chaos.

* * * *

Rock Chick Reawakening: A Rock Chick Novella
By Kristen Ashley

From *New York Times* bestselling author, Kristen Ashley, comes the long-awaited story of Daisy and Marcus, *Rock Chick Reawakening*. A prequel to Kristen's *Rock Chick* series, *Rock Chick Reawakening* shares the tale of the devastating event that nearly broke Daisy, an event that set Marcus Sloane—one of Denver's most respected businessmen and one of the Denver underground's most feared crime bosses—into finally making his move to win the heart of the woman who stole his.

Rough Ride
A Chaos Novella
By Kristen Ashley
Now available!

From *New York Times* and *USA Today* bestselling author Kristen Ashley comes a new story in her Chaos series…

Rosalie Holloway put it all on the line for the Chaos Motorcycle Club.

Informing to Chaos on their rival club—her man's club, Bounty—Rosalie knows the stakes. And she pays them when her man, who she was hoping to scare straight, finds out she's betrayed him and he delivers her to his brothers to mete out their form of justice.

But really, Rosie has long been denying that, as she drifted away from her Bounty, she's been falling in love with Everett "Snapper" Kavanagh, a Chaos brother. Snap is the biker-boy-next door with the snowy blue eyes, quiet confidence and sweet disposition who was supposed to keep her safe…and fell down on that job.

For Snapper, it's always been Rosalie, from the first time he saw her at the Chaos Compound. He's just been waiting for a clear shot. But he didn't want to get it after his Rosie was left bleeding, beat down and broken by Bounty on a cement warehouse floor.

With Rosalie a casualty of an ongoing war, Snapper has to guide her to trust him, take a shot with him, build a them…

And fold his woman firmly in the family that is Chaos.

* * * *

Chapter One
Atone

Rosalie

I stood staring at myself in my mother's bathroom mirror.

I was going to have scars. Three of them.

Men with scars on their face were considered interesting, like they lived adventurous lives or were tough guys.

Women with them were looked on as pathetic, like some traumatic life event happened to them that they didn't survive without being marked and because of that were objects of sympathy.

Another discrepancy between the sexes which was absolutely not fair.

Like the difference in physical strength.

I was top heavy. Slender, long legs, slim hips, thin arms, but I had big boobs in a way they looked fake.

They weren't.

My mother had given me a number of good things, including her thick dark hair.

And her big tits.

My father had lamented this.

"Already hard enough to keep the men off you, gorgeous," he'd say to my mom. "And you got my ring on your finger and it's sat there for years. Now I got my baby girl to worry about."

Man.

I missed my dad.

I stopped thinking about my dad and stared at my torso in the mirror.

I'd learned over the span of my twenty-eight years of life that large breasts had awesome powers.

Helping you handle yourself when eight men were intent to beat the snot out of you was not part of those awesome powers.

I lifted my gaze and studied my face in the mirror.

They'd kept me in the hospital for two days, considering I'd taken a number of blows to the head, and thus had a serious concussion, and they tried to be cool about it, but I could tell they were concerned about the number of times I'd blacked out.

Now I'd been out of the hospital for two days, as, apparently (and thankfully) all systems were a go.

The swelling had decreased significantly but only that morning did I note that the bruising was starting to recede, some of the edges of the purple going yellow.

My broken nose was still taped and would be for some time.

I'd had a total of twenty-nine stitches sewn into my face. My eyebrow would never be the same. The jaw scar wouldn't be easily seen. But the gash on my nose would stand out.

I had been pretty, not beautiful, but definitely pretty. And I knew it.

This was not vanity. This was being real. I could see myself in the mirror and I'd had a mom and dad who adored me and told me how proud of me they were for a lot of reasons, and they'd done this all my life. My looks just were what they were and I was grateful for them.

I also used them.

I used them to get guys I was attracted to.

I used them to get good tips at Colombo's.

I used them to jump the line at clubs I wanted to get into.

And I used them to get out of that speeding ticket that time that cop pulled me over.

Mom had taught me, if God gave you something good, you didn't waste it. You used it (for good, obviously—I mean, it *was* God bestowing these gifts).

So I'd used them.

But as I stood there, looking in the mirror, I knew that Beck and his brothers had concentrated on my face, thinking that they were taking the most important thing I had away from me.

Men were so stinking stupid.

In the last few days, when there wasn't a lot to feel good about, I felt good about the fact that they hadn't raped me.

That was my silver lining.

My boyfriend kidnapped me, delivered me to his buds, they beat the heck out of me, but they didn't rape me.

If they'd done that to me, it would have taken away something that meant something.

But they hadn't.

Yeah.

Awesome silver lining.

Still, for sure it was one.

But, to my way of thinking, they didn't do any lasting damage. They didn't break anything but nine ribs (since I had twenty-four, that could have been worse) and my nose. When Muzzle's fist connected with my schnoz, I felt the cartilage give, and that hadn't been fun, but it would heal. Eightball had sprained my wrist, but he didn't snap it, and it had been tender but it was already feeling better.

I'd recover.

I could walk, talk, eat, breathe. I could definitely still deliver pizzas to diners' tables (or would be able to in a week or two, after the bruising and swelling were gone and I had less pain due to the broken ribs).

I might even be able to learn to live with the fact that a man I trusted and thought I loved had not only brought me to that hell, he'd also delivered his share of it.

Sure, I'd broken his trust. I'd informed on him and his brothers' activities to Chaos, setting them up to be taken down by the cops.

But let us not forget, they were able to be *set up to be taken down by the cops.* This meant they were doing felonious crap. That felonious crap being providing transport for illegal substances and firearms, offering this service to really bad guys.

So sure, I could see, if he found out, Beck being really freaking pissed at me. Yelling at me. Breaking it off with me. That was, if he didn't give me the chance to explain *why* I'd done it in the first place, that being for *him.*

Well, not so much for him, I'd realized.

But I couldn't think about that right then.

I had to think about the fact I survived. I was alive. Walking, talking, eating breathing, and someday soon I'd again be laying pizza pies on tables for tips.

What I would not be doing was getting involved with a man, maybe ever again.

Seriously.

That might seem dramatic, but the first man I fell for, Shy Cage of the Chaos Motorcycle Club, had shown me a window to a world I wanted and the doorway I wanted to use to get to that was Shy because Shy was Shy. He was beautiful to look at and fantastic in bed, but he was also funny and sweet and protective and affectionate.

He was my dad (not that I knew about the "fantastic in bed" part with my dad, but from the time I understood the concept of sex, mom's dreamy looks and dad's cat-got-his-cream moods were not lost on me—gross, but not lost on me).

So Shy was all that...including having all of it on a bike.

But he dropped me like a hot brick the minute Tabitha Allen gave him indication that her doorway was open. He slammed the one on me and waltzed right through hers without a second thought.

Looking back, I knew as I fell deeper and deeper for him that he wasn't doing the same.

That didn't make it any better.

Now, also looking back, I knew as I got deeper and deeper into things with Beck that I was trying to find what I'd hoped to get with Shy.

They both belonged to motorcycle clubs, for one.

And Beck looked a lot like Shy for another (which, not so by the by, was a lot like my dad looked). Beefier, maybe. A bit rougher around the edges. But I definitely had a type.

And then came Snapper.

God, Snapper.

Nope.

No.

No more men for me.

Seriously.

About Kristen Ashley

Kristen Ashley is the *New York Times* bestselling author of over seventy romance novels including the *Rock Chick, Colorado Mountain, Dream Man, Chaos, Unfinished Heroes, The 'Burg, Magdalene, Fantasyland, The Three, Ghost and Reincarnation, Moonlight and Motor Oil, Dream Team* and *Honey* series along with several standalone novels. She's a hybrid author, publishing titles both independently and traditionally, her books have been translated in fourteen languages and she's sold over three million books.

Kristen's novel, *Law Man*, won the *RT Book Reviews* Reviewer's Choice Award for best Romantic Suspense. Her independently published title *Hold On* was nominated for *RT Book Reviews* best Independent Contemporary Romance and her traditionally published title *Breathe* was nominated for best Contemporary Romance. Kristen's titles *Motorcycle Man, The Will, Ride Steady* (which won the Reader's Choice award from *Romance Reviews*) and *The Hookup* all made the final rounds for Goodreads Choice Awards in the Romance category.

Kristen, born in Gary and raised in Brownsburg, Indiana, was a fourth-generation graduate of Purdue University. Since, she has lived in Denver, the West Country of England, and now she resides in Phoenix. She worked as a charity executive for eighteen years prior to beginning her independent publishing career. She currently writes full-time.

Although romance is her genre, the prevailing themes running through all of Kristen's novels are friendship, family and a strong sisterhood. To this end, and as a way to thank her readers for their support, Kristen has created the Rock Chick Nation, a series of programs that are designed to give back to her readers and promote a strong female community.

The mission of the Rock Chick Nation is to live your best life, be true to your true self, recognize your beauty and take your sister's back whether they're friends and family or if they're thousands of miles away and you don't know who they are. The programs of the RC Nation include: Rock Chick Rendezvous, weekends Kristen organizes full of parties and get-togethers to bring the sisterhood together; Rock Chick Recharges, evenings Kristen arranges for women who have been nominated to receive a special night; and Rock Chick Rewards, an ongoing program that raises funds for nonprofit women's organizations Kristen's readers nominate. Kristen's Rock Chick Rewards have donated nearly $145,000 to charity and this number continues to rise.

You can read more about Kristen, her titles and the Rock Chick Nation at KristenAshley.net.

Discover 1001 Dark Nights

SOME WAY by Jennifer Probst ~ TOO CLOSE TO CALL by Tessa Bailey ~ HUNTED by Elisabeth Naughton ~ EYES ON YOU by Laura Kaye ~ BLADE by Alexandra Ivy/Laura Wright ~ DRAGON BURN by Donna Grant ~ TRIPPED OUT by Lorelei James ~ STUD FINDER by Lauren Blakely ~ MIDNIGHT UNLEASHED by Lara Adrian ~ HALLOW BE THE HAUNT by Heather Graham ~ DIRTY FILTHY FIX by Laurelin Paige ~ THE BED MATE by Kendall Ryan ~ NIGHT GAMES by CD Reiss ~ NO RESERVATIONS by Kristen Proby ~ DAWN OF SURRENDER by Liliana Hart

COLLECTION FIVE
BLAZE ERUPTING by Rebecca Zanetti ~ ROUGH RIDE by Kristen Ashley ~ HAWKYN by Larissa Ione ~ RIDE DIRTY by Laura Kaye ~ ROME'S CHANCE by Joanna Wylde ~ THE MARRIAGE ARRANGEMENT by Jennifer Probst ~ SURRENDER by Elisabeth Naughton ~ INKED NIGHTS by Carrie Ann Ryan ~ ENVY by Rachel Van Dyken ~ PROTECTED by Lexi Blake ~ THE PRINCE by Jennifer L. Armentrout ~ PLEASE ME by J. Kenner ~ WOUND TIGHT by Lorelei James ~ STRONG by Kylie Scott ~ DRAGON NIGHT by Donna Grant ~ TEMPTING BROOKE by Kristen Proby ~ HAUNTED BE THE HOLIDAYS by Heather Graham ~ CONTROL by K. Bromberg ~ HUNKY HEARTBREAKER by Kendall Ryan ~ THE DARKEST CAPTIVE by Gena Showalter

COLLECTION SIX
DRAGON CLAIMED by Donna Grant ~ ASHES TO INK by Carrie Ann Ryan ~ ENSNARED by Elisabeth Naughton ~ EVERMORE by Corinne Michaels ~ VENGEANCE by Rebecca Zanetti ~ ELI'S TRIUMPH by Joanna Wylde ~ CIPHER by Larissa Ione ~ RESCUING MACIE by Susan Stoker ~ ENCHANTED by Lexi Blake ~ TAKE THE BRIDE by Carly Phillips ~ INDULGE ME by J. Kenner ~ THE KING by Jennifer L. Armentrout ~ QUIET MAN by Kristen Ashley ~ ABANDON by Rachel Van Dyken ~ THE OPEN DOOR by Laurelin Paige~ CLOSER by Kylie Scott ~ SOMETHING JUST LIKE THIS by Jennifer Probst ~ BLOOD NIGHT by Heather Graham ~ TWIST OF FATE by Jill Shalvis ~ MORE THAN PLEASURE YOU by Shayla Black ~ WONDER WITH ME by Kristen Proby ~ THE DARKEST ASSASSIN by Gena Showalter

COLLECTION SEVEN
THE BISHOP by Skye Warren ~ TAKEN WITH YOU by Carrie Ann Ryan ~ DRAGON LOST by Donna Grant ~ SEXY LOVE by Carly Phillips ~ PROVOKE by Rachel Van Dyken ~ RAFE by Sawyer Bennett ~ THE NAUGHTY PRINCESS by Claire Contreras ~ THE GRAVEYARD SHIFT by Darynda Jones ~ CHARMED by Lexi Blake ~ SACRIFICE OF DARKNESS

by Alexandra Ivy ~ THE QUEEN by Jen Armentrout ~ BEGIN AGAIN by Jennifer Probst ~ VIXEN by Rebecca Zanetti ~ SLASH by Laurelin Paige ~ THE DEAD HEAT OF SUMMER by Heather Graham ~ WILD FIRE by Kristen Ashley ~ MORE THAN PROTECT YOU by Shayla Black ~ LOVE SONG by Kylie Scott ~ CHERISH ME by J. Kenner ~ SHINE WITH ME by Kristen Proby

Discover Blue Box Press

TAME ME by J. Kenner ~ TEMPT ME by J. Kenner ~ DAMIEN by J. Kenner ~ TEASE ME by J. Kenner ~ REAPER by Larissa Ione ~ THE SURRENDER GATE by Christopher Rice ~ SERVICING THE TARGET by Cherise Sinclair ~ THE LAKE OF LEARNING by Steve Berry and MJ Rose ~ THE MUSEUM OF MYSTERIES by Steve Berry and MJ Rose ~ TEASE ME by J. Kenner ~ FROM BLOOD AND ASH by Jennifer L. Armentrout ~ QUEEN MOVE by Kennedy Ryan ~ THE HOUSE OF LONG AGO by Steve Berry and MJ Rose ~ THE BUTTERFLY ROOM by Lucinda Riley ~ A KINGDOM OF FLESH AND FIRE by Jennifer L. Armentrout

On behalf of 1001 Dark Nights,

Liz Berry, M.J. Rose, and Jillian Stein would like to thank ~

Steve Berry
Doug Scofield
Benjamin Stein
Kim Guidroz
Social Butterfly PR
Ashley Wells
Asha Hossain
Chris Graham
Chelle Olson
Kasi Alexander
Jessica Johns
Dylan Stockton
Richard Blake
and Simon Lipskar

Made in the USA
Las Vegas, NV
01 March 2021